BOOK 4 IN THE CERBERUS SERIES

FORRESTAL

JOHN FILCHER

© Copyright 2023, John Filcher

All rights reserved. No part of this book may be reproduced, distributed, stored in any retrieval system, or transmitted in any form by any means, including photocopying, recording, or other electronic or mechanical means, without express written permission from the author or the publisher.

ISBN: 978-1-955622-08-0

Published by

Fideli Publishing, Inc.
119 W. Morgan St.
Martinsville, IN 46151

www.FideliPublishing.com

SOLARA

Characters

Dan Ronin – Captain, *Cerberus*

Diane Mueller, Cmdr. – Commanding Officer (XO), *Cerberus*

Elvis Lazarus, Lt. Cmdr. – Chief Engineer, *Cerberus*

Pierre Delacroix, Lt. – Sensors, *Cerberus*

Kristoff Alphonso, Lt. – Fabrication, *Cerberus*

Matt LeCroy, Lt. – Tactical, *Cerberus*

Marcy Anzio, Lt. – Weapons, *Cerberus*

Maria Delgado, Lt. – Communications, *Cerberus*

Hirohito Taketa, Lt., Chief Medical Officer – Medical, *Cerberus*

Chrizanne "Anne" Abara, Nurse – Medical, *Cerberus*

Antonio Perez, Lt. – Helm, *Cerberus*

Kelvin Sunderland, Lt. – Commander Air Group (CAG), *Cerberus*

Adam Taylor, Deck Chief – *Cerberus*

Erin Johnson, Pilot Officer – Bulldog 1 pilot

Hal Patterson, Chief – Bulldog 1 rearseater

Helmut Meyer, Pilot Officer – Bulldog 2 pilot

Sophie Schmidt, Chief – Bulldog 2 rearseater

Antonio Russo, Pilot Officer – Bulldog 3 pilot

Michael Jonsey, Chief – Bulldog 3 rearseater

Gary Chanson, Pilot Officer – Bulldog 5 pilot

Akira Nakamura, Chief – Bulldog 5 rearseater

Lt. Adolph Gustav – Marine Commander aboard *Cerberus*

Brett Mackey – Marine Bravo team

Carlos Guthrey – Marine Bravo team

Terry Allison – Marine Bravo team

Steve Cupper – Marine Bravo team

Toshi Kanagawa – Marine Echo team

Adrian "The Pirate" Longman – Marine Echo team

Rhee Lee – Marine Echo team

David Danfries – Marine Echo team

Julio Gonzales – Marine Echo team

Nancy Dos – Marine Echo team

Hiro "Gung Ho" Gozen – Marine Echo Team

Jagr Bloodbane – Marine Echo team

Barqhest – Marine Echo team K9

Brett Blackwater – Marine Gamma team

Jefferson Langley – Marine Gamma team

Louis "Fireman" Caron – Marine Gamma team

Juan Diaz – Marine Gamma team

Aldo Pena – Marine Gamma team

Rick "Rickgun" Desantos – Marine Gamma team

Dr. Winston Wright – Protocol Officer, *Cerberus*

Jessup Rodding, Admiral – Wayside Station

Frida Enginnsdottir – Ullrian Shieldmaiden, spouse of Captain Ronin

Edward Ronin – Son of Captain Ronin

Sarah Ronin – Son of Captain Ronin

Karl Mueller, Dr. – Scientist, *Cerberus*, spouse of Commander Mueller

Perun – Surviving AI from the Asiatic Collective.

Leonid Petrov – Captain, *Pytor the Great*

Igor Kuznetsova – Commander and First Officer, *Pytor the Great*

Ivan Gretski – Chief Engineer, *Pytor the Great*

Alissa Gusev – Comrade-Recruit, *Pytor the Great*

Gregor Diski – Shipyard Foreman

Nikolai Ollo – Friend of Shipyard Foreman

Andrei Kirov – Fleet-Admiral, Soyuz

Sergei Drago – First Officer (XO), Soyuz

Dmitry Sidorov – Lieutenant, Soyuz

Aden Dyke – Lieutenant, Forrestal Particle Beam Installation

Dominick Blakely – Commanding Officer, Forrestal Particle Beam Installation

Hu Nagun – Captain, *Kitty Hawk*

Steve Fisher – Commanding Officer (XO), *Kitty Hawk*

Samuel Nortan – Chief Engineer, *Kitty Hawk*

Michelle Rodgers – Captain, *Ceres*

Alfred Jurgenson – Captain, *Cygnus*

Tomias Miller – Captain, *Cerberus*

CHAPTER 1

TIME IS SHORT

PYTOR THE GREAT

148 DAYS UNTIL IMPACT

Leonid Petrov shifted in his command seat again. His restlessness grew with each passing day of this miserable, pointless tour of duty captaining the last, old picket ship guarding a long dormant jump gate. *Patience. I took this duty station because it gave us access to a ship that isn't assigned to the evacuation, and because of that, Perun won't be able to stop us. Running off with this ship in a mutiny is the best, and only, option left among the bad choices available to us,* he thought angrily.

His train of thought was interrupted by the young, new crew member who cautiously approached. *What's this comrade-recruit's name? Alissa Gusev, I think.* He looked into Gusev's eyes and waited for her to speak. Petrov already knew what she was going to say, but he followed through with the charade of appearing to treat it as important anyway. The comrade-recruit was angling to get some face time with the ship's captain instead of merely forwarding the latest report to his desk.

"Comrade-Captain, the latest sensor readings of the jump gate indicate no changes or fluctuations. All ship systems are functioning within the known operational parameters. No threats have been detected in our vicinity," reported Gusev.

Even though the grooming regulations of the fleet permitted shoulder-length hair, the comrade-recruit obviously preferred her very black hair cut short in a flattop. The hairstyle accentuated her black, almond-shaped eyes and very pale skin, but not in a good way. She came across as rather harsh and unforgiving, which was unfortunate in the yellowed, dim lighting of the ship. That harshness contrasted sharply with the desperation and sadness in her demeanor.

Petrov merely nodded his acknowledgment of Gusev's report, and she quietly returned back to her station. He pulled up the latest progress report about the fleet's emergency shipbuilding program from the old screen at his station. By now, Petrov no longer noticed the aged, yellowing plastic bevel of the screen anymore. Nor did he any longer fixate on the brittle, yellowed plastics that were all over the ship. The colony's AI didn't factor in aesthetics when determining whether equipment functioned, or recognize the effect these constant reminders about the ship's great age and fragility had on the crew. The thought, *We've become numb to the signs of atrophy all around us,* sprang unbidden to his mind.

Reading the report, Petrov's interest quickened when he noticed the number had finally increased. Slightly. *There's now 125 hulls under construction. Only 125!* Petrov returned to brooding angrily. *We need millions of hulls if our people are going to have a chance at survival. Why wasn't Perun building more? Why didn't Perun start building hulls long ago? It's not like this End of Days wasn't predictable.*

Perun, the AI responsible for operating Forrestal, didn't seem inclined to throw all available resources into the evacuation after the orbital wobble of the other planet in the system finally evolved and threw the planet into a collision course a century ago. The ancient AI's seeming lack of urgency over the past 100 years was as unsettling as its vague promise to reveal the final destination for the colony's refugees after they depart the planet.

For the umpteenth time, Petrov reviewed the rescue plan in his head. His plan, not Perun's plan. *Pytor the Great* was an old ship, a relic built before the jump gate was shut down during the ancient war centuries ago. Countless repairs overseen by Perun over the course of that time had kept most of the ship functioning well enough. There were always critical gaps because of a chronic lack of resources. The ship's missile magazines hadn't been refreshed for centuries because Perun had other priorities than building new missiles for an enemy that hadn't been seen in the better part of a millennium.

Missiles become less important than cargo capacity with each passing hour that brings us closer to the End of Days, noted Petrov sourly. *Life support systems and the engines have been maintained in optimal condition, but once we rebel against Perun to rescue our families, the clock on those life support systems will begin to run out quickly due to the added stress,* he thought. The irony of a slow moving, centuries-long disaster and lacking time to respond to it wasn't lost on him.

We don't have enough time! The last pass of that wayward planet caused worldwide earthquakes on Forrestal and stripped away some atmosphere. Forrestal won't survive the next approach, regardless of whether it's a near miss or a direct hit, Petrov fumed. And Perun hasn't revealed the rest of its plan yet, so even if civilians were evacuated, the fleet had no obvious place to permanently relocate them.

Not unless we're relocating them to a mass graveyard, Petrov thought gloomily. He stood up and traded glances with the ship's first officer, Cmdr. Igor Kuznetsova. Petrov tilted his head slightly towards his office door, which was located to starboard side of the ship's command bridge, to indicate the commander should join him there. Kuznetsova likewise rose and they both entered the office. The sliding door to the office automatically swooshed open to admit them, and it closed behind them the same way.

Petrov spoke first. "Still nothing?"

Kuznetsova shook his head. "No. Engineering has been trying to learn how to activate the jump gate for months. They've gotten nowhere. Again."

They could speak freely in Petrov's office because the audio and visual pickups for the ship, and Perun, had mysteriously malfunctioned when Petrov spilled his tea onto the room's circuitry. It had taken Petrov several attempts before they shorted out. They hadn't been repaired since then because all resources were being prioritized for the evacuation.

Petrov sighed dejectedly. He had really hoped the latest idea from the ship's engineers would succeed. "Once we onboard our families, we will have to put them somewhere before the added strain wears down the ship's life support systems. Our only option is to finish the Enclave before they get there."

It was Kuznetsova's turn to look dejected. "Even if we finish it in time, the Enclave is only temporary. Without assistance, it lacks the resources to be a permanent facility beyond the first couple of years."

Petrov snorted. They'd been through these arguments repeatedly. "I know, I know. And yet it's still more than Perun seems to have made available for us and our families. If we can't get that jump gate open, where do we go? What shall we do? We don't have an FTL drive that can get us out of this dying system. The earthquakes from the last few passes destroyed all infrastructure that was devoted to building a permanent home for the refugees. There's no place left for us to run to anymore."

They fell into a gloomy silence for a few moments before Petrov spoke. "Unless something changes, we stick to our plan. We'll continue to perform our duties to Perun and our comrades by guarding this gate until it's time to evacuate our families. By then, hopefully Engineering will have found a way to sever Perun's command and control uplinks to *Pytor the Great*, and we run."

Kuznetsova nodded. What else could they do? "I can't help but imagine Perun's reaction when we go dark and rescue our families instead of the party leadership Perun had assigned for us."

Petrov's mouth quirked into a half-smile that masked his doubts. *Yes, but will be able to escape Perun's control uplinks to do all this? Or did we miss something?* he wondered, keeping those unsettling thoughts to himself

CHAPTER 2

SOLARA JUMP GATE

CERBERUS

135 DAYS UNTIL IMPACT

"**R**eady to initiate gate opening sequence, Captain," announced Lt. Pierre Delacroix from his scanning station on the bridge. He had turned to face Capt. Dan Ronin as he reported, his slightly Gaelic-accented American providing a lilt to his speech. By now, the Confederacy had made enough discoveries for them to know the language they spoke was originally called English before The Fall had wiped out civilization on Earth but, for reasons no one knew for sure, the language was now called American.

All eyes on the bridge were locked onto the two of them. Ronin nodded to acknowledge the report, then he traded "here goes nothing" looks with the executive officer of *Cerberus*, Cmdr. Diane Mueller.

Mueller raised her eyebrows as she wisecracked to Ronin, "Either it works, or it doesn't. It's not like anyone's been stopping by to change the access codes lately."

Ronin half-smiled and tilted his head slightly towards Mueller. "Yeah…*lately.* The histories originally told us The Fall was over 750 years ago, and newly obtained records indicate it may have taken as many as 25 years to unfold. Who knows what happened during that quarter century of chaos?" he replied.

"They used to think the destruction of human civilization in The Fall occurred swiftly, but historical records that had survived on Ninebase and Solara told a different story," he continued. "It took nearly a quarter of a century for civilization to completely collapse from successive waves of death and destruction inflicted by war, plague, nuclear weapons, and famine.

"Historians in the Confederacy have been rapidly filling in many gaps and improving their grasp of the ancient calamity, which their species had inflicted upon itself. Either way, it was a very long time ago and someone could've changed the locks to try to keep the waves of disasters out of the next system."

Just then Ronin's wife, Frida Enginnsdottir, walked onto the bridge. Her warm, dark brown eyes and raven-colored hair contrasted sharply with her pale skin and highlighted both her soft features and her strength. The civilian contractor's uniform she now wore aboard *Cerberus* did little to mask her origin as an Ullrian shield maiden from the 1.5G world of Solara. Ronin found her aura of beauty and danger intoxicating.

Enginnsdottir's eyes met her husband's, and she raised her eyebrows with a slight tilt of her head. Her unasked question was the same as everyone else's at that moment.

Nodding back at her, Ronin accepted that it was time to roll the dice. This was the reason why they had returned to Solara so quickly. They needed to find out whether the object they discovered on their last exploration mission to Solara was really a jump gate or not.

"Lieutenant LeCroy, sound action stations," Ronin ordered.

Lt. Matt LeCroy had been waiting for the command. The alarm klaxon began its cycle and after a few moments LeCroy responded to Ronin. "Captain, all stations reporting manned and ready for combat."

It was an unusually fast confirmation of the crew's readiness status, but everyone had been lurking near their combat posts anyway in anticipation of this moment.

Ronin nodded to LeCroy and turned to look at Lt. Antonio Perez. "Lieutenant, engage engines and bring us within the navigational funnel mapped out by Bulldog 1 when it discovered the gate."

"Engaging jump drive now, Captain," Perez responded crisply. The ship jumped closer towards the gate at the edge of the Solara system, and *Cerberus* suddenly reappeared with an unusually large jump flare. Large amounts of energy radiated in all directions due to the odd arrival.

"Captain, the navigational funnel worked as per the testing of the science teams that have been studying this structure the past few weeks. We are positioned dead center in front of the gate. Distance, 500,000 miles exactly," Perez reported.

Ronin looked at Delacroix and said, "Lieutenant Delacroix, have our AI transmit the opening code to the jump gate."

Now it was Delacroix's turn to look like they were just winging it. He was more than a little dubious an old code that had survived by being copied from papers that themselves would eventually become brittle and stained by age before being recopied again and yet again by the Solarans was somehow still accurate. *Cerberus'* AI estimated that each cycle of copying to aging to recopying was at least 150 years, so the code given to them had already been recycled for several generations. Delacroix was also acutely aware that no one knew who had created the jump gates, or how old they actually were, or much of anything else about them. Even the ancient records from Ninebase and Solara were silent regarding that information.

Putting away his misgivings, Delacroix pressed a tab on his screen. "Aye, Captain. Initiating now." His blue eyes quickly scanned his screens. "Sequence is complete. Scanning now," he said, somewhat distracted as he was busy. Suddenly he leaned forward in disbelief.

"Captain! Scans indicate there is a ... something inside the gate. Our AI is analyzing," Delacroix stated, very intent now.

Before Delacroix could speak further, the voice of the ship's AI spoke over the bridge audio. "Captain Ronin, I'm not sure how to describe what we are witnessing, but perhaps the closest analogy is either that of a temporal distortion, or perhaps a space and time vortex. Scans indicate the anomaly has stabilized in the precise center of the probable jump gate. None of the Confederacy science teams have successfully replicated any anomaly like this."

Eyebrows raised, both by the content of what the AI said, and the fact that the AI spoke at all because it was so rare, Ronin glanced over to the navigator. "Lieutenant Perez. Take us through the gate," he ordered.

Perez swallowed his nervousness. "Aye, Captain. Moving forward now at sublight speed, one quarter power." He kept his eyes glued to his instrumentation as the ship accelerated.

Delacroix began calling out a countdown. "Contact in fifteen seconds. Ten seconds. Five seconds. Three. Two. One."

Just before Delacroix could say "contact," everyone suddenly felt like something had triggered a funny bone in their nervous system for a moment. Nervous glances were exchanged.

Delacroix was too busy to do anything but read his screens for several moments. "Gate transition complete, Captain," he finally announced from his scanning station. "Sending navigation scans to Lieutenant Perez now."

Ronin nodded in acknowledgment. He was seated in the center of the bridge, and the bridge crew had all buckled into their seats in anticipation of being the first humans to travel through a jump gate in well over 700 years. No one knew quite what to expect, so they prepared for the worst. Buckling in helped with disorientation, rough passage or worse.

Seconds crawled by as Perez tried to establish just where *Cerberus* actually was. It was a big universe, after all.

While the scans worked to figure it out, everyone on the bridge could clearly see that the stars on the forward viewscreen had changed.

CHAPTER 3

FORRESTAL JUMP GATE

PYTOR THE GREAT
135 DAYS UNTIL IMPACT

Comrade-Captain Petrov was in his office. He spent a lot of his time in there now, chiefly because Perun's eyes and ears inside the office had been disabled.

"Are you sure this will work? We only have a week remaining before we bug out for the evacuation," Petrov asked. He was intently watching his chief engineer, Ivan Gretski, while they plotted.

Gretski was under a lot of stress, and it was showing now in his nervous demeanor and beads of sweat on his forehead. It did not help that the ship was too warm. The life support system needed an adjustment again, so they just had to live with it.

"Yes, Comrade-Captain. As sure as we can be. We've discussed the unknown variables derived from Perun's technology. It's an ancient AI that existed before the People's Great Revolution and War Against Western Aggression. No human being has had any knowledge of its design and programming for as long as 800 years. Maybe more. Maybe less. We don't know how it thinks, how it was trained, its cultural influences, nothing. We are simply guessing when it comes to Perun's capabilities."

Gretski was right, and Petrov was irritated about it. Not at Gretski for being correct. At himself, for letting his impatience lead him into a rabbit hole where he already knew nothing would be accomplished.

Petrov grinned when he realized what had been happening. "Yes. All true. And I find it ironic that our colony is about to be overwhelmed by chaos when it is run by an AI named after an ancient thunder god and overseer of right and order."

Gretski broke into a sardonic grin and was about to reply when they were interrupted by the ship's battle klaxon. Trading suddenly worried looks, both of them scrambled out of the office. Gretski was headed down to Engineering, while Petrov merely had to step onto the adjacent bridge.

"Report!" yelled Petrov as he swiftly moved to his command seat.

"Comrade-Captain, there is activity in the jump gate. Energy readings match what the ancient records specify is that of an incoming ship transiting the gate," said Comrade-Recruit Gusev from her sensor station. She said it loudly as she was a little too shocked from the sudden activity in a gate that had been dormant since before her ancestors could remember.

Gusev suddenly peered intently at her sensor readout. "Comrade-Captain! Updated scan returns coming in now. There is a ship in the gate! Unknown configuration. Energy readings indicate she is powered by dark matter!"

Every pair of eyes on the bridge suddenly locked onto Gusev, who was so intent upon her screens that she didn't notice. Petrov quickly walked over to her station.

"Confirm that last item. Dark matter, you say?" Petrov asked, concern quickly turning to fear. Forrestal's historical archives taught them that dark matter wasn't used by the Collective in the ancient war against the Capitalists; it was their ancient enemy's signature power source.

Seconds ticked by. "Confirmed, Comrade-Captain. We are seeing dark matter energy readings!" Gusev never looked away from her screen the whole time.

Stunned, Petrov thought hard for a moment. Dark matter. The Capitalists. They've returned. Why now? It must be because we are about to evacuate as many colonists as we can and are at our most vulnerable!

Their duty was clear and their AI would make them obey their duty. It was why they had been serving aboard an ancient picket ship and keeping watching on the ancient gate, even though they had been making ready to abandon their post to rescue their families before the end of the colony arrived. The expression on Petrov's face hardened into resolve when he noticed the orders on his screen that had arrived directly from Perun. The AI ordered them to destroy the mystery ship.

"Our enemy has returned to finish off what they started," Petrov stated aloud. He glanced over to his weapons officer and nodded gravely. "Lock missiles onto that ship and fire when ready."

With Perun retaining control over their ship, Petrov's order to launch missiles was basically redundant since Perun would have launched them if the human crew had failed to act. Petrov knew that, but he did not want to tip their hand about attempting to wrest control of the ship too early and give Perun time to deploy some sort of countermeasures.

The weapons officer nodded curtly and looked down at his board while he carried out Petrov's order. In a few moments, he looked back at Petrov.

"Missiles away, Comrade-Captain."

CHAPTER 4

A HEATED WELCOME

CERBERUS

135 DAYS UNTIL IMPACT

Lieutenant Perez looked at his boards in confusion. "Captain, Engineering just advised the gate transition took our FTL jump drive offline. It'll take a few minutes to spin it up again." Perez never looked at Captain Ronin while he making his report because he and Lieutenant Delacroix were simultaneously attempting to determine what their current position was.

Several minutes passed before Perez finally got a tentative position for wherever it was they were now at, and he turned in his seat to face Ronin. Before he could speak, a Tacnet alarm began shrilly blaring at Lieutenant LeCroy's tactical scanning station. Perez whirled back to look at his screens, because a Tacnet alarm was never good.

"Missile launch! Multiple inbounds. Acceleration is off the charts. Time to impact, 30 seconds!" LeCroy yelled.

As soon as LeCroy finished, Lt. Marcy Anzio announced, "Point defense systems are hot. We have no target data for our primary weapons."

Commander Mueller activated her commlink. "All hands, this is the First Officer. Brace for impact. Repeat, brace for impact. Missiles inbound."

"Perez, emergency jump!" Ronin ordered, loudly. He was hoping their jump drives were ready.

Perez turned his head only slightly to respond while he thumbed the tab to fire the ship's sublight drive at full thrust. "Captain, jump drives are slow in spinning up for some reason. Maybe it's due to the gate transition? Inbound birds will arrive before then!" Perez didn't add that he was attempting to increase the ship's velocity and attempt some evasive maneuvering because he knew Ronin could already both hear and feel the obvious.

Despite *Cerberus*' newly improved gravity compensator using Solaran technology, the thrust from the sheer power in the ship's sublight drive was still starting to press everyone into their seats. The new gravity compensator improvement enabled *Cerberus* to accelerate much faster than it could prior to the original mission to the Lost Colony of Solara because it dramatically reduced the stress on both the ship's superstructure and on the crew members.

LeCroy kept an eye on Tacnet to see if the ship's sudden acceleration and maneuver would affect the missiles streaking their way. It only increased the time until impact a little bit. "Time until lead missile impact now 45 seconds. Missiles still accelerating hard. They're much faster than anything we have in our arsenal except jump bombs," announced LeCroy. "Our acceleration has increased the time until impact by a dozen seconds."

"If they're that fast, we have to assume they pack a punch corresponding to the level of tech in those engines," Mueller noted. The concern in her voice was clear.

"Releasing countermeasures. Missiles will enter *Cerberus*' firing solution in ten seconds. Counter batteries are hot and released to AI control. 112 inbounds in four waves," Anzio said. Her voice sounded grim, but at least the wall of harm from the inbound missiles was coming in waves rather than arriving all at once. The ship soon vibrated slightly from weapons fire.

From the outside, it seemed as if the black hull of *Cerberus* had suddenly lit up. In addition to the blinding brilliance emanating from the full thrust of the ship's sublight drives, bright dotted lines seemed to spring from her hull. The glowing lines represented both kinetic energy "bullets" fired from the gun batteries, and Shrikers from the anti-missile batteries. Invisible, short range disruptor beams lanced outwards towards the nearest of the missiles.

Dozens of small explosions bloomed in the near space outside their hull. The first wave had been quickly eliminated, although several missiles had nearly made contact with the ship.

"Wave one, eliminated. Wave two is…changing course?" LeCroy sounded confused as he reported what he was seeing on his screens. "Waves three and four now altering course to the same position as wave two. Waves are merging now."

"What are they doing?" Mueller wondered aloud.

Ronin glanced at Mueller worriedly. "Wave one was sacrificed to test our defenses, and we proved we could stop it. Now they'll try to overwhelm our defenses with a much larger cloud of hurt coming our way."

LeCroy added to that thought. "Combined missile cloud is inbound again, 84 birds in this group. Coming at us from all points of the compass. Revised ETA is one minute, 17 seconds."

Ronin looked at Perez. "Lieutenant Perez, how soon until we have the jump drives spun up?"

Perez shook his head. "We don't have that much time. Jump drives will be back up in one minute, forty-nine seconds."

Ronin's expression was grave. "Jump us out as soon as they're online. Don't wait for any further orders from me."

Perez nodded. "Aye aye, Captain. I have emergency jump coordinates preselected now." He didn't add that he hoped they would still be around long enough to actually use their jump drive.

"Captain! Scans returning a possible ship. Range, 6…" Delacroix suddenly said loudly when Ronin interrupted him.

"Lieutenant Anzio, target that vessel and launch jump bombs at it!"

Ronin didn't have to repeat himself as Anzio was happy to have a target to shoot at. "Jump bombs away!" Anzio said, which was both an update and a confirmation that Captain Ronin's order was carried out.

Delacroix kept his eyes glued to his scanning screens and his fingers crossed that their return fire would work.

CHAPTER 5

JUMP GATE DEFENSE POINT

PYTOR THE GREAT

135 DAYS UNTIL IMPACT

"First wave destroyed, Comrade-Captain. We nearly overwhelmed that ship's defenses with it, so our missile's artificial intelligences combined the remaining three waves for the next run at them." Cmdr. Kuznetsova didn't look away from his screens as he reported to Petrov. There was too much information to process to waste time on unnecessary courtesies like looking at a person right now.

Comrade-Captain Petrov nodded and glanced towards Comrade-Recruit Gusev. She noticed his gaze and reported what she had learned from her scans. "Comrade-Captain, the enemy defensive and drive systems are rather primitive. We are not reading any form of shielding other than hull plating and some sort of energy-neutralizing, black hull coating. Their acceleration seems weak, as does its maneuvering capabilities and their scanning. Much of their point defense was by a combination of kinetic energy slugs and extremely short range disruptor rays."

Petrov's eyebrows suddenly furrowed in disbelief because he couldn't believe what he was hearing. First it was the dark matter, now it seemed this unidentified vessel was equipped with even more ancient technologies than he thought possible in the modern age.

"Are you sure?" Petrov asked Gusev.

The incredulity in his voice now caused Commander Kuznetsova to look away from his screens for a moment. Petrov returned Kuznetsova's startled look. "It's a mismatch. Kind of like a three-masted schooner taking on a guided missile cruiser," Kuznetsova muttered, but loud enough for the bridge to hear. Petrov was shaking his head in disbelief.

Kuznetsova's station suddenly beeped an alarm and he looked back at his screen. "They've finally seen us. Enemy missile launches detected. Three inbounds. Acceleration is…rather slow, actually," Kuznetsova dryly noted. He glanced over to confirm *Pytor the Great's* defensive systems had gone fully active. "Our shields are up and defensive counter batteries are hot."

Petrov nodded in acknowledgment. Moments later, Kuznetsova suddenly leaned closer to one of his screens as another alarm began bleeping. "Enemy missiles have disappeared from our scopes!" he nearly shouted.

Just then, *Pytor the Great* shuddered from a near-simultaneous, triple hammer blow. The lights went out on the bridge while sparks showered from several shattered screens and relays.

Decompression alarms began sounding throughout the interior darkness aboard *Pytor the Great*.

CHAPTER 6

SHOTS FIRED

CERBERUS

135 DAYS UNTIL IMPACT

"Impact!" Lieutenant LeCroy said loudly. He didn't have time to look away from his screens as Tacnet was tracking the storm of harm headed their way in the form of a cloud of missiles streaking towards them from every direction.

"Telemetry indicates all three jump bombs detonated, but only one actually reached the enemy vessel. The other two were broken up by some sort of shield or something. It wasn't registering on our scans until the first two bombs detonated and breached it for the third bomb." Just as LeCroy reported this, *Cerberus* began vibrating slightly as its point defense systems went hot again.

"Thirty seconds! Our jump drive field is reforming now," Lieutenant Perez yelled. He was eyeing a countdown timer he had set at his station.

Ronin nodded. He didn't bother to ask about refocusing the ship's jump drive fields into a frontal shield to protect the ship since death was approaching from everywhere.

In a matter of seconds, dozens of explosions erupted all around the space near *Cerberus* as the point defense systems did their job. The explosions quickly began occurring ever nearer as the sheer number of missiles began to overwhelm *Cerberus'* ability to keep them back.

Green lights suddenly replaced red and yellow lights on a portion of Perez's screen and he thumbed the command to jump the ship. He wasn't quite quick enough. The ship shuddered from multiple impacts just as the jump drive sent the ship to the coordinates selected by Perez.

Alarms were blaring aboard *Cerberus* so Perez had to yell again. "Jump complete, Captain. The jump drive is still spun up so we can jump again if need be," he said, checking his instruments as he did so.

"Damage report," Ronin ordered as he stood up from his command seat and walked over to Delacroix.

"Multiple impacts near sickbay, Captain. I'm not registering much physical damage from them," Delacroix responded as Ronin arrived at his scanning station.

Ronin looked at Lt. Maria Delgado, who was busy managing the incoming flow of communications to the bridge. "Lieutenant Delgado, away the damage control parties to the impact sites." Ronin didn't order any security to accompany them because he figured it was unlikely that the missiles carried anything but an explosive payload based on their attack profile.

Ronin and Delacroix looked at each other. "Why aren't we more damaged?" Ronin wondered aloud. Mueller had joined them by now as well.

Delacroix shrugged and pointed to his screens. "We'll know in a minute when a damage control party arrives. The way those birds flew, it seems pretty clear they weren't just kinetic energy weapons."

Mueller raised her right eyebrow. "Lots of conjecture goes into guessing the motives of an enemy we don't know anything about," she said quietly.

Both Delacroix and Ronin nodded. They could guess all they wanted to about what happened and why they were attacked, but without more context those guesses wouldn't be reliable.

Ronin's commlink chimed with a direct message. "Ronin here," he said after thumbing it open.

"Captain, this is Chief Lazarus. Engine room and main drives are undamaged."

With that, Ronin's eyebrow now rose questioningly. "Chief, why was our jump drive inoperable after the gate transition?"

Ronin could almost see the shrug by Lazarus on the audio commlink. "I dunno, Captain. I don't have an explanation for that. I don't even have a theory about it, either, so we'll be looking into it ASAP. They were spun up when we entered the gate, and completely shut down when we exited. It was like someone turned off a switch."

"Acknowledged. Ronin out."

Delgado turned to look at Ronin. "Captain, casualty reports are in. No deaths, only minor injuries to a dozen crew."

Mueller and Ronin looked at one another. "This day just keeps getting weirder and weirder," Mueller said quietly.

Ronin nodded. Something was definitely off.

Delacroix suddenly bent closer to study his screens. Both Ronin and Mueller noticed his intent look.

"What is it, Lieutenant?" Mueller asked.

With a somewhat confused look on his face, Delacroix cast the video feed he had on his screen to a larger screen. "Commander, take a look at this. The two missiles which penetrated the hull near sickbay failed to detonate and are in relatively good shape, considering they just slammed through our hull."

The live video showed one of the now-arrived damage control parties cautiously examining the missile. They were wearing exosuits to protect them from the vacuum of space until the missile could be removed and the hull patched so the damaged compartment could be resealed.

"Captain, the damage control parties have called in the ship's armorers. It appears both missiles were duds. Scanners are showing a live payload on one of them, but it appears the detonator was faulty. The other missile's payload is inert. It's dead," Delacroix said. His look of confusion began to increase. "Analysis of the live payload suggests the explosive is a form of antimatter."

At the mention of antimatter, every head on the bridge suddenly turned to look at Delacroix in surprise, and more than a little fear.

The ship's protocol officer, Dr. Winston Wright, who up until now had quietly watched the battle unfolding from an out of the way position on the back of the bridge, rolled his eyes in exasperation. "C'mon!" he said, drawing the word out in annoyance. "Everybody knows antimatter isn't real!"

Up until then, the rest of the bridge crew had been unaware of the man's presence and too busy to notice that Wright had graciously gone to the bridge to make himself available to oversee establishing friendly relations with any aliens they might encounter after the jump.

Ronin turned his head and side-eyed Wright, who was standing off to his left. His facial expression darkening into a mask of concern, Ronin didn't say a word as he very slowly shook his head slightly to indicate Wright was dead wrong.

Wright caught Ronin's look, then stammered, "It isn't real. Is it? How can that be?" Wright paled at the shocking realization that *Cerberus* had nearly been erased from existence. It did not help Wright's mood that their demise would have been from a super weapon that shouldn't even exist, and they had no idea who was shooting at them.

CHAPTER 7

DAMAGE ASSESSMENT

PYTOR THE GREAT

135 DAYS UNTIL IMPACT

"**D**amage report!" Petrov yelled. As he inhaled the smoke drifting through the bridge, he broke out coughing. The only response was a weak coughing from the other side of the compartment.

Petrov pulled himself to his feet from where he had been thrown and looked around while the fog inside his head cleared. As he started becoming more aware of his surroundings, Petrov suddenly realized the ship's gravity system was still operational. *So, there's that,* Petrov thought to himself as he stumbled around checking on his crew members. Comrade-Recruit Gusev was still strapped into her seat, but her eyes were closed and her head lolled. Petrov placed two fingers on her neck, checking for a pulse. It was weak, but steady.

Next, Petrov looked at two technicians who normally occupied stations near the entrance to the bridge. Petrov didn't bother with them beyond a glance. Not because he didn't care, but because it was obvious there was no point in checking. One was facing away from Petrov while strapped into her seat and slumped down with her head folded to the right. Judging from the impossible angle of her neck, she was already gone. The other was a male technician. It didn't take a medical degree to assess the man's health status as he had been impaled by a long piece of debris through the center of his chest. His sightless stare told of a violent, painful end.

Movement caught Petrov's eye, as a hand suddenly reached up over a crash seat and pulled its owner up into view. It was Kuznetsova.

Kuznetsova blinked away some of the wooziness in his face and dabbed at the blood running down the side of his head. Shrugging off the injury, his eyes met Petrov's eyes for a moment. There was fear there, but Kuznetsova's training took over and he lurched forward to get closer to the scanning station as there was one screen there that somehow had remained operational. The others had been shattered.

Petrov left Gusev in her seat for now as she was securely strapped in and safe for the moment, and continued his sweep of the bridge crew while Kuznetsova tried to figure out what was still working on the ship. All the others were dead.

Kuznetsova's voice interrupted the eerie quiet on the bridge. "Comrade-Captain, damage control crews are beginning repairs to critical ship systems. Replacement bridge crew are on their way here, as are graves personal to collect the corpses. The medical unit is reporting mass casualties. Many dead and severely injured. Numbers will follow after the counts have been made."

Petrov nodded to acknowledge Kuznetsova's report and the act made Petrov woozy because of his concussion. "What happened?" Petrov asked.

Kuznetsova shook his head slightly. "Best I can tell, our shields recorded three impacts, all in the same location. The shield failed after the second strike, which cleared the way for the third. And Comrade-Captain…" Kuznetsova paused for a moment, "Whatever hit was moving incredibly fast. The enemy ship has also disappeared."

"Theories?" Petrov prompted. They needed something to work with, and there wasn't much to go on.

"Enemy missiles are my theory. They launched three, which appeared to be accelerating at a slow rate until they suddenly vanished off our scans. We were then hit by three objects that were moving impossibly fast. That can't be a coincidence. We don't know how they went from the relatively slow speeds they were at initially to the high speed at impact that fast. And to cover the distance that fast, our scans suggest they were traveling at FTL speeds upon impact."

Petrov's eyebrows rose as he tilted his head forward towards Kuznetsova in disbelief. "You're thinking we were hit by faster-than-light missiles? Without them being affected by relativity? How is that possible?"

Kuznetsova shrugged and he shook his head slightly. "I have no answers, Comrade-Captain. The enemy ship seems to be a strange mix of primitive and ancient technology, paired with some inexplicably advanced weaponry. In boxing terms, what appeared to be a feather-weight amateur unexpectedly packed the punch of a heavyweight pro-fessional. The enemy ship appeared to vanish the same way as did their missiles. Presumably it, too, went to FTL speeds."

"And now they're loose in our star system. Who are these people?" Petrov asked.

No one had any answers to that question.

BOMB SQUAD

CERBERUS

134 DAYS UNTIL IMPACT

"How do we know we can safely transport the payload?" Delacroix asked without taking his eyes from the screens in front of him at his scanning station.

"We don't," replied Lt. Kristoff Alphonso, who was standing slightly to the side and behind Delacroix. The unusually terse assessment from Alphonso caused Delacroix to look directly at him now. The closest thing to a mad scientist on board *Cerberus*, Alphonso ran the ship's Fabrication section along with his staff of mad scientists.

Alphonso just shrugged. "Neither the Confederation nor our former Collective adversaries had measurable success in creating enough antimatter to study it because of its extreme volatility. Based on precious few surviving records, we know it exists, it blows up with amazing force, and that's about all."

Ronin overhead the end of the conversation as he approached the two of them, so he added his thoughts. "Our working theory here is if the high speed impact didn't trigger the weapon's payloads, we're probably safe enough to move them. And it's not like we have a lot of choice. We can't just fly around this system with a couple of holes in the hull and unsecured antimatter missiles rolling around the interior."

Expressed that way, Ronin's logic was irrefutable, but Delacroix wasn't exactly pleased with Ronin's explanation. "How many kilotons of explosive force are in those birds?" he asked.

Alphonso shrugged again. "Best we can do is extrapolate based on those fragmentary scientific records. And it wouldn't be kilotons. It would be megatons. Possibly as many as ten megatons."

Delacroix's eyes bugged out. "Megatons!" he said, louder than he should.

Ronin half-smiled, but there was no humor in his expression. "Enough explosive power to end *Cerberus* and reduce the ship to its component atoms."

Delacroix swallowed hard and tilted his head to the side slightly as he shook his head. His lips had formed a colorless straight line while he did so. He decided to change the subject. "Captain, I was reviewing our scanning data about the missile exchange. Both myself and our AI concur that only one jump bomb impacted with the target."

Ronin's eyebrows shot up in surprise, for he had assumed the initial assessment about some sort of shield was in error. "Are you still thinking there was something in the way?" he asked.

"That's where it gets interesting. Both detonated at precisely the same distance from the ship's hull, and they were consecutive impacts at the same site instead of concurrent hits," Delacroix said.

"How 'precisely' are we talking?" Ronin followed up.

Delacroix responded, "To the millimeter."

Cerberus' AI startled them when it unexpectedly joined the conversation. "Captain, as you are already thinking, the chances of that ship's point defense system shooting down two jump bombs at exactly the same distance are extremely remote, to say the least. My scans also detected a secondary energy distortion near the hull after each detonation. Almost like a ripple in a pond. Notably, the ripple after the second detonation was significantly larger before it suddenly collapsed."

"You're also thinking that ship had some sort of defensive shields?" Ronin asked. He had to know as it could be very important.

"Yessir, that we are," Delacroix said, casually drawling together the "yes" and "sir" into one word, as was commonly done among the ship's crew. "It's the most likely explanation that we've got so far."

"A working jump gate. One that's guarded by a hostile, highly advanced warship with antimatter missiles and defensive shields. Neither of which we have. And they're on their home turf, while we don't yet know what we don't know. This just keeps getting better and better," Ronin said ruefully. He looked over at Delacroix for a moment, who was busy at the tactical station. "You better bring Lieutenant LeCroy up to speed on these shields so he has some time to devise solutions based on our data."

Delacroix nodded. "Yessir, I was just about to send it to him."

"Have we figured out where we are yet?" Ronin asked.

"Interstellar-wise, or in this system?" Delacroix asked in response.

"Interstellar-wise," Ronin clarified.

"Yessir. We're a VERY long way from home. Again. This system is located well outside the Baidam constellation by over 200 light years. A totally different interstellar neighborhood than where Solara and Terra Station are," Delacroix stated.

"Unless we can use that jump gate, it's going to be a long ride home," Alphonso noted.

Before he could continue, Ronin's collar commlink node chimed. "Ronin here," he said after opening the commlink.

"Captain, the armorers believe they have secured the missile payloads, and the damage control crews are moving into position to effect repairs," said Mueller. She was down near where the missiles had entered the ship to keep a close eye on the situation.

"Acknowledged. Thank you, Commander," Ronin said, and Mueller closed the commlink.

Alphonso had a faraway look on his face as he was thinking hard. Both Delacroix and Ronin noticed.

"What's on your mind, Lieutenant?" Ronin asked.

Alphonso looked directly at Ronin. "Captain, I'd like to study the live antimatter payload to see if we can learn its secrets."

Ronin's eyebrows slowly rose in a mix of surprise and disbelief. "That's a BIG ask, Lieutenant!" It seemed sensibly prudent to question the sanity of anyone who wanted to keep an enemy missile's antimatter payload on board.

Alphonso was not deterred. "Yessir, I know. But this could be a once-in-a-lifetime opportunity for the Confederacy to learn about antimatter. And I believe we can study it in a completely safe manner."

Ronin thought about it for a few moments. Alphonso had a very good point. They might never have this chance again.

"Granted, Lieutenant. Don't make me regret this," Ronin finally said.

Alphonso smiled sardonically, tilting his head to the side slightly as he did so. "No worries, Captain. If this goes sideways, it'll end us so quickly we won't know what happened."

Now it was Ronin's turn to flash a grin. "True enough." His eyes flicked back to Delacroix after Alphonso saluted and left for Fabrication. "What have your scans told us about this system?"

"So far, a fair amount. It's a relatively empty system, with a slightly redder sun than Earth's. And if we stick around for another 134 days, we'll have front row seats to the collision of both the system's planets into one another," Delacroix reported.

"Walk me through it," Ronin ordered.

Delacroix had expected the command. "We've observed the system has two planets of comparable size located in the temperate zone that would support human life. One obviously has an atmosphere and is a blue and white planet with large bodies of water. The other is in an unstable orbit and appears to be a dead rock with very little atmosphere or water. We ran the numbers on the unstable orbit to try to sort out the story there. Get this, the orbit only became unstable between 750 and 775 years ago," said Delacroix, pausing to let the implications of that particular window of historical significance sink in.

It definitely sunk in as Ronin's eyebrows shot up in surprise. "A planet's orbit on the far side of a guarded jump gate suddenly becoming unstable during The Fall? That's way too many things for this to just be a big coincidence. Assuming whoever attacked *Cerberus* can detect our jumps, how long until they would see our jump flare from our arrival at this location?"

"A bit over six months as Perez jumped us slightly outside the system, and assuming there isn't anyone closer than our initial attacker. Are you thinking of designating this spot as Foxtrot Station?" asked Delacroix, referring to the Confederate Navy's convention of designating fixed locations outside a system from which to conduct reconnaissance flight operations and long-range scouting of a star system.

Ronin nodded imperceptibly, more of a slight tilt of his head to the side. "Maybe. But we don't have much time for long-range scouting before the system becomes a mess of broken planetary pieces. Do you have enough scanning data to pick a Dixie Station instead?"

Ronin didn't need to explain that Dixie Station was the Navy's designation of a fixed location inside a system to basically serve the same function as a Foxtrot Station, plus possible combat operations. The difference was that one was outside a star system, the other much closer.

Delacroix nodded. "Yesssir, we can designate both. I suggest we keep this position designated Foxtrot if any of our scouts or *Cerberus* need a place outside the system to run to, in case we have to abandon a Dixie station. And I can designate multiple Dixie Stations if you like."

Ronin was satisfied with that answer. "Let's do it. Designate Dixie Alpha and Beta. If both those have to be abandoned, then all forces fall back to Foxtrot. Once we've finished repairs and securing the missile payloads, we'll jump to Dixie Alpha."

Ronin then opened a commlink to the ship's air group CAG. "Lieutenant Sunderland, this is Captain Ronin. I have a job opportunity for you."

"Sunderland here, Captain. Skulking or shooting?"

Ronin snorted. "Skulking. In light of our hostile reception, we're going to designate Dixie Alpha and Beta, and a Foxtrot Station. Lieutenant Delacroix will send you his scan data on this system. We have a serious time crunch here as the system's two planets will collide in 134 days. Get your Bulldogs ready to recon a hostile system from Dixie Alpha and they need to be prepared to jump to Beta or Foxtrot if trouble appears. I want to know more about these two planets, and get some long-range observations of the jump gate."

"Very well, Captain. We'll be ready," Sunderland replied.

"Ronin out."

CHAPTER 9

SCOUTING

BULLDOG 3

130 DAYS UNTIL IMPACT

"Jump complete. We're in the pipe, five by five," announced Pilot Officer Antonio Russo over the command commlink in his slightly accented speech. Russo and all the passengers were buttoned up in their exosuits as a precaution.

Chief Michael Jonsey, the rearseater in Bulldog 3, didn't even glance towards the cockpit where Russo was when he replied in his exceptionally deep voice, "As my mama used to say back in Yazoo City, don't jinx us by saying stuff like that."

Jonsey's eyes were locked onto his screens as he surveyed the incoming information from their passive scanning. "We're receiving telemetry from the drones we seeded in orbit."

"Sweet baby Jesus, NEVER say everything is hunky dory right away! You'll put a hex on the whole damn mission!" thundered Bravo 1, GySgt. Brett Mackey over the command commlink. Confederate Marines were a superstitious lot, and the gunnery sergeant certainly was that.

Because of the similarity of their accents, it was obvious both Mackey and Jonsey were from a region of North America that was referred to as the Old South. They had only recently discovered why it was even called that. Like so much of their history, the reason had long been lost due to The Fall, when civilization collapsed as a result of a terrible war and a plague over 750 years earlier. The historical records that had survived on the Lost Colonies of Terra Station and Solara were just now being used to fill in the gaps.

"All right, all right. Duly noted!" Russo replied. He didn't bother to hide his amusement.

They fell silent for a while as they gathered data. Mackey glanced at the other three Marines. Each of them was highly experienced, and all prudently appeared to be sleeping. If things went sideways, Marines never knew when they could catch some sleep, so they were getting what sleep they could right now.

Russo broke the silence after about an hour. "Ugly planet. All sorts of scars are visible on the surface like it had repeatedly been hammered by meteors. You can see the ejecta blankets from orbit. It's very dark and foreboding, much like your taste in women, Gunny."

Even though Mackey's grin wasn't visible beneath his visor, he was certainly up to the task of responding. "At least my girlfriends aren't inflatable like yours."

Jonsey's deep, booming laugh filled their ears. "Inflatable! I don't care who you are, that's funny right there." His voice suddenly turned serious, which killed their banter. "I'm getting a bad vibe from these scans."

Russo's humor had vanished as he clicked on. "How bad?" Marines weren't the only superstitious people onboard this Bulldog.

"Preliminary scans indicate this planet once had a breathable atmosphere and sizable landmasses and oceans. There's evidence there once was life all over down there." Chief Jonsey's voice died down as he leaned forward to peer intently at his screen.

"Gunny, Russo, look at this!" Jonsey exclaimed as he cast the video feed to Russo's screen in the cockpit and Mackey's visor.

They sat in stunned silence, watching the video feed from the drone Jonsey had taken direct control over. Skyscrapers were clearly visible in the gloom. As the drone neared the skyscrapers, it became obvious they were seeing the ruins of a major metropolis. The dark superstructures of several of the tall buildings jutted skywards like the exposed skeletons of corpses that had been left in the sun for too long.

"This planet was once heavily populated," Jonsey said quietly, stating the perfectly obvious.

Mackey shook off the reverie. "Chief, is it safe to land down there?" he asked.

Jonsey shrugged. "Whatever blasted the place happened long ago. Our scans suggest the ejecta blankets from the impacts have been there for centuries because there aren't any dust clouds still floating around down there. We also aren't reading any unusual radiation or other energy signatures. That's the best I can tell you." Jonsey didn't explicitly say it, but the tone of his voice made it pretty clear that he preferred Jonsey's Bulldog to remain in orbit.

Mackey refused to take Jonsey's hint. "What do you think, Mr. Russo? Can you drop us off somewhere downtown for a few hours?"

Russo was already figuring out that very thing. "I believe I can, yes. But you be ready for extraction in two hours. We'll survey this position and wait for your call when you kids are done with play time."

Nodding, Mackey said, "Good. We'll activate a recall beacon. If we run into trouble," he said, pausing for a moment, "we'll run from it if we can. If we can't and the balloon drops, we'll try to shoot our way out of trouble."

Russo nodded and steered towards the city center where there appeared to be a large rectangle without buildings. "See this area without buildings? Let's call this Central Park. Arrival is in five minutes, so get ready. Departure from the same location unless you call for an alternate extraction location."

"Acceptable. Five minutes, departure or alternative," Mackey confirmed. He switched over to a common commlink for the Marines to brief them now that they had awoken. "Marines, gear up! We're landing in a ruined downtown in five minutes. That's one minute for each finger on your hand for those of you who can't count. The area looks long dead, but keep your heads on a swivel and keep alert for crumbling walls, floors, and anything else that might bring some hurt. This is a scouting mission, not a combat drop. If we encounter hostile forces, don't engage if you can evade instead. Questions?"

"How are we gonna tell if we find something important or not, Bravo 1?" asked Bravo 4, Pvt. Carlos Guthrey. His voice clearly indicated it was a serious question and that he wasn't being a smart ass right then.

Mackey privately was wondering the same thing. What were they looking for? "If it gives us clues as to who the residents were, or what happened to them, grab it or take pictures or something depending upon what it is. Use your judgment and send video of any objects to me if need be," he ordered. Despite the vagueness of the order, it would have to do. He didn't know how he could get more specific.

Even though they were buttoned up in their black exosuits, the other Marines traded glances anyway. There were a few shrugs in response.

There were no other questions.

CHAPTER 10

TASTE OF FREEDOM

PYTOR THE GREAT

130 DAYS UNTIL IMPACT

"**R**epairs are on schedule, Comrade-Captain. We've restored essential ship's functions, and will finish major patching within three days," reported Gretski. Even through the ancient video screen at his desk, Gretski's grease and sweat-stained face showed the strain of working around the clock to make the ship ready.

Sitting in his office, Petrov was likewise exhausted. The entire crew was. They had been scrambling to both repair their ship and stay on guard against that mysterious vessel which had somehow activated a jump gate which had otherwise lain dormant for centuries. That same vessel then survived a huge salvo of antimatter missiles which should have turned it into dust. Instead, the mystery ship threw a hard counterpunch at *Pytor the Great* and then simply vanished.

"What about our connection to Perun?" he asked. He scarcely dared breathe the name of the all-powerful AI that ran Forrestal.

"It's as gone as free vodka on shore leave, Comrade-Captain. It permanently severed our link to Perun far more thoroughly than we ever could have. We're unquestionably on our own now." Gretski's voice did not conceal his amazement that the connection he'd been trying to figure out how to disable so they could wrest *Pytor the Great* away from the control of the AI named Perun had just been blown away in combat. "The entire section of the ship where the Perun's uplinks and downlinks resided was destroyed from the enemy missile," added Gretski.

Along with over two hundred of our crew, thought Petrov. He didn't need to say that part out loud, though. Gretski's engineering crews had been uncovering bodies, or parts of them, for days as they went about making repairs.

"The enemy counterfire appears to have been a blessing in disguise, then. The last data Perun received was that we engaged with an unknown ship, which somehow transited the jump gate, and we took heavy damage before dropping off the grid entirely. Perun has to assume this ship was destroyed," Petrov said instead. "We're a ghost ship now," he added.

"Aye, Comrade-Captain. Once we finish repairs and get underway again, we can move ahead with our plans to rescue our families instead of following Perun's orders to guard the jump gate," Gretski noted.

"Agreed. I would like to have possessed the command and control of *Pytor the Great* to make first contact with the ship that came through the gate instead of firing upon it like Perun ordered. I have Kuznetsova working on a second contact plan to establish peaceful communications with them if we encounter them again. That's ship's ability to transit the gate and travel at FTL speeds may be the only way out of this system after the End of Days," Petrov noted.

"I hope he comes up with something good. Hard to imagine they'll be open to sitting down and sharing some vodka while we get acquainted after we tried to blow them out of the skies," Gretski commented wryly.

Petrov snorted softly. "Agreed. But now that we've suddenly gotten our freedom weeks earlier than when we hoped we would, we need to make friends now and that ship is the only game in town. Petrov out."

After closing the video connection to Gretski, Petrov leaned back into his seat at his desk and closed his eyes for a few seconds. His office was dimly lit at the moment, offering a brief respite from the stress beyond its door. Petrov's thoughts were worrisome.

Where is that other ship? And who are they? he wondered.

CITY OF THE DEAD

BULLDOG 3

130 DAYS UNTIL IMPACT

Mackey and the other Marines quickly ran down the rear ramp of Bulldog 3 and bounded forward to the nearest cover of a fountain located in a huge plaza surrounded by tall buildings and the remains of a crumbled statute next to the fountain.

"Bravo 1, Bravo 5. No movement. No threats on Tacnet. Awaiting orders," reported Bravo 5, Pvt. Terry Allison, in his Alabama accent. He was crouching near the bridge with a Buzzsaw rifle in his hands. Allison was using the cover instead of pointing his Buzzsaw downrange in search of targets since they weren't here to engage in a firefight.

Allison cranked up the optical resolution on his exosuit's visor as he briefly surveyed the surroundings from behind the cover. Mackey was likewise looking around while Bulldog 3 lifted off and departed. Their surveying was done with one quick look, and then they replayed the video they had taken with their look about while they remained behind cover.

Mackey's gaze was suddenly drawn to one of the tall buildings surrounding the plaza with the fountain. There was clearly an entrance on the ground floor facing them. It was dark inside the building, and he could just make out many shattered windows leading into the gloomy interior. His gaze swept upwards, noting dozens of floors of shattered exterior windows that did nothing to hide the foreboding gloom that seemed to emanate from the interior. Mackey then looked at the other buildings around the plaza. They were crumbling and seemed to be in even worse shape.

Mackey made up his mind and spoke over the commlink. "Bravo, I got a feeling our best bet is to investigate that building over there with the visible ground floor entrance. We can egress through the building exterior if we need to get out quick."

"Bravo 1, this is 5. I'll take point," Allison said by way of reply. Acknowledgment clicks from the others answered for them.

Mackey nodded for Allison to lead the way, and the rest of them trailed behind, quickly moving between scattered bits of rubble and other bits of cover along with way. They covered the distance to the entrance quickly. Nothing moved except the Marines and small bits of dust stirred up by their passage.

After a slight pause at the shattered door at the entrance, Allison's voice over the commlink broke the silence that had settled over them. "Bravo 1, this is 5. I'm entering the building," Allison reported.

Seconds later, Allison's voice again filled the team commlink while the rest of them entered the building behind him. "Dark, creepy building in the middle of a ghost town on a doomed planet. Marines without adult supervision. Lots of guns. Any of this seem familiar?" His exosuit video was streaming live to the rest of the team following him.

Mackey grinned inside his inky black exosuit. "This is the part where the scary aliens jump out and bite our faces off, isn't it?" he remarked dryly.

"That's affirm, Bravo 1," Allison replied. The tension in his voice eased somewhat with the joking around.

They moved further inside the building, passing badly scorched walls and the remains of furniture that looked like it had been made for humans. The main floor had a central hallway that led to a large chamber towards the rear of the building. Allison stopped for a moment as he was passing through a doorway that bisected the hallway, and he activated his light to shine on the doorway.

"Bravo 1, Bravo 5. I'm passing through a doorway in the central hallway that I swear is made out of bars," Allison reported.

"Bravo 5, this is 1. Bars of what? Gold or something?" Mackey asked.

"Negative, Bravo 1. Bars, like the kind of cages they lock you up in after the local sheriff has had enough of your crap on shore leave," said Allison. "I'm continuing on," he added.

Seconds later the rest of the Marines reached the bars while Allison moved forward again with his weapon raised. As he entered the large chamber, the hairs on his arms rose in alarm. It was two stories high, thirty yards long, and forty yards wide. There was a row of offices on the left, and long counter running along the right side. Scorch marks were everywhere as if a firestorm had quickly passed through. Some of the glass partitions on top of the counter still remained because they had melted into place instead of being shattered like the glass everywhere else in the large room.

As they entered, the Marines looked in every direction, pointing their weapons as they did so even there obviously wasn't anything to actually point them at. All of them noticed their arm hairs and hackles raising from the ghostly chamber.

"This place is as dead as my love life," Allison said, still looking around over the sights of his weapon.

"Bravo 5, your love life makes this place seem like a crowded night club," Mackey snorted. None of them were looking at each other as they wondered where to start. Mackey noticed a heavy door made of thick metal that was set on a massive hinge on the right side. It was located behind the counter in the far corner.

"Bravo 5, is that a blast door down there in the corner?" Mackey asked, seeing that Allison was closer to it.

Allison turned around to look at where Mackey was motioning. "Sure looks like it, Bravo 1. I'll check it out."

Allison reached the thick metal door in seconds. "The door is open just enough for someone to slip through it. Looks like the firestorm that blew through here didn't penetrate inside. You want I should look in there, Bravo 1?"

"That's affirm, Bravo 5. And watch out for face-eating aliens," Mackey responded.

Allison slipped past the entrance and stepped into a windowless room that was pitch black inside and poorly illuminated by his visor's starlight enhancement. He turned on his exterior exosuit light and looked around. There were hundreds of identical metal drawers, all locked into place. "Ah, I may not be a rich man yet, Bravo 1, but this looks like a bank vault in here. Little metal drawers, a few tables with privacy dividers, and a skeleton in a uniform."

"Wait one, Bravo 5," Mackey quickly replayed the visor feed from Allison's exosuit inside his own suit's visor screen. "That skeleton looks human," he commented.

Allison bent down over the skeleton to take a better look. "That's affirmative. Think we ought to take a few bones back with us?" he asked.

"Affirmative. Grab a couple, and the skull while you're at it. We'll give them to Doc Taketa to run some tests on," Mackey said as he slipped inside the vault.

Allison glanced over at Mackey and shrugged. "What else should we be looking for while we're here?" he asked.

"Let's break into some of these drawers here. See if there's something in them that might tell us where we are," Mackey said over the commlink. "The rest of you start looking around for anything that might indicate what planet this is."

A small chorus of affirmatives and clicks acknowledged his order.

Mackey and Allison began using the strength of their exosuits to tear out drawer after drawer. They quickly looked inside each one to verify whether the contents had survived whatever calamity had befallen this world. Most of the contents had been reduced to ash, but they found several pieces of jewelry with diamonds in settings, and a small rectangular box. It was locked. Suddenly Mackey froze after brushing some soot from the top of the box's diamond-like black exterior.

Allison noticed Mackey had stopped moving. "What's wrong?"

"There's lettering on top of this container. And it's in American," Mackey replied.

"WHAT?" Allison exclaimed.

"It says, Fireproof Personal Safe," Mackey replied. His voice rose, somewhat in panic.

"Boss, we need to take that back with us. And these gemstones," Allison noted.

Allison sensed Mackey's confusion about the diamonds, which weren't valuable in the Confederation, due to their easy availability—the Confederation had the ability to manufacture diamonds as well as mine for them. "Boss, I was reading about pre-Fall gemstone practices," Allison explained. "They used to place micro marks on them for identification and to help determine their value," he added.

Mackey couldn't help tilting his head somewhat to the side in his surprise. "YOU can read?" he quipped.

"Cripes, don't tell anyone!" Allison said. His body language clearly said he didn't want that little secret to get out.

"Next thing you're going to tell me is that you can do the maths, too," Mackey noted, deliberately mangling the syntax of the sentence. Then he turned serious, saying "All right. Let's grab what we got and bail outta here. We're running out of time." Mackey kept to himself the feeling that his skin was crawling from poking around what seemed to be a giant mausoleum.

CHAPTER 12

SHIPYARDS

FORRESTAL SHIPYARDS

130 DAYS UNTIL IMPACT

Sparks were flying as man and machine were busy as far as the foreman's eyes could see. Gregor Diski liked to start his days in his office next to the massive control room at the business end of the orbital shipyard. From the window in his office, he could see dozens of ships that were nearing completion. It gave him a feeling of accomplishment. A feeling that he had done something to help save his people. Some of them, at least.

"Surveying your domain, Gregor?" asked a friendly voice behind him. The blues and greens of the surface of Forrestal could be seen beyond the shipyard's edge.

Startled, Diski turned to look at his friend who was leaning against the open doorway. "Aye, Nikolai. Just thinking about our priorities for the day. Shut the door, would you?"

Nikolai Ollo forced a wan smile. They were both exhausted.

"These are the last ships that will join the Grand Fleet, yes?" Ollo asked. He knew the answer, but asked anyway to keep Diski's mind busy.

"Yes, you know that as well as I do, Nikolai. But see over here," Diski said, motioning with his hand to direct Ollo's attention to one particular hull under construction. "See this unusual hull?" Diski's voice started showing some signs of life despite his fatigue and despair.

Ollo looked in the indicated direction. "What kind of hull is that? Why is it so small?" he asked as he approached the window and got his first look at what Diski was talking about.

Although they'd been building identical, ponderous-looking evacuation ships one after another for the past several years, Diski was pointing to a much smaller hull mixed in with the evacuation ships. It was sleek and built for speed. It also featured multiple launch tubes like the warship that it was.

Suddenly recognizing the type of hull, Ollo was confused. "Why are we building a warship for the navy now? I thought all our resources were devoted to evacuation ship building?"

"That ship will carry Perun and some of the leading families away before the End of Days," Diski replied calmly.

Ollo looked stunned, then horrified. "I … I shouldn't know such things!" he finally stammered.

Diski rolled his eyes slightly. "Relax. Perun has no eyes or ears in here."

"You're sure about that?" Ollo asked, fear still coloring his voice. Perun was everywhere, and stories of retribution being carried out against careless citizens were well known.

"Actually, yes, I'm quite sure. And Perun isn't going to waste resources to make us disappear with the End of Days so near," Diski replied. He turned his attention back to the window.

Ollo's expression began to look confused again as he also looked out of the window. "So, why build a warship now? Who is Perun trying to protect?"

Diski shrugged. "I've been asking the same questions since we started building that hull. I don't like the answers I keep coming up with."

Glancing over at Diski, Ollo asked, "What answers?"

A pensive expression came over Diski's face, as his blue eyes suddenly looked sad. "There is no enemy out there to guard against that we know of. Not since the ancient war shut down the jump gate. And Celestra is extinct. That leaves one possible answer. This warship is meant to guard its passengers against our own people."

Shaking his head slightly, Ollo murmured "Unless we can find some-place to go, even that ship won't have to worry about us all that long."

Diski nodded slightly. All this effort would only buy their people a few more months of life before the Grand Fleet began to run out of breathable air, food, and water.

CHAPTER 13

CELESTRA

ABOARD CERBERUS

130 DAYS UNTIL IMPACT

"What did they find on their scouting mission to the planet?" Ronin asked, from his seat in the ship's conference room near the bridge.

Lt. Adolph Gustav shrugged slightly. "I dunno for sure. A ghost town. A relic or two. Their message was pretty cryptic," he responded.

Mueller looked thoughtful. "And they're sure this ghost town is on the dead planet that's on a collision course?"

Gustav nodded. "Yes, they're sure. Bulldog 3 was to scout that planet only. Other Bulldogs were disbursed throughout the system, but that planet was Bulldog 3's sole objective."

A few moments later Mackey entered the conference room and saluted. The gunnery sergeant was still wearing his exosuit, but his helmet had been removed and he was holding a small, rectangular box which had a diamond-like black exterior.

"Report, Gunnery Sergeant," said Gustav.

"Yessir. This is a BLUF report," said Mackey, knowing that everyone in the room knew BLUF stood for Bottom Line Up Front. "We scouted the second planet in the system. Scans determined it had once been habitable. Atmosphere, surface water, ecosystems. All gone. Something stripped away all that centuries ago. We also located a major city."

Eyebrows that had been already raised suddenly shot higher at learning the ghost town was something more than some outpost. "A city?"

Dr. Wright asked. He had slipped into the room behind Mackey and was taking his seat.

"Yessir, that's correct. We scouted the ruins of a major metropolis and scans found several other metros on the surface after that. Skyscrapers. Parks. Buildings like you'd expect to find on Earth. The works. All destroyed by a cataclysm of fire and impact craters."

Ronin glanced at Mueller briefly before speaking. "Sounds like you're attributing human characteristics to an alien city."

Mackey nodded his head to the side slightly. "Perhaps not as alien as you'd think, Captain. I retrieved this box from a facility that gave the impression it was a bank with a vault. The writing on top is in American and clearly says, Fireproof Personal Safe."

Mackey handed Ronin the box as he spoke. Wright, Ronin and Mueller studied it closely.

Mueller began speaking first. "Doesn't that look just like…" she began.

Ronin finished the thought. "Just like the protective hull skin on *Cerberus*." He touched the commlink node on his collar. "Lieutenant Alphonso, this is Captain Ronin."

The response was immediate. "Go for Alphonso."

"Lieutenant, the Marines on the Bulldog 3 mission brought back some sort of relic I'd like you to look at. We think its exterior coating is similar to the ship's diamond black metal skin."

Alphonso didn't reply for a few seconds while he checked Ronin's location using the node, and for a moment Capt. Ronin thought the commlink might have been closed. Then he heard Alphonso's response, "Captain, I'll be right there."

After Ronin nodded towards Mackey, the gunnery sergeant continued his BLUF report from where he left off. "We were scouting for materials which might indicate which planet this was, looking for evidence as to who the population was, and so on. We did locate a skeleton which certainly appeared human, and retrieved a skull and a few bones for analysis. We…"

Alphonso burst into the conference room with two of his techs in tow. The three of them came to a sudden halt when they spotted the small box on the table. Nodding to his companions, Alphonso ordered, "Run your scans."

Raising his hand, Ronin motioned for Mackey to stop and grab a seat while Alphonso took over. They didn't have to wait long.

"Captain! You are correct. This is the substantially the same composition as the ship's diamond black metal skin. It's extremely heat resistant. I think we can even jigger the lock open if you'd like," Alphonso noted.

Nodding, Ronin indicated to proceed.

The lock on the box was no match for Alphonso, and within a minute the mechanism popped. Alphonso opened the lid, which was hinged from the inside. The box then revealed its secrets.

"Actual, yellowed papers and a small electronics device," Alphonso said. After handing the papers to Ronin, Alphonso returned his attention to the small device.

"I think this answers the question whether this was an alien colony," Ronin said as he read the ancient papers. "It's written in American."

"What's it say?" Wright asked, his curiosity already at a high level.

"It's a legal form. From the Celestra Colony Company. For valuable consideration, the Celestra Colony Company as Grantor hereby conveys and warrants to Allen McLanahan, as Grantee, real property on Celestra Colony, legally described as follows: One hundred acres, Block 7, Lots ten through fifteen, of the Second Planetary Survey," Ronin read. He looked up. "There's some other legalese in here about being signed before someone, etc."

They sat quietly for a few moments until Gustav finally broke the silence. "It's a land deed for Celestra Colony?" He didn't hide his surprise.

Nodding, Mueller's attention was suddenly drawn to a light that began shining in Alphonso's face.

"I've got it!" Alphonso said triumphantly. The entire face of the device had lit up.

"That thing works?" Mueller asked incredulously.

"It's charging based on ambient power in the area around it," Alphonso said, still peering at the screen. "It says to enter a password, PIN, or use facial recognition to open." He fiddled around with it further. "None of those worked since we don't have access to any of that information."

Before anyone could say a word, the voice of the ship's AI filled the room. "Lieutenant, may I ask you to hold the device still for a moment?"

Trading glances with Ronin and Mueller, Alphonso carefully set the device down on the table. Its screen was dark again. Nothing appeared to happen for several seconds until the screen lit up and they could see data rapidly scrolling on it.

"Scan complete. I have accessed the data on the device. It's a personal communication device whose function is similar to a commlink with a data screen." the AI said. The table's holo suddenly lit up. "I am streaming video recorded on the device to the holo now."

"Narrate what we're seeing, please," Ronin requested as he settled back into his seat to watch the show.

"There isn't much video or data on the device. It appears it was primarily intended to serve as storage for data about several different land transactions," the AI noted. "There is one internal folder with two videos that I recommend you see first as it does not pertain to selling land."

Without waiting for Ronin's response, the video began scrolling with the AI's voice narrating in the background. "We are watching the first video taken from the surface of the planet that Gunnery Sergeant Mackey and a detachment of Bravo team Marines explored. I have time-compressed the playback."

Everyone silently watched the video of a night sky from centuries ago. Every few seconds, a faint streak of light could be seen in the distance. Suddenly, there was a bright flash of light as seen from far away, followed by several more flashes. Ronin got a sinking feeling that he was watching a battle in orbit.

"Now I will magnify the images and replay those flashes in slow motion," the AI announced. The holo zoomed in until the slightly grainy image of an advanced warship in space could clearly be seen. Then the AI split the screen and showed another warship. The process quickly repeated itself several times until there were a half-dozen screens visible. The videos began playing forward, more slowly this time, and showed the moment of impact where a missile struck each vessel. The split-screen videos then were replaced by still pictures of each warship.

"As you can see from these video stills, we are looking at warships of two competing design philosophies," the AI noted. "There is also a video that explains the fate of the planet."

The holo shifted again. This time it was day, with a few wispy white clouds off to the left side of what was an otherwise brilliant, late afternoon blue sky that seemed to surround a large moon that was visible on the right side of the video. A strangely accented voice speaking American began narrating instead of the AI.

"The Collective refused to surrender and claims they'll use a Doomsday weapon to destroy Celestra. I just don't see how. Celestra wiped out the fleets controlled by their AI in orbit around Forrestal. We've won. And the closing of the jump gate has stopped reinforcements from arriving to save Forrestal. It's only a matter of..."

The unseen narrator was interrupted by a bright flash on the side of the visible moon. The video continued while the speaker remained silent before exclaiming in horror, "My God. The moon!"

The video had re-centered to place the moon in the middle of the image. Instead of the clear, white lunar image that can be seen rising before sunset from time to time, the new image was now mostly obscured. Several large chunks of the moon were visible where a whole moon had previously existed. The narrator spoke again.

"I...I don't know what's going to happen. I think the Collective just killed us all! Maybe that was the Doomsday weapon they threatened us with. I'm going to place this video into a vault for safekeeping. If you're watching this and I'm not there, remember us and what we fought for."

The playback ended after the narrator's last words. There was silence in the conference room while Ronin, Mueller, Mackey, Wright and Gustav processed what they had just seen. The incredible scale of the destruction had left them speechless.

The AI spoke first. "Captain, we witnessed an ancient record of the destruction of Celestra Colony by Forrestal Colony through the use of an antimatter weapon. The Fall did not spare this system, and we are facing a dangerous situation."

Ronin asked, "What's your evaluation of the dangers here?"

"The surviving colony in this system is Forrestal, and that colony was founded by the Collective. The destruction of Celestra's moon pushed Celestra into an unstable orbit that slowly brought it into a collision course with Forrestal, which will occur in 130 days. Most life on Forrestal will already be dead prior to impact due to the gravitational effects of both planets. And Forrestal is likely still run by an enemy AI that existed prior to The Fall," said the AI.

That last sentence concerned Ronin even more than the others. "Any sense of whether the Collective's AI poses a threat to you?"

The *Cerberus* AI seemed to ponder the question before answering. "I believe there will be a danger, especially if the level of technology for that AI exceeds our own. We currently lack sufficient data to do more than make educated guesses based on the information our Bulldog scouts are collecting."

Almost simultaneously as the AI made the reference to the Bulldogs, Ronin's commlink node chimed with an incoming commlink. He opened the channel.

"Ronin here."

The voice of the ship's CAG, Lt. Kelvin Sunderland, was clearly audible to the four of them. "Captain, this is Lieutenant Sunderland. Bulldog 1 has returned with one of Echo team's scouting elements. They're already on their way to your location."

Ronin raised his eyebrows in surprise. "They're back early, Lieutenant!"

"Aye, Captain. They found some answers for what's going on in this system," Sunderland said.

Moments later, there was a knock at the hatchway of the conference room that preceded the entrance of GySgt. Toshi Kanagawa and Bulldog 1's rearseater, Chief Hal Patterson.

Pvt. Jagr Bloodbane, one of the newest Marines on the ship, opened the hatchway. The young Ullrian private had joined the Marines and finished boot camp in record time so he could join the crew on *Cerberus*. Like all Ullrian youths from the 1.5G planet of Solara, he was exceptionally strong and agile. Also, like the other surviving young men from the warlike Ullrian Faction, he was an experienced combat veteran and slayer of a Hellcat. The Hellcat teeth dangling from a chain around his neck was proof of his deadly prowess.

Bloodbane snapped to attention along with Kanagawa and Patterson. After rendering salutes, Ronin motioned for them to sit. He couldn't help but notice that, despite his youth, Bloodbane's blue eyes were cold, like an experienced killer.

"Report," Ronin ordered. He didn't engage in idle chit-chat because the body language of Kanagawa and Bloodbane indicated they already were in "All Business Mode."

Kanagawa spoke first. "Captain, our Bulldog scouted the primary planet in this system. It's definitely populated, and is located in the Goldilocks Zone for habitation. We chanced a closer look and jumped into maximum orbit while keeping our FTL drive spun up for an emergency jump out. We were quickly detected and were forced to jump out again by an orbital defense net, but Bulldog 1 was able to acquire the intel that Chief Patterson is going to show you now."

While Kanagawa was speaking, Patterson had readied the feed to the table's holo unit. It suddenly showed a picture taken from high orbit of the planet that the Captain, Commander and Marine Lieutenant now knew to be Forrestal. There was also an object in orbit.

Patterson spoke for the first time. "As you can see here, Captain, there is a heavily guarded object in orbit around the planet. We weren't able to jump in for a closer look due to several security satellites that went into active scanning mode to acquire weapons lock on us. The good news is this picture was taken with ultra-high-resolution optics." As the Chief mentioned the hi-res optics, the picture zoomed in onto the orbiting object.

In orbit was the largest shipyard any of them had ever seen. "Captain, our brief glimpse of this shipyard yielded an educated guess of at least 110 hulls under construction, and probably a few more that are hidden from view at this angle."

Ronin stood up and walked closer to the holo to get a better look. Seconds passed in silence.

"Most, or all, of the visible hulls are of the same type," Ronin noted.

Patterson briefly looked startled. He hadn't realized they were all the same ship type in his haste to bring the intel here. "Yessir. Seeing as this planet is about to collide with the planet that Bulldog 3 scouted, we concluded this might be an evacuation fleet. Captain, we also detected this as well."

Patterson cast the next image to the holo and zoomed in. "We also found this fleet parked in outer orbit."

They were all startled when the AI spoke. "My analysis of this image confirms this fleet is of hulls that are identical to those being built in the orbiting shipyard."

Ronin's eyebrow rose at the unusual chattiness of his AI as he spoke. "My assumption is this is the rest of the evacuation fleet. If Forrestal has a decent-sized population, this fleet is far too tiny to save most of them," Ronin said.

Kanagawa, Patterson and Bloodbane were startled that Ronin already knew the name of the planet. as they hadn't been in the conference room during that earlier revelation.

"We can also make some other deductions from the existence of this fleet," Ronin continued.

Mueller was certainly curious to know what Ronin was thinking. "What deductions?" she asked.

Ronin smiled slightly, without humor. "Because that fleet appears to be preparing for a long journey in terms of travel time, so they must lack two important technologies. They have no FTL drives, nor do they have the ability to traverse a jump gate. They're stuck in this system, and we learned upon our arrival that their sensor tech is very advanced, and that their AI is hostile."

Heads nodded around the table. Ronin focused on his Marines, Lieutenant Gustav, and Gunnery Sergeants Kanagawa and Mackey. "Hard to say what's going to happen, but my sense is you should be prepared to deal with refugees. Both aboard *Cerberus*, and possibly aboard other vessels. Some of them will panic," added Ronin.

Gustav looked at Bloodbane, who thus far hadn't said anything. "Private, you're by far the most experienced with the Monoshields and

Monosabres. Are you up for training the rest of us in their use so we can do some crowd control if the need arises?"

Bloodbane nodded. "Yessir," he said, drawling the words together like the rest of the crew normally did. "I can teach the others the techniques used by Ullrians when they captured large numbers of slaves during raids. They'll work well for crowd control."

Mueller's face briefly betrayed some of her shock at Bloodbane's matter-of-fact mention of having participated in Ullrian slaving raids, but she quickly masked it with a neutral expression. The Confederacy vehemently prohibited slavery, and the Factions of Solara had finally ended the practice when Solara recently joined the Confederacy.

Gustav nodded. "Good. We've got work to do, and time is running out for the people in this system."

With a nod from Ronin, the Marines filed out of the conference room along with Patterson. Mueller then glanced at Ronin and Wright. Eyebrows raised, she said, "The casual mention of having engaged in slaver raids was a surprise."

Ronin nodded. "Indeed. The Navy is becoming even more of a cultural melting pot than we'd ever have imagined a few years ago." Ronin's face then turned thoughtful. "I'm thinking of sending a long range jump drone back to Earth to call in reinforcements while we continue to send Bulldog scouts into this system."

"Through the jump gate? It might still be guarded," Mueller noted.

"No. I'd use its jump drive to return and avoid the gate defenses. It'll be a long trip though," Ronin said, massively understating their distance from Earth by merely saying it's a "long trip."

Mueller nodded. "I agree. Those are good ideas. The situation in this system is volatile and rapidly deteriorating. We need more ships and information to deal with it."

"The problem is, once the drone has arrived, there is no guarantee of any ships being in the home system to get the message and return here in time," Capt. Ronin said. He was right. They had no way of knowing who might be around to help before the big show.

"Captain, I'm concerned about our assumption the denizens of Forrestal will be hostile to our arrival," Wright said. He had been uncharacteristically quiet until now, which both Ronin and Mueller had been thankful for. "We don't know what their thinking is, or what motivates them. Assumptions aren't our policy. They have the right for us to assume peaceful intent."

Ronin just looked at Wright for a few moments while he decided whether to engage civilly with the good doctor, or just cut him off at the knees. Sighing in disappointment because civility won, Ronin cocked an eyebrow. "Well, Doctor, when we're ambushed with antimatter missiles, I shoot the bastards. That's my policy."

Shaking his head, Wright pressed his point. "You established intent from *that*?"

Growing angry now at Wright's shockingly obtuse view of their earlier engagement, Ronin retorted in a gravelly voice, "When they hit *Cerberus* with antimatter missiles that should have blown us from the skies, I figure they weren't too interested in welcoming us to the neighborhood."

Savagely grinning at Ronin's blunt retort, Mueller snorted. "Irrefutable logic, *Doctor*. If they had been interested in making friends, they would have made a phone call instead of trying to light us up like that."

Wright pursed his lips in frustration. The two officers made good points, but he didn't have to like it. Wisely, he decided not to push the issue further.

CALM BEFORE THE STORM

ABOARD CERBERUS

128 DAYS UNTIL IMPACT

"**E**dward Ronin! Leave your sister alone!" said Frida Enginnsdottir. Her voice sounded annoyed, and the 15-year-old Edward Ronin couldn't resist Enginnsdottir. She had grabbed Edward by the wrist and pulled his hands away from Sarah to stop him from tormenting his sister. Enginnsdottir's 1.5G muscles ensured the skinny teenager couldn't resist.

Eddie burst into a huge, but mischievous, grin, as Sarah erupted into gales of laughter at the incident. It wasn't everyday that someone tried to get her to drink a cup of salt that looked like a cup of milk. Eddie was so busted, but he knew he'd get busted anyway. Eddie did it for the laughs.

As the three were roaring with laughter, the hatchway to the family's quarters opened for Dan Ronin. At the sound of all that laughing he looked up at his family, a half-smile quirking the corner of his mouth. "Normally the sound of laughter doesn't make me suspicious…unless it's you three. Then I KNOW something's up!" he said as Eddie paused to sip some water while unsuccessfully trying to look innocent.

Eddie forgot to completely stop chuckling first, so he slightly choked while trying to take a drink and it ended up spraying in the opposite direction. This just caused them to laugh even harder. It took a few minutes for them to settle down and for Eddie to clean up his mess.

"So what's the story on this system, Dad? Did the Bulldogs find anything?" Eddie asked as Dan sat down with them at the small table.

Dan looked thoughtful for a moment as he glanced at Eddie. "Well, it's a case of good news/bad news. The good news is we found the system with BOTH Celestra and Forrestal. The bad news is Celestra was destroyed during The Fall and it is on a collision course with Forrestal. The other bad news is that Celestra was a pre-Confederacy colony, and Forrestal was a colony of the old Asiatic Collective that was controlled by a hostile artificial intelligence which may still be running things."

Everyone's faces froze at Dan's summary of the situation. He continued on. "There's more bad news. The hostile AI only built a grossly inadequate evacuation fleet that has nowhere to go because they lack the tech. Our latest scouts have determined they have some superior pieces of technology, but don't have FTL or the ability to go through the jump gate."

Frida's eyebrows had shot up while she listened. Her black hair framed the pale skin of her face and matched the dark brown of her eyes as they looked incredulously back at her husband. "That's a lot more bad news than good," she remarked. "How long do those people have?" she asked.

Dan shook his head slightly while Eddie and Sarah looked intently at him. "Not long enough. Our AI says the planets will collide in 128 days, assuming the competing gravitational wells don't break them apart before then."

Sarah looked perplexed. "Dad, why don't we jump in to try to rescue them?"

Frida and Dan's eyes met as they traded a brief glance. "Remember the hot reception when we arrived through the gate? The AI controlling things here isn't too friendly, and seems to have excellent scanners that easily can detect us. We've also been met by aggression every time any of our Bulldogs get too close. And our own AI isn't sure whether attempting to talk is a good idea, which is an assessment I agree with."

Frida just shook her head. It was a bad situation that they found themselves in.

The conversation continued on for a few more minutes before the kids left to go see some of their friends in other compartments. After they left, Frida looked at Dan and said, "You'll need to be extra careful for this mission." She wrapped an arm around her husband as they stood in the small kitchenette.

Nodding slightly, Dan replied in a very somber voice. "Yeah. This is a pretty scary situation we're in. No matter what we do or don't do, a lot of people are going to die."

"There's more lives at stake than you realize," Frida said simply. Her voice had taken on a very different tone.

Dan's right eyebrow rose as he processed Frida's last remark. "Are you saying what I think you're saying?"

"Yes," Frida said simply, as Dan pulled her tighter within his arms. The stakes had just shot up from Dan's perspective.

CHAPTER 15

BREAKAWAY

PYTOR THE GREAT

120 DAYS UNTIL IMPACT

"We're being hailed, Comrade-Captain. Perun is requesting system access to the ship," announced Gusev. Her voice betrayed her nervousness at what they were attempting to do.

"Disregard communication," ordered Petrov. Other than white knuckles gripping the hand rests on his chair on the command bridge, Petrov betrayed no other signs of stress.

Minutes passed in tense silence, broken up only by the sounds of the ancient ship as it maneuvered itself into orbit around Forrestal. It was night down on the surface below them. Few lights were visible because this was a sparsely populated side of the planet. Finally, an alarm beeped at Gusev's station.

"Captain, the shuttles are launching from the surface now. ETA is 20 minutes," Gusev said. Dozens of surface to orbit shuttles were launching from a huge, remote forest where they'd been hidden to await the arrival of *Pytor the Great*.

Kuznetsova's excited voice interrupted Gusev. "Orbital gunboats are diverting and approaching our location on an intercept course. They are broadcasting a hostile challenge and ID." He was keeping a sharp eye on the threat board.

With a nod, Petrov indicated that Kuznetsova was to transmit their pre-recorded message to the gunboats. Petrov had expected some opposition.

Per Petrov's prearranged orders, the reply message also had been pushed onto the speakers in the command bridge. The message was filled with static and intentionally garbled. "This is the *Pytor the Great*. We have [static] damaged [static] assistance. Do you read us?"

Kuznetsova was still glued to the threat board. "They're within weapons range now. Shields dropping." He was hushed by the incoming message from the gunboats.

"*Pytor the Great*. You are not authorized for the orbital exclusion zone and are ordered to submit to inspection under the authority of Perun. Do you comply?" said the unidentified voice from one of the gunboats.

Petrov's expression turned angry. "They're trying to determine if we're actually damaged as badly as we've made it seem and are wondering why the ship went to the exclusion zone instead of a shipyard. Guide them into an auto-landing pattern, and blow them out of the sky when they get too close to escape," he ordered.

Kuznetsova relayed the landing instructions to the gunboats, which took several attempts because he and Gusev randomly kept spiking the gain on the static filter to drown out his voice. Professional as the gunboat captain was, there was no mistaking the sound of irritation as he finally managed to decipher the instructions and confirm their receipt.

More minutes passed when Kuznetsova suddenly exclaimed, "Initiating firing sequence for the secondary batteries now. They haven't seen it yet!" Seconds passed, then he yelled, "Targets destroyed!"

"Did they get a warning off before they were knocked down?" Petrov asked. There had been three gunboats, so it was unlikely they would have destroyed all of them before a warning was sent.

Kuznetsova shook his head. "If they did, it was on a secure frequency to Perun that we couldn't detect. We'll know…" he was saying before interrupting himself. "Hold on. I'm reading an All Forces Alert! It's being broadcast to every unit in the system. Perun is advising that *Pytor the Great* has been captured and is ordering any available unit to shoot us down on sight!"

Petrov sighed. They had anticipated this and had timed their arrival to coincide with the largest gap in coverage window for the planetary defense network, but he had hoped for a larger time window in which to act. "There's our answer. How soon can the nearest units reach our position?"

Kuznetsova hadn't torn his eyes from the ship's threat board. "It is somewhat less than we predicted. The window closes in 45 minutes as the nearest gunboats are well beyond the planetary horizon, and the surface on this side of the planet has no defensive systems. The first shuttles arrive in 8 minutes. All the shuttles should be aboard within 20 minutes."

A 25-minute escape window was too short for Petrov's comfort. "Then we will go with the first alternative plan. Advise the shuttles we are moving the ship to increase the distance the enemy force must cross, and the shuttles will have to make combat landings on the ship while we are accelerating."

Kuznetsova nodded and sent the message to the fleeing shuttles. There was no artificial interference now that he had dropped the pretense of damage to *Pytor the Great's* communications array.

As the ship broke orbit and began to accelerate along a preset course that had been given to the shuttles in advance, Gusev updated the times for the bridge crew. "Shuttles begin arriving in 75 minutes. Final shuttles to be aboard in 95 minutes. Enemy units will not arrive until…165 minutes!" Her voice clearly communicated her excitement that they had gained that much additional lead over the incoming warships by having charted a course that diverged from their path more than it impacted the shuttles from the surface.

Petrov nodded in acknowledgment. His impassive face hid his discomfort at how naturally both he and his crew had accepted Petrov's labeling of their own people's ships as an "enemy force." Once they destroyed the first gunboats, that die had been cast. They were openly in rebellion now.

The bridge fell silent as they minutes passed, the somber crew lost in their own thoughts while they performed functions required by their duty stations. Petrov couldn't help but notice the pit in his stomach as he worried whether they'd be able to pull this off. There were so many unknowns that could stop it, so it was fitting that his current mood matched the darkness cast by the planetary shadow. *Pytor the Great* wouldn't be able to hide in the shadows much longer now that they were accelerating out of orbit.

CHAPTER 16

A TIME FOR CHOOSING

CERBERUS

120 DAYS UNTIL IMPACT

"Captain, incoming commlink from Bulldog 8. They've detected the ship that fired on us back at the jump gate. It's entering orbit around Forrestal in the area we thought was an exclusion zone," said Delgado from the Communications station." Bulldog 8 was the new replacement for Bulldog 7, which had been destroyed in the Solaran system in an ambush by the Ullrian ship named *Warspite*.

Ronin andMueller exchanged brief glances. "Perhaps our conclusions about that side of the planet being an exclusionary zone weren't correct?" Mueller asked, somewhat rhetorically. They had been observing and tracking orbital traffic patterns of the planetary defense network for a couple of days.

"Lieutenant Delgado, tell Bulldog 8 to maintain observation and report any developments," Ronin ordered.

Delgado responded with a nod, saying "Aye, Captain." Then she passed the orders along to Bulldog 8's crew.

With a tilting nod towards LeCroy at the Tactical station, Ronin indicated for Mueller to join him there. They walked over.

"Lieutenant, what does your gut say about this ship going where no one else has been allowed?" Ronin asked LeCroy.

LeCroy leaned back in his seat as he thought a moment, breathing in a breath and slowly exhaling it. Furrowing his eyebrows, he said, "Captain, I'm thinking this ship decided to break some serious rules. I'm thinking they went off the reservation because it left its post guarding the jump gate and traveled all the way here, only to enter orbit where no one else has been permitted. Something's changed, but I don't have enough information to make a solid guess as to what."

Nodding, Ronin answered that guess for LeCroy. "My working theory is this ship figured out a way to break the control of the AI in this system, and has gone rogue."

Mueller looked thoughtful. "Rogue ships are pretty dangerous. Wouldn't we want to stay far from this ship?"

Nonplussed, Ronin answered her question. "Not if they've gone rogue to rescue their families."

LeCroy and Mueller looked surprised. "How do we know they intend to effect a rescue?" LeCroy asked.

Before Ronin could respond, Delgado interrupted with another incoming message from Bulldog 8. "Captain, Bulldog 8 reports orbiting ships from the defense network are diverting to intercept, and that dozens of shuttles are launching from the planetary surface."

Ronin, Mueller and LeCroy all looked at one another. "What's going on? Is it the rescue you guessed would happen?" LeCroy asked.

Looking at Tacnet, Ronin noticed the smaller orbital defense ships would arrive first. "My gut says we are looking at two groups of vessels who are both racing to reach the big ship in orbit first, and that only one group knows for sure whether the big ship has switched its allegiance."

Mueller was quick on the uptake. "That 'group in the know' has to be the shuttles from the surface! They're launching with no other place to go, unlike the gunboats already in orbit, and they lack the means to remain in space for long before their resources will be exhausted."

LeCroy looked at her quizzically so Mueller explained the rest of her thinking to get him caught up. "There also isn't any reason for those two smaller ships from the defense network to approach the larger ship other than for security purposes. They're too small to be helpful if the larger ship needs aid and the shuttles from the surface will arrive soon afterward anyway."

LeCroy nodded in understanding and finished connecting the dots. "And a cloud of shuttles arriving almost en masse probably wouldn't be a resupply run because they'd get in each other's way and it would be terribly inefficient compared to docking the ship at their shipyard on the other side of the planet."

That wasn't all. Ronin noted, "This is all occurring over the unpopulated side of the planet while it's nighttime at exactly the same moment the defense network ships are furthest away from their current position in orbit. There are too many coincidences for this to all happen by chance. We're watching a jailbreak and rescue mission." His voice hardened as he said this.

A Tacnet warning bleeped at LeCroy's station. "Captain, the bigger ship just destroyed the ships from the defense net!" LeCroy announced. "They've engaged main drives, and are slowly pulling out of orbit. Shuttles from the surface are still gaining on them."

Mueller keyed on the change in Ronin's tone. "What do you want to do?" A decision had been made, and she had a feeling she knew what it was.

Ronin looked at Tacnet, then at her. "They're running now to buy time, but letting those shuttles catch up so they're all fleeing something we haven't seen yet. Designate the large ship as 'Ship Alpha.' Let's go make some new friends if we can."

Ronin turned to walk purposely over to his command chair on the bridge. As he sat down and Mueller took her seat, Ronin issued decidedly new orders in a loud, commanding voice. "Lieutenant Perez, plot a jump to a point close enough where we can communicate with Ship Alpha. Also plot addition micro-jumps to defend them against possible pursuit and to jump *Cerberus* away from danger."

Perez nodded and turned back to his instruments, saying "Aye aye, Captain." Seconds later, he reported, "Jumps laid in."

"Sound Action Stations." Ronin ordered. The muted alarm began calling the crew to their combat posts.

"All stations report manned and ready for action, Captain," reported LeCroy shortly thereafter. The sound of the alarm faded away a few seconds later.

Ronin thumbed open a commlink. "All hands, this is the Captain. We're about to jump into a possible combat and potential rescue situation near Forrestal's orbit. Be prepared to endure emergency micro-jumps if necessary. Ronin out." Closing the commlink, Capt. Ronin looked to the helm. "Lieutenant Perez, jump the ship," he ordered.

"Aye, Captain, jumping the ship in three. Two. One. Jump!" Perez announced.

Cerberus vanished with just a tiny jump flare.

CHAPTER 17

NOT THEIR FIRST RODEO

PYTOR THE GREAT

120 DAYS UNTIL IMPACT

"First shuttles arriving now, Comrade-Captain," said Gusev, tilting her head only slightly towards Petrov as she spoke because she couldn't spare the time to look away from the display screen at her station. She was too busy to be scared or to watch the main view screen.

Kuznetsova was standing next to Petrov, who was still sitting in chair. Leaning over slightly and speaking in just over a whisper, he said to Petrov, "Simultaneous shuttle landings has never been tried before, Leonid." Kuznetsova couldn't take his eyes from the image on the main view screen.

Nodding, Petrov glanced at Kuznetsova. Although he was sitting on a starship's bridge, his gray-streaked beard and the wizened wrinkles around his gray eyes made Petrov look like a throwback to the weathered sailing ship captains of several millennia earlier. That image was only enhanced by Petrov's gravelly voice, when he snorted a reply. "Igor, we've never even simulated it before."

Humorlessly half-smiling, Kuznetsova nodded slightly and returned to his post. Minutes later, a small alarm clamored for his attention. "Missile launch from the next round of approaching gunboats. They timed their long-distance strike to arrive during the window when we are most vulnerable. Inbound missiles will arrive a few minutes before the last shuttle," he said dryly.

While attempting to land a shuttle was hazardous at the best of times and required straight and level flight from *Pytor the Great*, attempting simultaneous multiple shuttle landings under combat conditions was beyond reckless. It was also their only chance to save their families and escape before it was too late.

No one said anything, but the sadness in their expressions and body language spoke volumes. None of them were going to make it out of this alive.

Seconds later, a different alarm clamored for Kuznetsova's attention. "Proximity alarm! A large ship has appeared off our port bow. Instruments are reading the presence of dark matter!"

Petrov shot up from his command chair and quickly stepped over to Kuznetsova's station. "Where did they come from?" Petrov asked. The ship's sudden reappearance couldn't have happened at a worse time, and their scanning instruments should have given them plenty of advance warning. Now they were nearly trapped between the incoming missiles and this ship.

"I don't know. They just appeared out of nowhere. Should I launch a missile salvo? That ship matches the configuration of the one that appeared at the jump gate," Kuznetsova asked.

They were interrupted by Gusev. "Comrade-Captain! We're being hailed by that new ship."

Petrov's and Kuznetsova's heads both turned to look at Gusev with incredulous looks on their faces. At least the new ship wasn't shooting first and asking questions later. Trading glances with Kuznetsova, Petrov shrugged and simply said, "On speaker." Under his breath, Petrov then muttered so only Kuznetsova could hear, "Not like we have much to lose now." Kuznetsova nodded slightly in agreement.

The bridge speakers came to life, with a human sounding voice speaking an unintelligible language. "This is Captain Dan Ronin of the Confederate Naval ship *Cerberus*. Can we assist you in some way?"

Confused by the gibberish, Petrov barked "What did he say? Run that through the translation program!"

✲✲✲

"Captain Ronin, I will begin live-translation between that language and American. It is one of the known languages of the old Collective from before The Fall," announced the *Cerberus* AI over the bridge speakers.

Nonplussed, Ronin spoke again. Based on their observations the past couple weeks, Ronin had been expecting they would need to translate once a particular language had been identified. And the *Cerberus* AI could easily translate into natural speech that sounded like a human speaking.

"This is Captain Dan Ronin of the Confederate Naval Ship *Cerberus*. We are now translating our communications into your language. Can we assist you in some way?"

Long seconds passed with no reply.

***

Petrov's and Kuznetsova's eyes grew wide when the gibberish on their speaker suddenly turned into an oddly-accented, human-sounding voice which they could now understand. Kuznetsova motioned to mute their bridge microphones, then he looked at Petrov. "It's an unknown AI translating into our language," he said to Petrov. "Our translation program hasn't even gotten started on the translation yet."

Nodding, Petrov suddenly had an idea. "Igor, is that ship large enough to divert some of our incoming shuttles to?"

Surprised, Kuznetsova thought for a few moments. Nodding in return, Kuznetsova said, "Yes. It's certainly large enough, but they would need to confirm that since we don't know much about their capabilities or design. And based on their acceleration profile back at the jump gate, they'll never be able to outrun the missiles."

Motioning to unmute the microphones, Petrov waited until they were live again before speaking. "This is Comrade-Captain Leonid Petrov of the *Pytor the Great*. My sincerest apologies for the live-fire incident when first we met at the jump gate as our vessel was still under control of a hostile AI on the surface of the colony. Your ship's missiles severed that connection when you damaged our ship, and we are now free to act independently. We would be most appreciative if you could land some of the incoming shuttles of refugees and our families so we can have a chance at escaping before the missiles from the gun boats arrive. Does your ship have that capacity and can it outrun those missiles?"

Tense, Petrov and Kuznetsova waited for a reply.

***

"Is he telling the truth?" Mueller asked no one in particular.

Shrugging, Ronin glanced at her. "I suspect that he is. If he isn't, why would they allow potential family members aboard *Cerberus* when we could simply treat them as hostages?" As he said this, his eyes flicked over to where Wright had positioned himself.

Nodding slightly to Ronin, Wright silently signaled his agreement with Ronin's interpretation.

"Captain, we can just barely land about half of those remaining birds and jump away before those missiles arrive," Delacroix said from his scanning station. Both Ronin and Mueller looked at him, nodding.

Ronin made his decision. "We need to try. We're looking at the greatest catastrophe and loss of life since The Fall. Rescuing a few hundred won't have a huge impact on that outcome, but even saving these few will be something." He thumbed his commlink node at his neck. "Lieutenant Gustav, this is the Captain."

"Gustav here, Captain."

"Lieutenant, we're going to attempt to rescue refugees arriving from some incoming shuttles and jump away before a wall of harm arrives. Make sure your Marines are in their exosuits and ready for crowd control aboard the ship. Tie into the ship's AI to translate communications into their language," Ronin ordered.

"Aye, Captain. I'm on it. Gustav out." Gustav didn't waste Ronin's time telling him that the Marines donned their exosuits already because the ship was headed into combat.

Ronin motioned to Delgado with a head nod, and she reopened the commlink to *Pytor the Great*. "Comrade-Captain Petrov, we can land half of your remaining shuttles and still depart within a reasonable safety margin. Those missiles won't be able to catch this ship. Can you send us the navigational frequency for them so we can guide them into our landing bays? And where should we rendezvous?"

The response from *Pytor the Great* was nearly instantaneous.

"Captain, we're sending that data over right now. Based on the acceleration profile we saw at the jump gate, we'll await your arrival at the rendezvous coordinates. Your ship appeared to be much slower. I sincerely hope you factored in the need to depart early enough to evade the missiles," said Petrov.

Snorting softly, Mueller looked at Ronin. Speaking too softly for the commlink mic to pick up she said, "Won't he be surprised, then."

Smiling slightly at Mueller's comment, Ronin nodded and spoke aloud. "Thank you, Comrade-Captain. We did factor that in, although you might be surprised by our capabilities. When your ship is ready, just depart for the rendezvous and don't wait around for us. We'll catch up. Ronin out."

Before Ronin could say anything, Delacroix spoke first. "Captain, scans indicate half of the remaining shuttles are diverting towards *Cerberus*. They'll arrive after the last shuttles to *Pytor the Great* because we're further away."

"Thank you, Lieutenant." Looking over at LeCroy at the tactical station, Capt. Ronin then ordered, "Lieutenant LeCroy, put a dual countdown timer on our screens. One for the arrival of the last shuttle, the other for the incoming missiles. And designate the rendezvous coordinates as…Point Luck."

Looking around at his busy bridge crew, Ronin determined that no further orders were necessary. Trading glances with Mueller, he muttered softly, "Now we wait."

CHAPTER 18

CUTTING IT CLOSE

CERBERUS

120 DAYS UNTIL IMPACT

Their world had narrowed down to a fast-paced cycle of landings and preparing to receive the next landings. That cycle was finally drawing to a close.

"Captain, message from *Pytor the Great*. They've landed their shuttles and are departing for the rendezvous coordinates," said Delgado.

"Acknowledged. We'll join them after we land the last shuttles, Lieutenant," Ronin replied.

As Delgado passed Ronin's response to *Pytor the Great*, Capt. Ronin looked at Perez at the helm. "Lieutenant Perez, engine status?" he asked.

"Engines are spun up and my board is green. We're ready to jump," Perez answered.

Thumbing his commlink node, Ronin checked on the refugees. "Lieutenant Gustav, report."

Gustav was obviously buttoned up inside his exosuit because there wasn't any background noise. "This is Lieutenant Gustav. Refugees are being offloaded as they arrive and processed into temporary quarters in the ship's mess and part of the hangar bay. Count so far is 500-plus."

"Acknowledged. Ronin out." Switching to another commlink, Ronin used the CAG's call sign when he connected to Lieutenant Sunderland.

"Archangel, report," Ronin ordered.

Unlike Gustav, Sunderland was not in an exosuit. There was a lot of background noise. "This is Archangel. I'm in the hangar bay. It's getting crowded in here. Captain, we've secured the arrived shuttles, but I'd like permission to dump these excess birds as soon as possible."

Surprised, Ronin asked, "Dump them? Why?"

Sunderland had been expecting the question. "Captain, we need the space for flight operations, and for warehousing all these people. And because the shuttles are junk."

"Junk?" Ronin asked.

"Yessir, they're junk. They were thrown together as cheaply as possible to make them just barely flight worthy. I'm pretty sure they were only intended to make it through a one-way trip before being discarded," Sunderland said.

Ronin thought that made sense now. "Acknowledged. We'll start getting rid of them after we jump to safety. Ronin out."

LeCroy nearly interrupted the report from Sunderland. "Captain! Tacnet shows missile inbounds have suddenly accelerated and reoriented on *Cerberus*. Updated attack profile has them arriving before the last two shuttles."

Ronin's face paled slightly as many of the bridge crew stole glances at him. *Do we stand and fight for the last shuttles? Or do we run and condemn the passengers on the last shuttles to certain death?* Ronin wondered to himself.

"LeCroy, how many inbounds are there again?" Ronin asked.

"Hundreds. We're facing another missile cloud, Captain," LeCroy answered. The bridge crew had gone very quiet to listen to them.

"We can't fight that many while we're busy holding still enough to land those shuttles," Ronin noted. "Can we reverse the order of the final four shuttles? Jump to the tail end shuttles to land them, and jump back to land the two we skipped over?"

LeCroy quickly ran the numbers at his station, and frowned. "No, sir. There's just not enough time to do both," he reported.

Sighing slightly, Ronin made the only decision he could. "Then we don't have a choice. Lieutenant Perez, jump the ship to the rendezvous coordinates after the last pair of shuttles we can safely bring aboard. We can't risk being here when those missiles arrive."

Rather than risk the destruction of *Cerberus*, they had to abandon dozens of refugees. Innocent men, women and children would die, and there wasn't anything the crew of *Cerberus* could do about it.

"Aye-aye, Captain," acknowledged Perez somberly. The bridge remained quiet.

The silence was soon broken by Delacroix. "Updating our count now. Final shuttles arriving in one minute."

"Acknowledged," said Mueller. The terse expression on her face revealed some of the tension she was feeling inside.

They didn't have long to wait. "Shuttles aboard. Missiles arriving in 65 seconds," LeCroy announced loudly.

"Lieutenant Perez, execute jump," ordered Ronin.

Perez nodded. "Aye, Captain. Executing jump in three. Two. One. Jump!" His finger pressed the button on his screen as soon as he finished the countdown.

With a tiny jump flare, *Cerberus* vanished, leaving a pair of shuttles filled with desperate refugees behind to their doom.

CHAPTER 19

RENDEZVOUS

POINT LUCK

110 DAYS UNTIL IMPACT

"We're arriving at the rendezvous coordinates in a few hours. Still no sign of *Cerberus*?" asked Petrov. He was on the bridge and standing behind his command chair. As he often did, Petrov's arms were folded as he leaned on the back of the chair.

"Negative, Comrade-Captain. We lost sight of them because our acceleration flare blinded our instruments as we left orbit. The only thing we know is the missiles from the orbital gunboats destroyed something. Could have been *Cerberus*, could have been some shuttles. We couldn't gain more data than that about the impacts," said Gusev.

She was still reviewing what tactical data their ship had acquired from the escape, but there wasn't much of it. Nothing *Pytor the Great* carried could see through their main drive's acceleration flare. It was the one blind spot in their sensor 'net, yet all the action had taken place right in that blind spot.

Petrov snorted. "Could have been both *Cerberus* and the shuttles, too."

Gusev merely tilted her head to acknowledge the grim probability of Petrov's statement.

Eyes flicking over to land on Kuznetsova, Petrov furrowed his eyebrows for a moment. "Status of our guests, Commander?" he asked. The tone of his voice made it an order.

Kuznetsova had been busy with just that very thing the past ten days since their escape from Forrestal. "Supplies of water and food are better than planned for because we only took on about 60% of the total we were expecting. Breathable atmosphere is slowly degrading, but it is well within the parameters we anticipated for the same reason. Making a ship's manifest listing the refugees is now complete. I've forwarded the manifest to your tablet for review."

Petrov winced at Kuznetsova's use of the word "refugees." "Commander, seeing as we just are as much refugees as they are, I'm thinking a better way to refer to them is as our guests. Don't you agree?" Petrov kept his voice low, and friendly-sounding. They had all been pushed to their limits for a long time.

Kuznetsova nodded slightly, his tired eyes suddenly showing his weariness. "Yes, Comrade-Captain. I agree. My apologies."

Petrov's face softened. "Mine too, Igor. We're all exhausted, and we still have a long road ahead."

They were interrupted by Gusev. "Comrade-Captain, we're being hailed by a tight message laser. It's the *Cerberus!*"

Exchanging glances with Kuznetsova, Petrov muttered "It seems they survived." Looking over at Gusev, Petrov asked, "How far behind us are they?"

Gusev shook her head. "They aren't, Comrade-Captain. They say *Cerberus* is already waiting for us at the rendezvous coordinates."

Petrov and Kuznetsova exchanged shocked looks now. "AHEAD of us, you say?" Kuznetsova asked in a perplexed tone of voice. His eyebrows had shot up.

Before Gusev could respond to Kuznetsova, Petrov ordered "Put them on speaker, Comrade-Recruit Gusev."

"This is Comrade-Captain Petrov, how did *Cerberus* arrive ahead of us?"

The reply was immediate. "Captain Ronin here. Welcome to Point Luck, Comrade-Captain."

Petrov looked confused for a moment. "Point Luck?"

"We dubbed these rendezvous coordinates 'Point Luck.' We were able to rescue all but the last two shuttles before the missile cloud arrived. I'm profoundly sorry we could not do more," Ronin replied.

A fleeting look of sadness crossed Petrov's face. "Thank you, Captain Ronin. Rescuing everyone was a long shot at the best of times. Once those gunboats appeared, the odds went heavily against us. You didn't answer my question. How did you get ahead of us?"

"*Cerberus* has a faster than light jump drive, Comrade-Captain. Your ship is faster in sublight travel, but ours can travel between stars," Ronin said in a matter-of-fact tone. "We are going to transmit a passenger manifest now. Comrade-Captain, now that we're here, where are we going?"

"Thank you for the manifest, Captain Ronin. We are sending the coordinates for our destination now." Petrov motioned to Gusev to send the new coordinates as he said so. "You should be receiving them now. We are going to a hollowed out asteroid on the rim of the system that our families have been preparing in secret for over a decade. We named it the Enclave. You and your ship will be most welcome."

"Comrade-Captain, I have also been asked to pass along a personal message. It's from your wife and daughters. They're safely aboard *Cerberus*."

Relief flooded Petrov's face. "Would you permit me to call them?"

"Of course. You can even come over and visit, or transport them to *Pytor the Great* if you like," Capt. Ronin answered.

Petrov looked at Kuznetsova, who shook his head and spoke too softly for the microphone. "Comrade-Captain, our shuttle hangars are full. We don't have any room to launch or land anything until we can offload."

Petrov then spoke up so the microphone could pick it up. "My first officer says we can't launch or receive shuttles until we create some room in our hangars, so I will have to settle for calling until our arrival in about two weeks. Will *Cerberus* stay with us throughout the trip?"

Ronin had been expecting that question. "Sort of. *Cerberus* will jump ahead and disembark our guests, then rejoin *Pytor the Great*. We just aren't carrying sufficient supplies of water and food to accommodate this many people."

Petrov nodded his head slightly. "That makes sense. We were just discussing our own supply situation when you contacted us. Where is *Cerberus*, anyway? Our scans aren't picking you up yet."

"*Cerberus* is both far away and running silent at the moment, which is why you can't spot the ship yet. We set up a message relay system using drones, because *Pytor the Great* is still far enough away for our ships to experience communication beam degradation. *Cerberus* is ready for departure, Comrade-Captain. We are going to shove off after you speak to your family, and will rejoin *Pytor the Great* soon. Ronin out."

After the message laser stopped, Kuznetsova traded glances with Gusev and Petrov. Kuznetsova spoke first. "The varying levels of technology aboard *Cerberus* defies explanation. And we didn't ask where that ship is from."

Petrov furrowed his eyebrows. "They're from Solara. According to our records, that's where our jump gate goes to."

Kuznetsova looked worried. "Solara sided with Celestra during that ancient war. They were the enemy."

Petrov almost looked annoyed. "I know the histories, too. And that ancient war was nearly 800 years ago. That's enough time for most aftereffects of a war to settle down."

"And yet we're fleeing one of those aftereffects right now. It might seem like a long time to hold a grudge, but some influences can last a startlingly long time," Kuznetsova remarked, referring to the impending collision of the dead colony of Celestra with the soon-to-be-dead colony of Forrestal. That collision course was a direct result of that ancient, catastrophic war.

Petrov could only nod thoughtfully. Then he noticed his personal screen suddenly announced he was receiving an incoming video call from *Cerberus*.

Time to check on his family, then return to the business of running his ship.

CHAPTER 20

COMPANIONS

PYTOR THE GREAT
108 DAYS UNTIL IMPACT

Despite the relative quiet on the bridge for the past several hours, Comrade-Captain Petrov was unsettled. *Maybe I really am getting too old for this*, he thought gloomily. His moodiness was interrupted by the approach of Chief Engineer Gretski.

"How long does it take *Cerberus* to offload our guests?" he asked. Gretski was wondering the same thing all of them were wondering.

Petrov merely looked at him for a moment. "Frankly, I have no idea. We don't have anything to tell us when or even if they've arrived at the Enclave yet, or what their other capabilities are. We don't even know if they went to the Enclave, for that matter."

Gretski was about to say something more when he was interrupted by Gusev.

"Contact! Scans are picking up a large ship in close proximity!" she shouted.

"Identification?" Petrov asked.

Seconds passed in tense silence as Gusev reviewed the data on her instruments. Every set of eyes on the bridge kept close watch on her.

"It's the *Cerberus*!" she cried in relief.

"Send a hail by focused laser," ordered Petrov.

Seconds later, Kuznetsova announced contact had been established. "It's Captain Ronin for you, Comrade-Captain. By video communication."

"Patch it through to me." Petrov said. Seconds later, his screen lit up with the incoming message.

"Petrov here. Captain Ronin, are we glad to see you."

***

Ronin was seated in his command chair on the bridge of *Cerberus* when the video commlink with *Pytor the Great* was established. Mueller was standing just behind him so she could get a clear look at the video as well.

"Petrov here. Captain Ronin, are we glad to see you."

Although the *Cerberus* AI was providing real-time translation between the two, the AI simply couldn't do anything about the difference between lips moving in a different language. It reminded Ronin of cheap movies from other continents that had been dubbed into American. Ronin smiled disarmingly. "The reverse is true as well, Comrade-Captain. It's good for us to get our first looks at one another."

Petrov's face formed a sheepish half-smile. "Captain, for a while, I must admit I harbored a fear that you and your crew were some sort of green-skinned aliens. It's a relief to see that is not so."

Both Ronin and Mueller's faces broke into large grins before Ronin barked a small laugh. "I hate to disappoint, but we haven't encountered any green-skinned aliens, either. I'd like to introduce my first officer who is standing over my shoulder, Commander Diane Mueller."

Petrov, having now been joined by his own first officer, nodded towards him. "Commander Mueller, it is a pleasure to make your acquaintance. Allow me to introduce my own first officer, Commander Igor Kuznetsova."

Both Ronin and Mueller said they were pleased to make their acquaintance.

Introductions over, Petrov's voice turned serious now. "Captain, are my people safe?"

Ronin nodded before speaking. "Yes, you have my word on that. We settled them on the Enclave and ensured the facilities were operational before we left. It was a bit of a challenge to overcome the linguistic and written differences, but we managed."

Petrov nodded thoughtfully. "Our histories don't mention what the written language of Solara was, but I am assuming as an enemy colony, they spoke English."

Petrov couldn't help but see the expressions of both Ronin and Mueller.

Mueller sighed and answered for the two of them. "Comrade-Captain, we really do have a lot to discuss. Have you opened up space on your hangar deck yet?"

Petrov nodded. "We have. Would you like to have the discussion on *Pytor the Great*, or *Cerberus*?"

Ronin answered now. "How about we do it aboard *Cerberus* in an hour? It'll help us get you up to speed."

"I'll be over forthwith with an away party. *Pytor the Great*, out."

CHAPTER 21

NEW FRIENDS

CERBERUS

108 DAYS UNTIL IMPACT

Shoulders sagging and a dejected look on his face, Petrov leaned back into his seat. The main conference room on *Cerberus* had gone deathly quiet after the ancient video from Celestra had played and the *Cerberus* AI had finished the translation.

"How could we have known?" Petrov whispered to no one in particular. Kuznetsova met his gaze and shook his head slowly. The unspoken message was agreement that they just could not have known they had been lied to by Perun all their lives.

"Comrade-Captain…Leonid. We've been lied to by a power mad AI our entire lives. All to keep us under control. Perun always taught our people that the Celestrians destroyed themselves rather than surrender to our peaceful fleets, but we can see this is entirely untrue. We've even proved Perun was lying to us in other ways. You said so yourself when you discovered the true number of hulls being built. Perun knew the End of Days was coming a long time ago, yet it deliberately failed to do what was needed to save most of our people."

Petrov's face had paled as he considered the full scope of the deception, and he sighed slightly. His gray eyes hardened with resolve. "You speak the truth, Igor. That's why we made the Enclave habitable when we found the old mine on that asteroid."

Petrov's eyes flicked over to Dr. Wright and spoke to him. "Perun also lied to us when it taught us Earth was a myth, and the jump gate to

Solara no longer worked. Among other things, the lies didn't square with oral histories passed down among families that said we all came from Earth, and there were some artifacts I have seen which corroborated the oral histories."

Wright nodded sadly. "Gentlemen, I'm very sorry. The Fall and destruction of our peoples are an ugly truth that we have all been dealing with for a long time. We've also been re-discovering much of our own history that had been lost because of The Fall. Some of those discoveries completely upended what we thought we knew. And even in this system, The Fall continues to affect everything."

Kuznetsova pursed his lips before speaking. "Calling the ancient war and disaster that followed by that name, The Fall, is much catchier than our name for it."

All eyes turned towards Kuznetsova. Mueller asked, "What's your name for it?"

Kuznetsova smiled slightly and tilted his head. In an ironic tone, he said, "We were taught to call it 'The People's Great Revolution and War Against Western Aggression.'"

Ronin snorted, while everyone else laughed. "That's quite a mouthful," Ronin said just as the hatchway opened to admit Frida Enginnsdottir. Ronin, Petrov and Kuznetsova stood as she walked in. The officers from *Pytor the Great* couldn't help but notice she was wearing the typical gray utilities of the crew aboard *Cerberus*, but that she also had a sheathed sword strapped to her back. Enginnsdottir's dark brown eyes looked at Petrov coldly.

"Comrade-Captain Petrov, Commander Kuznetsova, may I introduce my wife, Frida Enginnsdottir," said Ronin.

Ronin quickly evaluated his wife's body language and realized their guests were about to die unless he did something to stop it. In an even voice, he said to her, "Frida, our guests have explained their ship was not under their control when we emerged from the jump gate, which has also been confirmed by our own AI. There is a hostile AI in control of their colony that was in control of their ship until our counterstrike at the jump gate severed the connection and freed them."

Enginnsdottir looked at Ronin in surprise and disbelief. "Is this true?" she asked in her Solaran-accented American. Last she had heard, this was only a working theory.

Both Ronin and Mueller nodded that it was, and Enginnsdottir's demeanor suddenly became more neutral. Enginnsdottir's diplomatic training was serving her well as she masked her feelings about her family living through an attack. She tilted her head towards the two men in greeting.

Kuznetsova, who had noticed Enginnsdottir's different accent, stuck out his hand to shake with Enginnsdottir as he said, "Pleased to make your acquaintance, ma'am." He nearly yelped with surprise when Enginnsdottir gripped it far more firmly than he expected and completed the handshake.

"'Tis good that you were not in control or I would have had to challenge you both in a duel to the death for attacking me and my family," Enginnsdottir said.

Sensing how awkward this was becoming, Ronin offered some explanation. "Gentlemen, my wife is not from Earth. She is an Ullrian Shieldmaiden from Solara Colony. The Ullr are a volatile and warlike Faction on that heavy gravity world. A strong word of caution is needed here. Ullrians *always* strike back if attacked," he said, emphasizing "always."

Enginnsdottir slowly turned her head to look at her husband, cocking a dark eyebrow that contrasted with her pale skin. "Volatile and warlike?" she asked, somewhat teasingly.

Ronin half smiled now, rising to the bait. "Definitely volatile and warlike."

"I like it," Enginnsdottir noted, smiling sweetly in return. By now, calling her warlike was a long-running joke between the couple.

Petrov and Kuznetsova shared a somewhat confused look at what was obviously an inside joke. Neither of them was too sure whether Ronin and Enginnsdottir were being serious. Ronin noticed their unspoken confusion and decided to continue on.

"Comrade-Captain Petrov, the Enclave appears to be a mined-out asteroid that had been abandoned during The Fall. There is plenty of space to accommodate your families, and there already were crops being grown inside by various drones. It is my understanding that the long-range plan was to live there temporarily, unless no other options presented themselves. Then it would be permanently, correct?"

Petrov nodded. "Yes, you are correct. As you no doubt have already learned, we're trapped in this system. Our people did not know how to open the jump-gate, and we have no FTL drive technology. The Enclave is far enough from the interior of this system that we hoped to ride out the destruction of Forrestal and Celestra. It was also our only option." Petrov's frustration with their situation was plainly evident.

Kuznetsova had also turned serious. "Captain Ronin, the real question is where do we go from here? We can create a sustainable environment at the Enclave, but only if we don't face new disasters like having more people than resources, or the arrival of debris from the colonies."

Sighing and leaning back in his seat, Ronin thought through their options. There weren't many. "I'm not sure what to do either. That evacuation fleet Perun is still building doesn't have anywhere permanent to go because Perun failed to prepare a destination. The Enclave doesn't have the resources to sustain that large of a fleet anyway, and the fleet won't follow *Cerberus* because Perun is in control of the fleet. Perun also won't allow *Cerberus* to just show up and start rescuing civilians from the colony either."

Mueller glanced at Ronin, knowing his thought processes were leading him somewhere. "So, what do you propose?" she wondered aloud.

Returning her look for a moment, Ronin continued talking through the idea that was forming. "I'm thinking the constant stumbling block here always seems to be Perun. That AI is willing to condemn millions to death just to keep control of the few who survive, so we need to neutralize it somehow and rescue as many of the population as we can. We can send our last long-range jump drone back with instructions to set up refugee camps on Solara, and transport the refugees there through the jump gate. Our ship's AI estimated we can save many more than Perun had planned for."

Eyebrows shot up in surprise all around the table. "How are we going to take down a hostile AI we know nothing about?" asked Mueller. The tone of her voice clearly suggested she thought the idea was nuts.

Looking to Petrov, Ronin asked, "Comrade-Captain, your mere presence on my ship means you've already abandoned Perun in favor of saving civilians. Would your engineering people be willing to work with mine to develop a way to neutralize Perun?"

A slow smile broke out on Petrov's face as realization dawned. "Captain Ronin, it would be our genuine pleasure to work together!"

"I thought so. I'll get some coffee sent in here. You have a lot of planning to do," Frida noted before she left the room.

Ronin traded looks with Wright, who tilted his head slightly and cocked his eyebrows. Even Wright was savvy enough to realize he had just witnessed a close call for their guests.

"Yeah. Coffee would be good right now," Ronin said softly.

CHAPTER 22

STRIKEFORCE

THE ENCLAVE

100 DAYS UNTIL IMPACT

"**M**ake a hole!" roared Gunnery Sergeant Kanagawa through his exosuit commlink. He was running into a dark and narrow, rough-hewn passage with Echo team right behind him.

Three Gamma team Marines operating as a forward scouting element quickly parted to allow Echo team to pass and charge into the dark passage.

"Think they'll do any better this time, Gamma 7?" asked Pvt. Juan Diaz on a separate exosuit commlink just between the three scouts. His voice sounded skeptical.

Snorting, Pvt. Aldo Pena shook his head. "That'd be a negative, Gamma 6. There's just nowhere to hide and nothing to duck behind when the shooting starts."

Pena's mechanized left arm held a heavy container with various supplies they might need for the mission. Pena had elected to keep the mechanized replacement after his left arm had been sliced off by an Ullrian warrior, who had boarded *Cerberus* during an attempt to capture the ship in the Solaran system on their last mission out into The Dark. Although Lieutenant Gustav and the gunnery sergeants had banned him from participating in the ship's arm-wrestling contests, Pena really liked the extra strength the mechanized arm gave him. It also gave him colorful stories to tell when he returned home to visit his family in Barcelona, Spain.

They all could hear the sudden sound of automatic weapons fire down the narrow passage. The heavier sounds of the defensive weapons turrets quickly drowned out the small arms fire of the Echo team Marines.

"Different team, same result," announced Gamma 2, LCpl. Jefferson Langley, in a disgusted tone. The big man from Wisconsin was crouched alongside Gamma 6 and 7 and he was the third member of the scouting element for this exercise. Langley's piercing blue eyes, hidden by the visor of his exosuit, his body language and the tone of voice told the same message as the past four failed attempts. They just couldn't get past the defensive systems, and all of them were going to die in a futile assault.

Gustav's disembodied voice flooded the commlinks of all the elements in the exercise. "This is LT. All players, all players, mission stop. Repeat, all stop. All teams return to their team ready rooms aboard the ship. After-action review with team leaders in two hours."

***

"Lieutenant, every time we stage an assault on the objective, we get mowed down because our ingress is bottlenecked into a killbox. Unless another way into that building is located, we'd just be throwing away the lives of our Marines," Gunnery Sergeant Mackey said as he leaned back in his seat slightly. The frustrated look on his face spoke volumes more than his succinct statement of their rehearsals to breach a hardened facility.

Nodding his head, Gunnery Sergeant Blackwater said, "I concur, LT. Each team has rehearsed assaulting that facility to help devise a tactic for success, and each team was wiped out down to the last Marine before achieving mission success. The floors and walls are too thick to breach, so we're left with a straight ahead, single-file attack straight into auto-cannon turrets. Is the Captain sure that we can't skip attacking this particular target?"

Clasping his hands behind his head and blowing out a breath, Gustav leaned back in his seat to think out loud. "You guys look like someone kicked your puppy. We're Marines! We need to adapt and overcome." Inhaling sharply, Gustav continued, "Setting aside the 'rah rah' stuff for the moment, Petrov and Kuznetsova both confirmed that Forrestal's hostile AI, which is named Perun, has four alternate backup sites on the planet's surface. Any of these backup sites can independently keep the planet's defense network functioning. We can't rescue any civilians unless we take all of them down, and this one is the only backup site the Captain isn't willing to erase from space using the ship's weaponry because it's the only one located in a populated area. They're also all similarly defended, though, so these factors chose our target for us."

Kanagawa asked, "Can't the ship just toast it using the ship's shiny new pulse cannon instead so we can get inside through a burn-thru tunnel?"

"'Fraid not. I already asked," Gustav replied, shaking his head. "We can't achieve burn-thru due to distance, atmospheric interference and thickness of the building itself. *Cerberus* would be turned into a missile sponge before our fancy raygun could do its thing."

Blackwater furrowed his eyebrows. "Why does it matter if we pulverize the site from space? All the surrounding civvies are going to die soon anyway when the End of Days arrives."

Blackwater and the rest of the Marines had quickly adopted the handy term, End of Days, for the coming apocalypse as soon as they heard it during their planning sessions with the crew from *Pytor the Great*.

Again, Gustav shook his head. "Our new friends don't want any more blood on our collective hands, even if it soon won't matter anyway. They'd rather risk our lives instead. So we need new ideas."

The group fell silent for a while. Everyone's eyes stared off into time and space far beyond the walls of Gustav's small office as they mentally reviewed their inventory of gear and possible tactics.

Kanagawa's eyes narrowed as his mind began to wander, the seed of an idea beginning to sprout. "LT, what we need is some sort of portable shielding to withstand the rounds from the auto-cannon turrets, yes?"

Eyes refocusing on Kanagawa, Gustav nodded. "Yep. But the Solaran Monoshield's can't withstand the heavier caliber of those auto-cannon, and a thicker Monoshield is too heavy to carry."

"For a normal human in an exosuit, but what about abnormal humans?" Kanagawa retorted.

With a hint of a grin on his face, Gustav replied, "Going to need to be more specific than that, Gunny. We're Marines, which means abnormal by definition."

It was Kanagawa's turn to chortle with amusement. "True that. If any of us were right in the head, we wouldn't have joined the Corps, LT.

"But," Kanagawa continued in a more serious tone, "I'm thinking some of our Marines are even more abnormal than the others. In this case I'm thinking of two Marines in particular. Bloodbane and Pena. Our 1.5G and our mechanized arm Marines might be able to hold up a much heavier shield by working together. That combination, plus working in powered exosuits, should be the equivalent strength of at least three Marines…"

With his eyebrows slowly rising in surprise, Gustav exclaimed, "All those losing bets you make on arm wrestling matches might pay off for once, Gunny." He then opened a commlink to the ship's Fabrication department.

"Lieutenant Alphonso, this is Lieutenant Gustav."

The reply was immediate. "Go for Alphonso. What can I do for you, Lieutenant?"

"Kristoff, can you take a look at some specs I'm going to send to you, ASAP? Specifically, we need to determine if you can fabricate an especially heavy-duty Monoshield that would typically require three Marines to move it. More importantly, would such a shield be able to withstand the caliber of rounds fired by the auto-cannon turrets that I'm sending you some additional specs on. Lastly, the shield would only have carry handles for two persons," Gustav concluded.

There was a pause before Alphonso repeated the request back to confirm what he thought he heard. "Adolph, if I understand you right, you want a three-man shield, which would be too heavy for two men to carry, to nonetheless have carry handles for only two men, if it can deflect bullets of a certain size or below?"

Gustav nodded. "Yep. That is accurate."

There was another small pause before Alphonso spoke again. "Why is it Marines always have the weirdest requests? If I do this, will you keep your Marines out of Fabrication's secure area?"

Smiling broadly now, Gustav replied, "No promises. I'm sending you the specs now. How soon can you do all that?"

Alphonso was running the numbers as he replied in a distracted tone, "Checking now…yeah, the shield will hold, but no promises on how you plan on moving the thing."

Gustav exchanged brief glances with his team gunnery sergeants. "Leave that to us. We need it for the assault on the AI backup site, and we need time to practice with it. Say, two days for delivery?"

Alphonso snorted, "You insult me, Lieutenant Gustav. I'll send you a message to pick it up sometime tomorrow. Alphonso out." Alphonso's voice simultaneously betrayed both humor and feigned indignation at being asked to do something so simple.

Nodding brusquely to the gunnery sergeants, Gustav said, "You heard the man. The package is being delivered tomorrow. In the meantime, grab some cardboard and make a mock shield to practice behind. Echo team will be first up. And get Bloodbane and Pena in the loop."

Holding up his hand in a "stay put" motion, Gustav continued, "This isn't just an op to blow up a pretty building. Officially we are hitting this facility with a ground force to avoid mass casualties among the citizens who live nearby. Unofficially, Commander Mueller and our own AI think this is an opportunity to grab data from the primary data center of an enemy AI named Perun. That's why the brass ordered me to attach a hacking package to each team. We break in, hack as much data as we can, blow up the pretty building, then bug out. We got a lot of work to do, so let's make it happen."

A chorus of "Aye-aye, LT," answered Gustav.

CHAPTER 23

FORRESTAL

BULLDOG 1 AND 3

95 DAYS UNTIL IMPACT

"Jump complete! We're in the atmosphere. Altitude is rapidly falling. Bulldog 1 is one mile off to our port side," Chief Jonsey said rapidly in a detached, professional manner. The Bulldogs were plummeting like a pair of flaming comets over the city below, trailing plumes of smoke and flame while they fell through the bright blue sky.

"Chief, weapons are now at your discretion. All players prepare for rapid deceleration in three. Two. One. Decelerate!" announced Pilot Officer Russo from the cockpit over the common commlink. He was answered by grunts from both flight crews and shuttle loads of Marines as the G forces suddenly increased.

While they were slowing, Russo suddenly saw a bright flash, followed by a rapidly rising mushroom cloud off in the distance. The mushroom cloud seemingly was being pushed skyward by a straight column of flame linking the ground to the edge of the planet's atmosphere. Fighting to make his voice sound normal, he switched to the command commlink channel and pushed the video to the rest of the strike force. "Railgun strike from *Cerberus* just erased one of Perun's computing core sites."

Moments later, several more flashes began appearing even more distantly, the new mushroom clouds angrily rising to meet the sky along their own columns of fire that were barely visible in the growing distance.

The crushing deceleration eased off quickly, seemingly just in time for everyone aboard the shuttle to gulp much needed air.

"I thought you said this was gonna be a smooth flight, Russo," said Echo 1, Gunnery Sergeant Kanagawa. He had quickly regained his composure and sounded almost normal over the command commlink.

"That WAS smooth, Echo 1. A rough flight is when we crater into the surface," replied Jonsey in his deep Mississippi drawl. The rearseater sounded both amused and distracted because he was also scanning the vicinity for threats.

Inside his buttoned up exosuit, Kanagawa half-smiled in amusement. "Of course. Carry on then. Best flight ever," he quipped.

"Customer service not up to your usual standards, Gunnery Sergeant?" asked Echo 2, Cpl. Adrian Longman as he joined the banter.

Kanagawa had been waiting for Longman to pipe up. "That's a big affirm, Echo 2. No in-flight movie, no drink service and the food is a downright embarrassment."

Longman's mirth was evident over the command commlink. "On the bright side, no one's shot at us yet."

"Yeah, but the lads get bored and restless without quality entertainment. A gunfight might keep them out of trouble for a spot," Kanagawa quipped, suddenly imitating Longman's Australian accent.

Almost as if on cue, Chief Jonsey launched a missile from the weapons pod attached to the shuttle for this mission. He interrupted the joking around. "Missile launch. Target is an air defense unit that's spinning up."

While Jonsey made his announcement, Russo had finished dropping the Bulldog down to below rooftop height.

"Threat destroyed," the Chief said a few seconds later. His voice sounded flat while he was busy working.

From the video displayed on his exosuit's internal visor, Kanagawa could see they had entered the city that was their target. Longman and Kanagawa fell silent as they took in the video from the Bulldog's external cameras.

"Big, ugly, gray blocks of thoroughly uninspiring buildings we're seeing here, Echo 1," Longman commented.

"Yeah. The Collective and their philosophy of government control over the individual inevitably crushes humanity's normal motivation to create and build. Why go to all the extra work when government just ignores it or punishes you for initiative? No reward for working harder, no reason to improve yourself or anything around you. Conform and get in line, peasant, or line up against a wall and get shot," Kanagawa commented.

Heads all over the Bulldog nodded in agreement while Longman replied, "Amen to that Reverend. That hateful ideology almost destroyed our race once, and it nearly did it again a second time."

Russo interrupted their ruminations by opening the all-team commlink. "All players, we're approaching the target. ETA, 45 seconds."

Kanagawa immediately began speaking over the Echo team commlink. "All right, you apes, you heard the man! As soon as that rear hatch drops, we move. Fast and silent, leapfrogging and weapons hot. If something moves, it dies. Take no chances."

The Bulldog suddenly slowed, Russo raising the front of the shuttle briefly like he had pulled on the reins of a horse. While the rear ramp was lowering, the shuttle skids lightly settled down onto the rooftop of yet another, nondescript cement building that looked like hundreds of others around it.

"I sure hope our new friends were right about which building we needed to visit," muttered Jonsey over a commlink to Russo.

Nodding, Russo kept his head swiveling as the Marines swiftly exited the rear of their bird. The whining of their Bulldog engines was pretty loud and Russo was certain it would be heard for blocks around.

"Echo team is dirtside, away the Bulldog," ordered Kanagawa over the command commlink.

"Roger that. Bulldog 3 departing," responded.

"Bulldog 1, ETA two minutes. Clear the LZ." said another voice seconds later over the command commlink. It was Chief Patterson, the rearseater of Bulldog 1.

Weapons up and ready, Echo team rapidly spread out over the rooftop of the building while Bulldog 1 was inbound to the LZ portion of the roof. Echo team's war dog, Barqhest, sniffed around, scouting for telltale scents of recent human activity.

"Echo 6, Echo 1. Does Barqhest smell anything?" asked Kanagawa over the team commlink.

"Echo 1, Echo 6. That's a negative. He's not picking up anything," replied Echo 6, Pvt. Julio Gonzales. He was the handler for the team's Rottweiler, Barqhest. While every Marine came from somewhere they called "home," Gonzales seemed to be the exception. No one could recall the man having talked about where he was from, or relatives and family, or anything like that. It was as if Gonzales had appeared out of thin air at a Marine recruiting depot one day, and he wasn't interested in sharing his background. All Echo team knew he was particularly deadly in close quarters combat and didn't show remorse about killing if it were necessary. Only Barqhest knew Gonzales had been a mob hitman prior to joining the Corps, and for obvious reasons, Barqhest wasn't talking either.

Engines whining, Bulldog 1 set down moments later and Gamma team repeated Echo's rapid exit. Bulldog 1 left the LZ in less than a minute and the rooftop suddenly was quiet again.

While Gamma took up their own positions, both the team leaders briefly conferred. "Gamma 1, this is Echo 1. We have the door to the ingress point wired and ready to blow," Kanagawa said to Gunnery Sergeant Blackwater over the command commlink. Both of them were positioned on opposite sides of the massive roof.

Blackwater nodded to himself as he responded. "Roger that, Echo 1. The shield team is in position. I'll pass word along." He then switched to the all-team commlink. "All players, this is Gamma 1. It's showtime. Breach the entrance and follow the shield team in. For you knuckle draggers who can't remember who the shield team is, that would be Gamma 7 and Echo 12 and the oversized Monoshield they're hauling."

Blackwater was answered by a chorus of "Aye Ayes," clicks, and more than a few sniggers at his quip as every Marine on the mission knew exactly who the shield team was. Echo 5's voice suddenly flooded the all-team commlink. Being the first arriving Marine for this particular away mission with a specialty of breaching, Pvt. David Danfries had quickly wired the heavily shielded door with explosives.

"Boomstick detonation in zero three seconds. Fire in the hole!" Pvt. Danfries said loudly. The thunderous blast rocked the building and scattered debris over the entire rooftop. Far more explosive had been used than was actually necessary to breach the door.

Over the command commlink, Kanagawa laughed. "Hoo RAH! I LOVE the 'P' for Plenty formula!"

Blackwater snorted in laughter at Kanagawa's excited quip. While every explosive had a chemical formula where letters represented various elements, it was an old joke in the Marines that the most important element in blowing something up was to use "P," which merely means to use **p**lenty of explosive.

After the shock of the blast passed and they were cleared to enter, the shield team of Gamma 7 and Echo 12 stormed down into the narrow, dark stairwell. Pena and Bloodbane struggled to maneuver their heavy Monoshield to keep them covered as they nonetheless advanced quickly. Tiny butterfly drones streamed past their position and continued on scouting ahead. Echo and Gamma teams had kitted up with extra drones for this particular field trip as they figured they would need a lot of them.

Multispectral imaging from the scouting drones was displayed inside each Marine's exosuit visor. They did not travel down many floors before encountering the first obstacle that Commander Kuznetsova's intelligence briefing had pinpointed.

"Contact front! Target is designated as auto-cannon 1. Shield team is moving to engage," announced Echo 12 over the all-team commlink. Bloodbane's Ullrian accent when speaking American (the language that once had been known as "English" before The Fall) served to identify Bloodbane as the speaker as surely as his exosuit commlink system identifier.

Carefully, the shield team exited the stairwell at the bottom floor and moved into a creepy, dark, narrow hallway. Keeping their Monoshield between themselves and the auto-cannon they had spotted on the butterfly drones that were scouting ahead, Bloodbane and Pena exchanged nervous glances. Both of them were thankful to be wearing liquid black exosuits which concealed their facial expressions.

The view inside the exosuit visors was quite different than what the Marines would have faced with the naked eye. The multispectral light and scanning clarification provided by the exosuits and projected inside their visors made the hallway seem brightly lit. Their view was overlaid with Tacnet data, which could be accessed by focusing an eye on an object and blinking. To the Marines, exosuits and Tacnet had long ago become second nature due to constant training.

Breathing hard, Bloodbane and Pena pushed the heavy Monoshield forward several steps. "Why didn't they put some damn wheels on this thing?" grunted Bloodbane over the commlink Pena had opened between the two of them.

Pena snorted. "If we gonna pimp our ride with wheels, let's make it a low rider, paint some righteous flames on it. All the girls will dig it."

As if answering Pena's terrible quip, the auto-cannon suddenly opened up on them. It fired bullets so fast all the Marines could hear was something that sounded like the mutant lovechild of a giant chainsaw and a Solaran Hellcat. The shrieking noise was earsplitting and ended all possibility of communicating except by hand signals.

Grunting with effort, Bloodbane braced his shoulder against the lower part of the Monoshield to stabilize it against the sudden storm of bullets. Pena did the same as he kept his mechanical left arm clamped to the upper grip on the back of the Monoshield. Using his right hand, Pena reached behind him to where a Stinger rifle was attached and quickly pulled it free. Both of them had their exosuit power dialed up to maximum to help them move.

Pena synced the Stinger to the targeting information he was receiving from Tacnet and the tiny drone cameras. The Stinger was preloaded with explosive, armor-piercing rounds for this mission. Nodding at his partner, Pena dialed up the exosuit's targeting assist on his right arm and barely stuck the edge of the barrel over the Monoshield when it fired several times. The rifle targeting was entirely under the control of Tacnet for this motion because they couldn't risk exposing themselves to aim like they were taking a normal shot.

There was a muffled, thudding detonation and the deadly hail of bullets stopped. The sudden quiet was nearly as unsettling as had been the shrieking of the auto-cannon. Bloodbane glanced at Pena and grinned, which was unseen inside his exosuit. "I guess the locals don't think much of pimping our ride like that," he said with undisguised humor.

Shaking his head slightly, Pena grinned back. "These clowns just have no sense of style." The two began to move forward, carefully keeping their Monoshield in front of them. "Let's move to the next one," Pena said, suddenly serious again.

They didn't have far to travel until the next auto-cannon, which the tiny butterfly drones had already located, suddenly announced its presence. The shield team followed the same procedure and quickly dispatched the fixed emplacement. Once the noise of the weapon had been silenced, their external audio microphones picked up something new. It was a deep, strangely accented voice.

"You won't succeed, you know."

Behind their Monoshield, Bloodbane and Pena shared a troubled glance. Pena shrugged, and looked behind them to where Gamma 1, Gunnery Sergeant Blackwater, was positioned. Blackwater shook his head and motioned a non-verbalized question about where the voice came from. Pena shook his head to indicate he had no idea. The voice seemed to come from everywhere at once.

A few more steps forward were taken by the shield team before the deep voice spoke again. "You can't save them all. My children are too many, and the evacuation ships are too few."

Over the all-team commlink, Gamma 1 suddenly quipped, "Doesn't this stupid machine realize we're Marines? Math is hard."

Kanagawa chimed in, adopting a really bad imitation of a country boy accent. "I dunno 'bout you boys, but I figure them math's are why the Good Lord blessed me with fingers and toes. Need something to count on."

"Maybe those two missing fingers of yours explains why you always a cheatin' at cards, then?" drawled Gustav in a truly terrible imitation of a Texas accent because he wasn't able to suppress his German accent.

He was still aboard Bulldog 3, and running the operation from a multiscreen command center that had been set up on that shuttle.

Guffaws broke out over the commlink. Kanagawa waited a few moments for it to die down, then he said, "If you ain't cheatin', then you ain't trying, LT!" Kanagawa's imitation of a Texas accent was just as bad as Gustav's.

The wisecracking quickly died down when their external audio picked up a low, mechanical growling suddenly emanating from ahead of them in their direction of travel. Barqhest's growling to warn of approaching danger only added to the rising cacophony. Bloodbane risked a quick peek around the Monoshield to get a better look because the butterfly drones weren't delivering a clear visual.

"Danger front! Incoming, top and bottom!" yelled Bloodbane to alert the others about the flying and rolling dangers at the same time Tacnet plotted their positions almost simultaneously. Bloodbane and Pena ducked down low with their shield to minimize their defensive profile.

"Echo team, take the ground force. Gamma team the fliers. Fire at your discretion!" Blackwater ordered over the team commlink. His voice sounded relatively calm, despite the danger. His visor had detected many wheels and wings from a cloud of death headed their way.

Hundreds of small death machines darted down the hall at the intruders. The machines were of all types. Wheels, rotor blades, rockets, and even tracked drives. Many launched a hail of small needles, which did little other than to skitter off the tough exosuits of the Marines. The needles weren't enough to damage the Marines, so they merely served as a distraction.

The wall of projectiles hurled in return by the Marine teams was definitely not meant to distract. Dozens of the machines were ripped apart in seconds, but they continued pressing closer to the Marines due to sheer numbers.

"Echo 1, Gamma 1. This is a straight-up gunfight!" yelled Blackwater over the command commlink to Kanagawa. The noise level was high in the narrow hallway.

"Gamma 1, I gotta bad feeling about this. We can't maneuver, and we're limited by the progress of the shield team!" replied Kanagawa.

Blackwater's reply was drowned out by several powerful explosions. Two of the flying defensive machines had detonated over the shield team's position, funneling fire and overpressure in the two directions allowed by the narrow hall. The blast shook the massive building, and a thick cloud of dust and smoke obscured the enhanced vision provided by the Marine's exosuit visors.

Instinctively, the two gunnery sergeants, Kanagawa and Blackwater, checked Tacnet for the life signs of their shield team. Tacnet also showed the last of the mechanical defenders had died along with the blast. Bloodbane and Pena were still in the green.

Before either Kanagawa or Blackwater could even ask, Bloodbane reported in, "Echo 1, Echo 12. We're all right. Thanks for asking."

Annoyed at Bloodbane being a smart ass at an inappropriate moment, Kanagawa was about to adjust the Marine's attitude when Tacnet suddenly flashed an alert. Kanagawa changed his mind and opened the all-team commlink. "All players, be advised, we have more incoming. Targets are larger and slower this time."

Dozens of humanoid-shaped robots moved forward at a run. They were somewhat larger than the average human and had glowing red eyes staring out from a metallic, chromium-like skull. The robots carried far larger weapons from an over-the-shoulder sling that allowed the things to fire from the hip as they moved.

The robots and Marines filled the narrow hall with gunfire. Several Marine Buzzsaws opened up simultaneously, spraying heavier caliber bullets than the standard Mag-rail rifle round. Although both sides were armored, men and machines traded varying degrees of damage.

Unseen at first, a pair of huge robots joined the wild melee. These robots were twice the size of the others and towered over the Marines as they swiftly plowed into the strike force. Marines were mercilessly swatted aside.

"Echo 3, Echo 1. Shift fire to those jumbo robots!" Kanagawa ordered in response.

Echo team's heavy weapons specialist, Pvt. Rhee Lee, confirmed the order even as he shifted his Buzzsaw to the new threats. Lee unleashed a fusillade of heavy caliber rounds at the fast-moving machines. Bullets ricocheted off the armored skeleton of the jumbo combat units without causing significant damage.

Kanagawa was about to call in more heavy weapons when a painfully bright blue fire streak seemingly appeared from the middle of the melee. It moved far faster than the naked eye could follow, leaving everyone with a faint impression of having seen a powerful blue lightning bolt. The sound of it tearing through the air trailed well behind despite the small, confined space.

A projectile fired by the Firefly doesn't merely hit a target, it is more of an impact event. This particular impact event was remarkable because Echo 8, LCpl. Hiro Gozen, had positioned himself so that the two jumbo combat robots were briefly in line with each other when the Firefly impacted. The result was a catastrophic mix of torn metal armor, accompanied by the screeching sounds of metal being violently shredded and a low, metallic *whuumph.*

The first jumbo remained standing, although it now sported a large hole in the center of its torso. The ragged edges of the new hole were still glowing orange from the friction heat of the passage of the incredibly fast-moving projectile that punched its way straight through the jumbo's reinforced armor plating.

The effect of the impact on the second jumbo was another matter entirely. It wasn't a center mass strike like on the other jumbo. Ordinarily, missing the center of the armored torso would have left the machine somewhat combat effective. Ordinarily. But this was not the case here, as the streaking Firefly round had slivered from passing through the first jumbo. Instead of one projectile impact, there were dozens of them, still traveling too fast to see. In their wake was a broken jumble of melted and torn parts. The effect was that of a powerful shotgun blast at close range.

The shocked silence that had descended inside the hallway was broken by an all-team commlink remark by Gamma 8, Pvt. Rick Desantos. Gamma 8 was from a cattle ranch located near a ghost town once known as Boulder, Colorado, and he grew up riding horses and protecting the herd from predators. Desantos was nicknamed "Rickgun" by his Marine teammates when he served aboard the cruiser *Lancaster* because of his penchant of carrying pearl-handled, six-shooter revolvers into combat;

"Rickgun" sounded a lot like "six gun." Rickgun relished how cool and deadly his six-shooters looked.

"Hoo-e. Nice shootin', Tex! Looks like that second jumbo got holed by the world's biggest shotgun," drawled Rickgun. He was eyeing the wreckage of the second jumbo and when he noticed part of it was still attempting to move, he drew his revolver and shot the machine a few more times for good measure with heavy, armor-piercing rounds. The wreckage stopped moving.

Kanagawa rolled his eyes and privately commlinked Blackwater over the command commlink. "Our boy Gung Ho's got a hard-on for Fireflies or something." Kanagawa thought "Gung Ho" was the perfect nickname for Echo 8, who had earned the moniker during their last deployment.

Laughing, Blackwater had to agree. "He sure does. But he's a good shot. That was perfect timing!"

Kanagawa looked at Tacnet and took stock of their situation. "I see six wounded, four of whom are hurt too badly to continue. Their exo-suits have the injuries stabilized for now. I'm sending them back to the roof."

Blackwater nodded, even though he and Kanagawa couldn't see each other. "Concur. I'll send a corpsman element with them."

Blackwater switched to the all-team commlink. "Echo 7 and Gamma 6, this is Gamma 1. Escort the wounded to the roof and rejoin us ASAP. Make it happen!"

Echo and Gamma teams Corpsman, Echo 7, Pvt. Nancy Dos, and Gamma 6, Pvt. Aldo Pena, were already tending to the wounded. Gamma 6 definitely noticed Echo 7 had been ordered to escort the men to the roof with instead of himself. It was a new experience being part of the strike force shield team because of his mechanical arm.

While Echo 7 and Gamma 6 tended to their business for a few minutes, Kanagawa and Blackwater conferred over the command commlink.

"Tacnet can't pick up these combat 'bots until they exit their hidey holes and move on us in the hallway," Blackwater grumbled. He would much rather take the fight to the enemy than lure them out into the open, when that "open" was little more than a narrow, dark hallway.

Kanagawa nodded. "Agreed. It sucks being both the bait and the hammer at the same time. If the pre-mission intel provided by Commander Kuznetsova holds true, there are only two more auto-cannon turrets before we reach the objective."

The same, deep, menacing voice they heard earlier suddenly spoke again. "You will not stop me. All of you will be mine."

Kanagawa just rolled his eyes and shook his head. "Of all the AIs in the universe, the one we assault turns out to be a drama queen."

CHAPTER 24

ORBIT

CERBERUS

95 DAYS UNTIL IMPACT

"**B**ombardment damage estimates?" asked Ronin. He was leaning forward in his command chair in the center of the bridge, intently reviewing data as it came in.

"Computing core, sites one through three, totally destroyed, Captain," reported Lieutenant Delacroix without tearing his eyes from his scanner screens. His scans were making the extent of the damage from the surgical railgun strikes very clear. Not that something as powerful as the railguns on *Cerberus* could ever be accurately described as "surgical." They just didn't need to unleash many rounds to achieve target destruction from orbit.

An alarm sounding from the tactical station broke their concentration. "Tacnet showing 72 incoming enemy warships, from all points," announced Lieutenant LeCroy, indicating they're approaching from all directions. "They're launching missiles! Time until initial impact, 7 minutes, 12 seconds."

Immediately a countdown timer appeared on Ronin's screen at his chair as he appeared to be deep in thought. Folding his hands together in front of him with the fingers intertwined, he absentmindedly rubbed a thumb along the curve of his chin as he eyed the timer. *These next few minutes are going to go down fast*, he thought to himself.

"Hrrumph. I still think might have at least tried talking to the planetary AI before we started blowing up everything," noted Wright haughtily. Wright was standing next to Ronin's command chair, and imperiously cocked an eyebrow at him.

Ronin shot Wright an incredulous look. "Doctor Wright, the time to assume peaceful intent ended upon the ambush of *Cerberus* with antimatter missiles. That was only reinforced by everything we've since learned from Captain Petrov and the folks aboard *Pytor the Great*. Ignoring that would be foolish and deadly." As he finished speaking, Ronin traded glances with Mueller.

Wright was about to reply when Mueller cut him off. "Doctor, Captain Ronin is right. That AI isn't about to greet *Cerberus* with wine and roses. It's irresponsible and dangerous to attribute peaceful intent to an ancient entity we know very little about, especially when its actions have clearly been hostile."

Wright held back what he had been about to say. He knew Captain Ronin and Commander Mueller were correct, and he suddenly realized he made the age-old mistake of failing to believe actions instead of words. Sighing slightly, he nodded at Mueller silently.

After trading knowing glances again, Ronin and Mueller returned their attention to the countdown display.

***

"Enemy ship is surrounded and trapped against the planet in a low orbit, Comrade-Admiral," said the young officer aboard the warship *Soyuz* as he glanced up nervously at the high-ranking officer looming over his station at the front of the bridge.

Fleet-Adm. Andrei Kirov nodded in acknowledgment slightly before speaking to the crew on the bridge. "Now we will see what our ancient foe is made of. We don't know for sure where they originated from, but we know they arrived in Forrestal system from the jump gate to Solara and somehow avoided our picket ship guarding the gate. Time to end this threat once and for all!" After concluding his announcement, Kirov turned to face the large view screen at the front of the bridge.

If Kirov noticed the subtle looks exchanged between the dozen members of the bridge crew behind his back, he chose not to acknowledge them. The only thing that travels faster than light in the Forrestal navy is gossip, especially gossip about unidentified or missing ships. And the *Soyuz* crew had heard the fastest gossip of all because it involved a trifecta of intrigue with an unidentified ship, a missing ship from their own fleet, plus the long-dormant jump gate.

It didn't take a genius to conclude that the presence of the unidentified ship and the absence of their own missing ship probably meant that the unidentified ship might mean trouble.

***

"That's got to be *Cerberus* down there. Only Captain Ronin could stir up that much trouble," grumbled Capt. Hu Nagun without tearing his eyes from the tactical map currently displayed on the main viewscreen. He was sitting in his command chair on the bridge of the fast and sleek corvette, *Kitty Hawk*, as it approached the planet from several light minutes away. Nagun had ordered his Bulldogs to seed a scout drone 'net and otherwise look over the inner system before *Kitty Hawk* arrived. The drone data flowing back to Tacnet told them they came late to the party.

Standing next to Nagun's seat was the ship's executive officer, Cmdr. Steve Fisher. He snorted softly in response. "Outnumbered 72 to 1. Clouds of missiles and an orbital bombardment in the shadow of a celestial catastrophe. Where the hell else would Captain Ronin possibly be, except in the middle of that?"

Fisher's wry comment left little doubt that even though they were still too far away to locate the exact position of *Cerberus*, he didn't think they would have much difficulty figuring out where to look.

Nagun broke into a huge, lopsided grin as guffaws broke out around the bridge at Fisher's remark. "Just so, XO. I'm thinking we jump some Bulldogs to a closer position just outside that whole fracas and launch our communication drones. Use those to try to establish contact with *Cerberus* and tell them we've arrived. Based on Ronin's response, we'll join the fun or get involved in some other way."

"Concur. I'll pass the orders along," Fisher said with a nod before returning to his bridge station to get the drone mission underway.

Nagun leaned back in his seat with a pensive look on his face. "Cripes, Dan. What have you gotten mixed up in this time?" he quietly muttered to himself.

CHAPTER 25

GROUND ASSAULT

LAST REMAINING PERUN COMPUTING CORE — FORRESTAL
95 DAYS UNTIL IMPACT

"Shield team, you're cleared to engage," said Blackwater over the all-team commlink. His voice somehow didn't betray the heavy breaths he was taking due to the strain of combat. Echo and Gamma teams had already advanced deep into the building's interior. Inside his exosuit, sweat ran down Blackwater's face and he was now limping a little from an injury inflicted by one of Perun's mechanical terrors. The nasty thing had hit his leg like a maniacal bowling ball and sent him tumbling. Blackwater never saw which Echo team Marine ended the machine before it could harm anyone else. There was too much smoke and too many bullets flying everywhere at the time to ever have figured that out.

Underneath their now battered and dented super-sized Monoshield, Bloodbane and Pena shared a wordless glance that nonetheless spoke volumes. Weary was their body language. If they hadn't long been buttoned up in powered exosuits, exhaustion would have been plainly reflected in their faces. Both men were nearly spent with the effort of hauling the heavy Monoshield into combat, fighting for their lives the whole way. Even the powered assist from their exosuits didn't seem to make their burden any lighter at this point.

They had fought their way into a diabolically confusing maze of narrow, dark hallways. Shrieking mechanical defenders had repeatedly ambushed them and had been blown to smoking bits. Marines had fallen victim to automated defenses that shot bullets, slashed, stabbed, and otherwise tried to cut them down. Bloodbane even recalled seeing a bipedal machine swinging some sort of chainsaw sword. The combat unit wielding that terrifying weapon had badly injured a couple of Marines before Echo 3, Private Lee, had blasted it full of holes with his Buzzsaw heavy infantry assault rifle.

Grunting with the effort, Bloodbane and Pena hefted their oversized Monoshield and advanced to their next destination, the computing core of the AI named Perun. Paradoxically, the entrance to the inner sanctum where the highly advanced Perun was housed had a simple door, with a small keypad in the wall to the left. The two Marines pushed up to the door and set the edge of their Monoshield on the ground behind them. It stood tall, protecting their backsides while they prepared to breach the entrance. Reaching out, Pena grabbed the door handle with his mechanical prosthesis.

Before he tried the door handle, Pena suddenly grinned and spoke to Bloodbane over a separate commlink. "This is so crazy."

"How so?" Bloodbane asked, tilting his head quizzically.

"In the past few months, I lost my arm to an Ullrian from a lost colony, then assaulted another lost colony with an Ullrian Marine from the prior lost colony, all while using a replacement mechanical arm and tech that I never heard of a few months ago." Pena's voice clearly revealed his bemusement at how complicated things had become the past few months.

Bloodbane laughed. Pena's remark seemed funnier than it actually was because Bloodbane was so tired. "Age before beauty?" he asked, nodding towards the door handle.

Pena didn't bother trying to crack the code on the keypad. He simply yanked hard on the door handle and broke it by pulling it entirely through the door. Bloodbane and Pena shifted the Monoshield to their front before pushing the broken door open and entering the AI's inner sanctum.

Expecting more violence, they were only met with silence and what appeared to be a crystalline-based server farm in a chamber that was at least 50 yards long. Bloodbane glanced at Pena in confusion. "Aren't we supposed to be returning fire at something by now?"

Pena nodded slightly as he observed dozens of rows of servers and compared the tactical readout shown in his visor. "Tacnet scans say nobody's home." Both Marines could see that the rest of the invasion force had taken up defensive positions outside the door and down the hall leading from the inner sanctum.

They were interrupted by the same deep voice they had heard before. "My children will stop you all. We will prevail over you, Capitalist scum!"

Sighing, Pena and Bloodbane exchanged annoyed glances behind their Monoshield. Bloodbane snorted and shrugged, asking, "How does an artificial intelligence become such a drama queen?"

Pena shrugged. "I dunno. Let's take what we came for and bug out."

The two of them lifted the shield and swiftly moved to the center of the server farm. Most of the crystalline-based servers emitted a faint blue glow that was slightly brighter along the outer edges of each crystal card chip and bathed the room in a soft blue hue.

The center was easy to locate. Little more than a couple of workspace desks and screens arranged around a single, 6-foot tall tower that resembled a black filing cabinet in width and depth.

"Bingo! It's right where Commander Kuznetsova said it would be," Pena exclaimed.

Realizing the Marines were well aware the other computing cores had already been vaporized into dust clouds, Perun wisely stayed silent instead of threatening that it would simply shift into another core. Instead, Perun tried to beg.

"Why are you attacking me? I haven't harmed any of you!" Perun pleaded.

Bloodbane ignored Perun for a moment while he studied the core tower and located the access panel. Then he distractedly said over his external speaker, "Only because your missile attack on us at the jump gate failed."

"But I was protecting my children!" Perun said plaintively.

Not bothering with niceties like tools, Bloodbane simply ripped the access panel off using the combined power of his heavy gravity physique and the exosuit. "You failed to protect your so-called children despite having centuries to prepare. And then you simply planned to save only those you found convenient," he said, reaching inside the tower slowly and carefully grasping the first of the primary core cards that made up the AI's sentience.

Pena interrupted Perun's next statement. "Typically corrupt collective society. An elite class hypocritically making rules that only apply to the little people. Yet you always seem to have some who are more equal than others."

Perun never got the chance to continue as Bloodbane began pulling out the core computing cards of the AI. Putting a half dozen of the core computing cards into a ruck sack on his back, Bloodbane and Pena noticed that the soft glow of the server farm slowly began to die, along with the building's ventilation system and everything else that had been drawing power.

Pena's external mics also told him something else at the same time it appeared on Tacnet. "Heads up. Hostiles entering the far side of the inner sanctum!" he yelled on the all-team commlink.

A chorus of answering clicks from the Marines was drowned out by the explosions of synchronized grenades thrown across the room by Echo team. Their simultaneous detonations wreaked havoc among the unarmored human soldiers who had tried to crash the party.

"Shield team, bug out!" roared Kanagawa as he eyed the undisciplined soldiers. "Looks like half-trained Regulars!" he added so the Marines would be aware they weren't facing top notch troops.

OLD FRIENDS

CERBERUS

"**I**ncoming message from *Kitty Hawk*, Captain!" said Delgado as she turned to look at Ronin. "It's from *Kitty Hawk* Actual." The look of complete surprise on Delgado's face carried an entirely different message.

Raising his eyebrows and looking over at Delgado, Ronin responded, "Open a commlink, Lieutenant."

"*Cerberus* Actual, this is *Kitty Hawk* Actual. Your comm drones made it back home, and *Kitty Hawk* was available to respond. We see you've managed to set another world on fire. Again. How can we help?" asked Captain Nagun.

Despite the jovial tone, Nagun wasn't wasting much time now that the shooting had started without *Kitty Hawk*, but he still tossed in the obligatory jibe on his former Academy roommate, Captain Ronin. By now, it had become an inside joke among other fleet Captains that Ronin tended to seek out interesting new worlds, and then blow them up.

"Hu, welcome to the lost colony of Forrestal! How did *Kitty Hawk* even get here past the blockade at the jump gate? Never mind, I have to make this quick as we are short on time. We have two Marine teams on the surface who are about to do a fighting withdrawal to their exfil point.

"*Cerberus* is playing fox to the hounds in orbit. We'll be jumping out of missile range shortly. Forrestal is ruled by a hostile AI leftover from the pre-Fall Collective. We are taking down that AI to break its grip over the planetary society so we can begin rescue efforts and save more civilians than that AI had bothered to plan for. The hostiles lack FTL drives but have an incredible sublight drive system that we can't match, so I'm not sure *Kitty Hawk* should come any closer until after this blows over."

Nagun smiled. "Dan, *Kitty Hawk* was retrofitted with jump drives while you've been away. We used our FTL drive the whole way and bypassed the jump gate in the process."

Surprised again and because everything was happening too fast, Ronin snorted. "Well, in THAT case, can you lead some of that huge fleet away from the combat zone? We want them too far away to interfere, but close enough to recall for rescue efforts before the End of Days."

Nodding, Nagun didn't ask what "End of Days" meant. For anyone who had glanced at Tacnet recently, its meaning was glaringly obvious. "Good copy, *Cerberus*. *Kitty Hawk* Actual, out."

Nagun sat quiet for a moment and collected his thoughts before issuing his orders. "Helm, plot a course that takes us close enough to the combat zone to attract their attention. Keep the jump drive spun up in case they're faster than we anticipated. Weapons, load some railgun rounds into the primary batteries. I want them to come close and give them some chin music, but not hit those ships. Also, let's light up our running lights on our hull, make sure they can't miss *Kitty Hawk's* glorious arrival."

The Bridge crew made those orders happen very quickly. "Course laid in, Captain." reported the helmsman after a few moments.

"Execute battle plan." ordered Nagun. His entire demeanor was totally All Business Mode now.

***

"Comrade-Admiral! Scanners have detected an unknown ship approaching from the outer system!" reported the young officer on the *Soyuz* bridge. FAdm. Andrei Kirov frowned and walked over to loom over the young officer.

"You are sure?" he asked. He was perplexed that there might be a second unidentified ship lurking nearby.

In response, the young officer threw the visual image of the approaching ship onto the bridge view screen. It was black, but lit up with bright running lights.

The young officer studied the data coming in about the new ship. "Its profile is smaller than the ship we've been chasing, Comrade-Admiral, but the drive signature indicates it uses the same propulsion system."

Kirov looked at the tablet he was holding to get a different tactical perspective. He circled an outer grouping of capital ships on the tablet screen, which included the *Soyuz*. The tablet's screen image simultaneously was mirrored on the main view screen. "Order these ships to accompany the *Soyuz* on an interdiction. If we can't capture that ship, we'll shoot it down."

***

"Enemy ships turning to intercept *Kitty Hawk*, Captain. Sublight closure speed is very high," announced Commander Fisher. His eyes were riveted onto his scanning screens.

Nagun nodded. "How soon until they intercept?"

Fisher looked over at Nagun. "Ten minutes, Captain."

Capt. Nagun's eyes widened considerably. "TEN minutes?" he exclaimed softly and then whistled as he looked at Tacnet. "That's absolutely incredible acceleration!" he noted. His eyes flicked over to the helm and weapons stations. "Helmsman, I want a micro-jump at five minutes. Take us further away from our pursuers. Weapons! At four minutes, fire railguns and force them to take evasive action. I want them distracted so they don't realize we jumped and increased the distance between us."

A chorus of "Aye, Captain" answered his orders. Nagun leaned back into his command seat to watch the timer countdown. At precisely four minutes to intercept, he felt *Kitty Hawk* shudder from its railgun salvo.

"Enemy ships altering course. Most of them. One doesn't seem to have detected the salvo," Fisher observed. He was silent for a few seconds and then he exclaimed, "Impact! A round from the salvo hit the ship that failed to alter course. The ship appears adrift."

Before Nagun could acknowledge Fisher's report, *Kitty Hawk* micro-jumped. The helmsman then announced the obvious, "Micro-jump complete, Captain."

Nodding his head, Nagun looked at Fisher. Without taking his eyes from his screens, Fisher could feel Nagun's eyes upon him, silently asking for the new data as Tacnet updated with their new position. "Time until intercept has increased to 20 minutes," he said at last.

***

Amid the blaring of the ship's klaxon, "Comrade-Admiral, the interdiction window just increased to twenty minutes!" reported the confused young officer. His facial expression of confusion matched his emotions.

"What! How can that possibly be? Our maneuvering couldn't have extended the window by anywhere near that length!" roared Kirov as he stalked over to the young officer's station.

Before either of them could say anything else, a distress call demanded their attention. The young officer read it to Kirov. "Warship *Potemkin* is reporting its drive is disabled from a kinetic strike. Many casualties," he said, reading the message aloud.

Kirov shook his head in bewilderment at the sudden turn in events. "Forward the distress call to Perun. It will send the necessary aid. Our task force will continue pursuit of this new ship."

"It will be done, Comrade-Admiral," replied the young officer.

CHAPTER 27

FORRESTAL

ECHO AND GAMMA TEAMS

95 DAYS UNTIL IMPACT

"**C**overing fire!" yelled Kanagawa as he directed short bursts of rounds from his Mag-rail rifle at any target that exposed itself, while Echo team withdrew from the inner sanctum. The Marines had already claimed over 100 souls as their exosuits provided insurmountable advantages. The vastly inferior Regulars who were attempting to stop them from taking the essence of Perun's computing core next attempted a human wave assault.

Corpses, some of which looked remarkably intact, were soon strewn throughout the inner sanctum. The carnage was incredible. Small fires dotted the ruined server farm, with smoke obscuring much of the room. Burning plastic and broken metal and glass was everywhere.

Keeping the jumbo-sized Monoshield between them and Perun's human Regulars, Bloodbane and Pena grunted with the effort of moving backwards as quickly as they could. Occasionally a bullet would ricochet off their jumbo Monoshield, which only had the effect of encouraging their hasty departure.

As they reached the door to the inner sanctum, Bloodbane and Pena passed Kanagawa. Without moving his carbine sight from possible targets downrange, Kanagawa motioned with his head for them to pass by. As soon as the shield team passed, Kanagawa activated the proximity fuses of several anti-personnel mines that he had placed near the server farm entrance.

Jogging to catch up while he covered their withdrawal, Kanagawa kept his head on a swivel as he scanned the numerous doorways and hidden hidey holes for new threats all the back to the rooftop. He didn't have long to wait. Behind them there was a powerful blast that sent tongue's of flame and smoke curling into the smoky, darkened hall. Cries of pain and anger filled the hall.

"Keep moving! That was one of the mines I set. They're coming!" Kanagawa roared as he hurled his last grenade back towards the server farm entrance. The power and guidance system of Kanagawa's exosuit enabled him to accurately throw an otherwise impossible distance. Another detonation, and more cries of pain erupted before they were drowned out by the sound of a flood of the onrushing Regulars who were still alive.

Just as Kanagawa reached the stairwell, a fusillade of angry sounding bullets ripped through the air just before a rocket propelled grenade impacted the wall next to his current position. Kanagawa was blown off his feet and brutally slammed into the opposite wall with such force it would have turned him into jelly if he had not been in an exosuit. Grunting through the pain, Kanagawa checked his exosuit status and saw far too many red and yellow status indicators. Suddenly his pain began to ease, which Kanagawa knew was from the numbing agent administered by his exosuit. He slowly realized he was too badly hurt to stand up, and his suit was too damaged to effectively help him do so. At least, his exosuit wasn't too damaged to automatically report the injury on Tacnet. It was detected immediately by Gamma 1.

"Echo 1 is down!" roared Blackwater over the all-team commlink. Blackwater was at the center of their column and currently was two floors above Kanagawa. He was just too far away to help his friend, Echo 1, but Echo 8, LCpl. Hiro "Gung Ho" Gozen, and Gamma 3, Pvt. Louis Caron, were close and Blackwater redundantly ordered the two Marines to retrieve Echo 1. Gozen and Caron were already rushing to Kanagawa's aid before Blackwater issued the orders, and Blackwater could follow their progress on Tacnet.

Gozen and Caron leapt down a flight of stairs and landed near Kanagawa. Dust and smoke swirled around Caron's feet as he switched to his new secondary weapon. Caron was Gamma team's heavy weapon's specialist, and he detached a huge tube that had been magnetically linked to the rear of his inky black exosuit. Stepping from the dark stairwell with the giant weapon pointed downrange, the menacing Marine seemed to appear from nowhere through the swirling dust and black smoke in front of pursuing forces of Forrestal.

***

"Take him! We can trade him for Perun's primary core cards!" yelled the officer. He was a young man, and had been identified by Perun for rapid advancement due to his devotion to protecting the AI's control over the impoverished workers of Forrestal. Perun had long ago perfected its system of identifying and training soldiers to protect Perun first, above all other concerns. When Perun spotted the young officer, he hadn't seemed to have any qualms about shooting starving workers in another food riot a few years earlier. That was the sort of loyalty Perun rewarded. The young officer had been rewarded many times since then, as the number of food riots in the worker's paradise of Forrestal were increasing in frequency while the planet was slowly dying.

The young officer certainly hadn't been chosen for his tactical acumen since his experience mostly consisted of executing unarmed, starving workers who never shot back. When they saw the inky black apparition step out of the swirling smoke and fires caused by the RPG that injured Kanagawa, the young officer was so shocked he didn't know what to say and simply skidded to a stop.

Ghosts don't need guns. Marines do. And Marines like guns. A lot. Without making a sound, this ghastly looking Marine pointed the barrel of the huge tube at the pursuing security force and pulled the trigger.

A tight, angry beam of fire erupted from the tube that punched right through the officer and the Regulars he was leading. The heat was so intense, it immolated the Regulars and erased them from existence. The beam of fire shot down the hallway for at least a hundred yards before crashing through the far wall at the end, leaving behind a hallway that became a boiling hell storm of death and destruction that melted the stone construction of the walls. Glass and metal quickly liquefied and ran down to the floor in glowing rivulets. The heat was so intense, the oxygen in the air quickly super heated and ignited downrange from Gamma 3's position to create a vacuum that pulled in additional air to feed the fire.

Gamma 3 nodded slowly in satisfaction at the terrible conflagration in front of him, and he turned back to help Kanagawa into the stairwell to return to the roof. Even had there not been a temporary vacuum, the exosuit would have prevented him from smelling the tiny remaining bits of charred and smoking human meat that was left behind.

*****

"I got you, Echo 1," said Echo 8, Lance Corporal Gozen. He had wrapped Echo 1's arm around his shoulders and was helping Kanagawa stand up behind Gamma 3, when the world on the other side of Gamma 3 lit up in a blazing storm of angry fire. Gozen and Kanagawa stumbled a bit because their exosuit visors darkened to protect their vision. Both noticed their external scanners suddenly indicated the ambient temperature was like the surface of a sun for a few moments.

"Gamma 3, Echo 1, what in the hell was THAT?" barked Kanagawa through his pain. He hadn't noticed he used the all-team commlink.

Gamma 3, Private Caron, stooped to wrap Kanagawa's other arm around his shoulders, and he nodded to Gozen that he was ready to help haul Kanagawa up the stairs before responding. "That was…satisfactory."

"No, seriously, what was that?" Kanagawa grunted through the pain while Caron and Gozen hauled him up the stairs.

"Just a little something the El-Tee tactically acquired from the mad scientists in Lieutenant Alphonso's lab. I don't think it's even got a name yet," Caron said. In Marine parlance, "tactically acquired" was a euphemism for their well-earned reputation for stealing anything not nailed down, and El-Tee was simply a phonetic spelling of LT.

Kanagawa snorted, both at Caron's report and because of the pain that was nonetheless overwhelming his nanites and pain meds. "How 'bout we call it the GMG?" he asked.

Blackwater had already reached the roof by now, but he saw the replay of Caron's hell storm on his visor while he had finished the climb towards the roof. "What's GMG stand for?" Blackwater asked, since Kanagawa's, Caron's and Gozen's conversation was still on the all-team commlink. Using hand motions, Blackwater was busy moving Marines into place for the arrival of the three inbound Bulldogs whose locations were identified on Tacnet as Caron and Gozen finally appeared on the roof with Kanagawa. Clouds of dense black smoke now billowed from behind them and flowed up into the sky.

"It means God Mode Gun," Kanagawa said. "That thing is even scarier than a Firefly."

"Old Gung Ho is gonna be jealous of the Fireman's GMG. I gotta get me one of those now," quipped Echo 8. Gozen's third-person reference to himself by his nickname and simultaneously bestowing the nickname "Fireman" on Caron caused a chorus of guffaws by both teams over the all-team commlink as Bulldog 1 settled down on the roof and dropped its ramp.

Blackwater approved of the new nickname. "The Fireman. I like it. Totally fits Gamma 3's crazy take on providing 'covering fire.'" With that, Blackwater suddenly returned to All Business Mode and began issuing orders for their departure from Forrestal.

When Kanagawa was injured while the teams were ex-filtrating up the stairwell, Blackwater had assumed full control over both Echo and Gamma. The highly experienced Blackwater smoothly handled the loading and liftoff of both teams and all the Bulldogs. "This is Gamma 1, first team get the wounded on Bulldog 1. MOVE OUT!" he roared. The tone of his voice brooked zero joking around.

Echo team didn't need any more encouragement than that and they quickly bounded up the ramp, with most of them helping wounded Marines into the assault shuttle. The Bulldog's engine whine suddenly became a roar as the pilot lifted off before the loading ramp had even finished closing. Bulldog 3 landed seconds later, dropping its ramp as it lightly settled on the rooftop with its engines whining as the power was just barely dialed down low enough to allow it to touch the roof.

"Second team, load now. Shield team, here comes our ride," Blackwater ordered. In less than a minute, Gamma team was quickly away and Bulldog 2 replaced Bulldog 3 on the rooftop. "Let's go! And shut down all exosuit commo suites before boarding," Blackwater ordered, as he helped Bloodbane and Pena carry the jumbo-sized Monoshield into the third Bulldog.

Seconds later, Pilot Officer Helmut Meyer turned his head to nod at his new passengers and confirm they were buckled in as he lifted Bulldog 2 off the smoking rooftop. Meyer's face wasn't visible behind his exosuit visor. Thick smoke dimmed the light outside the Bulldog and darkened the interior. Fires were beginning to burn out of control on the lower floors of the massive, windowless gray building the Marines had assaulted and the building was in danger of collapse.

Mueller returned Meyer's nod. She was onboard with her husband, Dr. Karl Mueller, and was also wearing an exosuit, though like Meyer, she wore the Navy's version instead of an inky black Marine combat exosuit. Using hand signals, she motioned to her husband that their Bulldog was about to jump.

Dr. Mueller responded with a thumbs up and motioned for Bloodbane to hand over the primary core cards that Bloodbane had taken from Perun's processing tower. Despite being buttoned up in an exosuit, Dr. Mueller had no difficulty attaching universal power leads to the primary core cards that Bloodbane gave him, and the core cards lit up.

Commander Mueller looked at Blackwater and gestured with her hand that he should report using hand signals only as Bulldog 2 was under a strict EEQ (Electronic Emissions Quarantine) protocol. The EEQ and this third Bulldog was prearranged during their mission planning only if they had been successful in obtaining the hostile AI's primary core.

Blackwater nodded as Mueller's message was only a reminder. He signed back that the enemy resistance was lighter than expected.

Concerned, Mueller signed, *too easy?*

Nodding more emphatically, Blackwater signed back. It was too easy. Keep the Bulldog under strict EEQ. The AI let us take its core.

Mueller passed Blackwater's report along to the pilot and the rearseater, Chief Sophie Schmidt. It confirmed the worst danger Dr. Mueller had warned them about during the mission planning. That danger was the AI actually wanted to be taken because *Cerberus* was the only ship capable of leaving the Forrestal star system that had trapped Perun in it for centuries. The token resistance on the surface had been meant to lull the *Cerberus* crew into thinking they had safely taken the ancient technology onboard their ship.

Bulldog 2 jumped into space.

CHAPTER 28

ORBIT

CERBERUS

95 DAYS UNTIL IMPACT

"Missile cloud approaching, Captain. Looks like it's getting organized to strike all at once, so that's changing the attack profile and extending the time line a bit," reported LeCroy from the tactical station. LeCroy never took his eyes from his screens while he noted the change in the missile's flight patterns.

Before Ronin could do more than nod slightly, they were interrupted by Delgado. "Captain! Message from the away team strike force. They captured Perun's primary core cards and have been extracted by the three Bulldogs."

"Casualties, Lieutenant?" Capt. Ronin asked. No one on the bridge was surprised by him asking that first. Ronin's first question was always the same. It was because of how deeply he cared for and respected his crew and Marines that their welfare was foremost in his mind.

"No dead, about 30% wounded, including Gunnery Sergeant Kanagawa. Bulldogs 1 and 3 have jumped to the Point Romeo One One rendezvous point. Last message from Pilot Officer Russo advised Bulldog 2 about to initiate a complete EEQ blackout and jump to Point India two five for safety."

Cerberus suddenly rocked with an impact. "We're hit!" yelled Delacroix as he looked at his screens to assess the automated flow of damage reports. He activated a commlink. "Damage control teams to Engineering! The jump drive is down."

Ronin looked at his screen where the countdown timer on it had adjusted to account for the increased time the missiles were taking to arrive. "What hit us?" he asked loudly.

"A particle beam of some sort. Origination is on the planet's surface," said Delacroix. The main viewscreen changed to show the planet with a red highlight indicating the beam's origin. Tacnet had automatically back traced where the threat came from.

"Fire railgun turrets at that site. Heavy slugs. Take it out," Ronin ordered.

"Aye-aye. Firing solution has been loaded into port side turrets. Firing," LeCroy said. The ship shuddered slightly when the massive turrets opened fire.

***

"It's a hit!" yelled the young gunnery officer, a bit too loudly. His enthusiasm drew glances from the rest of the crew manning the giant weapon. It also drew a rebuke from the commanding officer.

"Calm yourself, Lieutenant. Comport yourself like an officer, not a new recruit," said Commander Aden Dyke. "How long until the particle cannon recharges for the next shot?"

While Dyke hadn't bothered to get to know his officer well enough to know that the excitable young gunnery officer actually WAS a new recruit, Dyke knew exactly how long it was until the next recharge but had asked the young officer anyway just to distract him. The particle cannon required an incredible amount of power merely to function, and that amount increased exponentially with distance. Firing through a planetary atmosphere at ships in orbit required an obscene amount of energy and a large infrastructure to generate it. Perun had never bothered to try to devise a way to shrink the system down enough to mount on a space ship because no external threats had existed for centuries.

Dominick Blakely, the young officer, blushed in shame at letting his emotions get ahead of him. Outside of simulations, Blakely had never expected to actually fire the giant weapon. It was too costly and would do nothing to save Forrestal from its End of Days meeting with the remains of Celestra in a few months.

"Recharge complete in…five minutes," Blakely said in a flat voice. He felt thoroughly chastised. Being located in a reinforced operations center deep inside the bedrock below a mountain located several miles away from the particle cannon had the odd effect of magnifying his shame. Interjecting youthful excitement into the cold, dignified quiet that pervaded the center at all times made for a jarring juxtaposition in vibes.

"Have the next target on that vessel loaded. We want to take that ship mostly intact, if possible."

Dominick was about to acknowledge the order when the ground shook violently. An otherworldly rumble from a massive impact drowned out everything for a few seconds while plunging the control center into absolute darkness. The ceiling partially collapsed and spewed a thick cloud of dust throughout the center. A few red emergency lights clicked on and cast their weak light into the heavy, dusty darkness, not enough of them having survived to do more than appear as a weak beacon of light to illuminate mangled corpses. There was no one left alive below the mountain.

The few survivors of the military stationed up on Forrestal's surface were shocked beyond words. Seemingly without warning, both the mountain over the control center and the particle cannon some distance away erupted into multiple mushroom clouds. Moving at over 37,000 miles per second, the six massive slugs fired by the *Cerberus* railguns slammed into both targets at one fifth the speed of light. There was no way for the naked eyes to follow objects with that kind of velocity. It was later reported that there was the brief appearance of six pillars of flame that seemingly blinked into existence and stretched from the outer atmosphere to the planet's surface. They preceded a sound so deep it was felt rather than heard.

There also was no way to miss the resulting impact events. Objects moving that fast transfer kinetic energy into whatever they hit. The greater the kinetic energy, the more heat and force they bring with them. *Cerberus* had fired its heaviest slugs, and they packed an incredible amount of force.

Two-ton, solid-core railgun slugs encased in titanium alloy shells traveling over 37,000 miles per second carry a load of kinetic energy that is an order of magnitude similar to an asteroid strike. The railgun slugs also pushed a massive shock wave ahead of them as they plowed straight into the surface. The inbound shock wave super heated the air by compressing the atmosphere between the surface and the slugs, which smashed trees into flaming toothpicks inside of ground zero.

An apocalyptic wave of incineration flensed leaves and needles from the surrounding forests for miles beyond each ground zero. The fiery destruction barely preceded the following impact shock waves that subsequently crushed the smoking remains of the forests. Ash and smoke from the inferno was lost amid the clouds of fire, dirt and debris launched high into the atmosphere by each impact. The mountain protecting the operations center was turned into a melted crater, with miles of molten ejecta blanketing the surrounding area for dozens of miles.

None of surviving witnesses were positioned anywhere near the destroyed targets.

CHAPTER 29

SLEDGEHAMMER

CERBERUS

95 DAYS UNTIL IMPACT

"Captain, damage control teams reporting in. That beam burned through a small chunk of Engineering and severed the jump drive control nodule. They're bypassing to the auxiliary now but it will take a few minutes," reported Delgado. Her voice remained professional, but Ronin could still detect the stress in her voice. Everyone on the bridge knew they didn't have minutes to spare before the missile cloud arrived.

Ronin also had orders to issue to try save his ship. "Lieutenant LeCroy, engage point defenses when ready. Buy the ship as much time as you can. Lieutenant Perez, take evasive maneuvers and jump the ship on your authority when the drive is back online. Don't wait for additional orders from me."

A chorus of ayes acknowledged his orders. Ronin looked at Delgado. "Lieutenant Delgado, have Sickbay get us a casualty count from Engineering."

Delgado quickly passed the order to Nurse Chrizanne "Anne" Abara in Sickbay. An eerie silence descended on the bridge while everyone kept an eye on the countdown timer heralding the arrival of the missiles. As hundreds of missiles were literally approaching from all points around the ship, Perez's evasive maneuvering could do little to buy *Cerberus* more time, so Perez focused on making the ship's aperture of exposure as small as possible.

The silence was broken when LeCroy released defensive control over the point defense counter batteries to the ship's AI. Soon, *Cerberus* shuddered as the point defense counter batteries opened up. A combination of disruption beams and kinetic gun turrets began destroying inbound missiles by the dozens in each sector that Perez was forced to expose the ship to during the maneuvering.

Two missiles got through the fiery wall of defense thrown up by *Cerberus*. LeCroy's voice echoed throughout the ship. "All hands, brace for impact! Brace! Brace! Brace!"

A pair of celestial sledgehammers slammed into the forward hull armor plating of *Cerberus*. Emergency lighting painted the bridge in a red pall accented by a light, smoky haze. The ship continued to shudder from the point defenses.

"Damage report!" shouted Ronin. He shook his head slightly to clear it as he rubbed his left shoulder where the restraining belt had dug in and prevented him from being thrown clear.

"Nuclear weapon impacts to the port side hull near the prow! Looks like the armor plating held and kept out the hard stuff," said Delacroix. "Casualty reports are being assembled and sent to your screen."

"We can't take many hits like that," Ronin muttered. He looked at his screen and noted the countdown timer, which had rolled over into the negatives by several minutes. "The DC team needs to get the jump drive fixed no-" he began saying when Lieutenant Perez jumped the ship.

CHAPTER 30

POINT INDIA TWO FIVE

BULLDOG 2
95 DAYS UNTIL IMPACT

In the silence pervading Bulldog 2, all eyes were on Dr. Mueller as he hurriedly hacked into the primary core cards that the Marines brought aboard. He was using a home-brewed, purpose-built hacking computer with retro-engineered programming language translation provided by the crew from *Pytor the Great*. Karl had built his hacking system while Echo and Gamma teams were training for the assault in the caverns of The Enclave. The assault shuttle's rearseater, Sophie Schmidt, was acting as Mueller's assistant. The two of them had repeatedly rehearsed their hacking plan prior to the mission going ahead.

As soon as Dr. Mueller hacked into the core cards, they lit up. Within seconds, the air inside the Bulldog suddenly drained out of the shuttle and the lights died. Inside, everyone turned on their exosuit external lights.

Perun is attempting to take control of the shuttle, signed Dr. Mueller to the others while he waited for the onboard computer to finish extracting the information that Ronin had wanted him to obtain. *It shut down our life support system*, he added unnecessarily.

Blackwater exchanged glances with Commander Mueller while her husband was occupied with hacking the core cards. Despite a strict EEQ quarantine that shut down everyone's data and commlinks, and the exosuit visorsobscuring facial expressions, Commander Mueller's body language still clearly communicated her worry about bringing a highly capable enemy AI aboard a Bulldog. Since this was now Dr. Mueller's show for the time being, Blackwater hated the feeling of uselessness that he was experiencing right now.

The shuttle lurched slightly as Perun attempted to penetrate the Bulldog's software firewall and gain control over the thrusters. PO Helmut Meyer swiftly flipped off a switch to power down the flight systems board that controls the shuttle's drive and thrusters. He turned to the others and signed, *We're adrift now. I tripped the hardwired power switch to cut the power for the drive engines.*

Dr. Mueller kept his exosuit camera trained onto his computer screen's readout while time slowed to a crawl as the darkened, airless shuttle drifted through space. He sat so motionless he appeared to have become a statute of a man in an exosuit.

To pass the time, Blackwater sat back and mentally reviewed the mission and made notes for the debriefing to come later. Despite the difficulty of assaulting a massive building and indoor close quarters combat in the confined spaces, Blackwater's Marine team would definitely hear about the mistakes he had spotted. It was always time to learn what his Marines could improve upon.

Blackwater hadn't kept track of how much time had passed while he was occupied, but Dr. Mueller's sudden motion caught his attention.

I've got it! signed Dr. Mueller after he stood up.

All eyes turned to the pilot, who shook his head. He had been forced to shut down all the shuttle's flight systems while Perun attempted to breach their software firewalls. Meyer signed to make the shuttle's status clear. *Negative on pilot control. All systems compromised by hostile AI. Time to abandon ship and scuttle it.*

Blackwater nodded. This was his show now. He stood up and pointed towards the airlock with a motion indicating everyone needed to leave and leave now.

Commander Mueller reached the airlock first since she was nearest to it and opened it up. Motioning, she sent Meyer and Schmidt out first, followed by her husband. She then nodded at Bloodbane and Pena, who quickly followed Dr. Mueller. Then she turned to look at Blackwater to make sure he was aware the crew had departed and she was about to depart as well.

Blackwater acknowledged he was aware and ready to take his next steps by giving Commander Mueller a thumbs up. She nodded, and pulled out her pistol. Taking careful aim at the airlock controls, she fired several shots into them. Sparks went flying from the bullet impacts as they smashed the controls into junk and effectively froze the airlock in the open position. Cmdr. Mueller then entered the airlock and jumped from the Bulldog out into space.

Alone now, Blackwater moved through the shuttle cabin to a large, metal container that had been bolted to the wall near the starboard engine firewall. The lights in the cabin began flickering, which was reflected inside his visor by his cold blue eyes that were flecked with gold highlights. Fresh sweat began trickling down his head with the effort. If his black hair hadn't been shaved nearly to his scalp, the cowlick his mother had always adored would have stood straight up.

Blackwater suddenly noticed the flickering light followed a repeating pattern while he opened an access door on the plain, crudely constructed hull colored metal container. The thing was bolted together, and it did not need to be pretty and refined to fulfill its purpose.

Probably trying to get my attention through some sort of light messaging code. Too bad, you stupid machine. Not today, he said to himself. Had Blackwater been born in an earlier era, he would have recognized the flashing as ancient Morse code. The AI named Perun had no idea that Morse code had disappeared on Earth centuries ago during The Fall, when the mother planet's civilization collapsed and no one from Earth was left who would recognize it.

Inside the access door wasn't the standard digital trigger; it was analog. There was nothing digital about it that Perun could interfere with. This simple analog timer had been deliberately chosen for that reason.

During the mission planning and prep, Blackwater had rehearsed everything there was to know about the old-school analog trigger he was about to set. It had been drilled into him by Lieutenant Gustav that Perun must be hacked to obtain the fleet access codes and then destroyed to stop the Forrestal AI from changing them. Failure to achieve either step would result in many lives being lost because Perun couldn't move refugees through the jump gate like *Cerberus* could.

As he grasped the trigger mechanism, the blinking lights suddenly went out and the interior of the shuttle was plunged into an inky darkness broken only by the exterior light beam from his exosuit. Blackwater began to shake his head slightly in exasperation when Bulldog 2 suddenly lurched to the side, which threw him across the interior and slammed him into the wall of the port side hull. In the vacuum of space, Blackwater hadn't been able to hear the whine of the shuttle's thrusters suddenly spinning up because sound can't travel without atmosphere. Perun had figured out how to reverse the hardwired kill switch and send power back to the thrusters!

Perun had infiltrated past the Bulldog's software firewall just enough to begin taking partial control of the shuttle's thrusters. Groaning in pain inside his exosuit, Blackwater scanned his visor's damage report on his exosuit status. Still green lights, he noted. Just then, the shuttle began to lurch again before the thruster suddenly cut out.

Blackwater knew he was now in a race against time. He had to start the trigger and bail out before Perun achieved full control over the shuttle's flight systems. Again, the shuttle lurched and Blackwater was thrown against the starboard hull near the trigger. Blackwater hit much harder than he did against the port side, but was ready for it this time and he managed to reach out with his arm to snag the container with the trigger. By the next time the thruster fired, Blackwater had clamped himself to the bolted down container.

Infernal computer, Blackwater thought to himself as he once again grasped the trigger. He twisted the mechanism to arm the timed chemical reaction of the trigger. Once it began, nothing would stop the reaction from running. *Ten minutes and counting. Time to look lively, he thought.* His dark mood began brightening with the thought of leaving the Bulldog behind. As far as Blackwater was concerned, hauling an enemy AI effectively meant the Bulldog was as good as actually being haunted.

The chemical reaction began and cast the shuttle in a hot green glowing hue. Inside his exosuit, Blackwater's eyebrows furrowed in alarm and he exclaimed to himself, "Gods, that looks scary!" He pushed off from where he had attached himself inside the Bulldog and moved to the still open airlock.

Before he entered the airlock, Blackwater got his first good look at Commander Mueller's handiwork. "Good shooting," he murmured to himself in approval. It was Commander Mueller's job to keep Perun from taking over the airlock controls and trapping Blackwater inside the shuttle. No matter what, Perun would have gambled that Blackwater wouldn't have committed suicide if he were trapped inside the shuttle because the enemy AI had no other options available. What Perun couldn't have known is that Blackwater would have followed through with arming the bomb detonator anyway, figuring that it made little difference whether he were killed by Perun or by the blast. Dead is dead.

Blackwater jumped free of Bulldog 2 using the power of his exosuit and firing his thrusters to get as clear of the shuttle as he could. Glancing around, he saw nothing. That could only mean those who departed earlier were now too far away to see because of the extra distance traveled after the Bulldog's thrusters had been partially engaged by Perun. Blackwater decided to angle his thrusters to change his direction of travel, just in case Perun had managed to turn on a camera or sensor to project his future position and intercept him. With the EEQ still engaged, no one would have any idea where Blackwater was, or where to look for him, so he was all alone in the void until he could emerge from the EEQ protocols.

Minutes later, as the timer on the inside of his visor approached zero, Blackwater turned around to look back at the shuttle far behind him. At this distance, it was no longer visible so he engaged his optical magnification. Suddenly the image of Bulldog 2 seemed as if it were only a few steps away instead of miles and he began to counting down out loud. "Six. Five. Four. Three. Two. One. Boom!" The seconds crawled by. "Boom! Dammit, go boom ya piece of junk!" he roared inside his exosuit. Still nothing. The silence seemed to be mocking him.

Another minute elapsed. Shaking his head, Blackwater continued talking to himself and decided to return to the Bulldog. "Stupid piece of junk. We should have just turned it into dust like I wanted to with a railgun, but nooooo. We have to get cute with ancient timers and stuff," he grumbled as he got closer. "Now old Blackwater's gotta go back and get himself blown up bec—"

Bulldog 2 suddenly exploded. It wasn't an ordinary self-destruction that left a few smoking holes in the hull. Bulldog 2 was obliterated, with a shock wave rolling away in all directions along with shredded bits of metal moving at the relative speed of bullets.

With only seconds to react, Blackwater quickly switched off his exosuit's EEQ. "Brace for impact. Brace. Brace. Brace!" warned Blackwater's exosuit as he curled into the smallest ball he could to reduce his exposed surface area as much as possible. A few seconds later, the shock wave impact slammed into Blackwater with so much force it knocked him out and sent him bouncing away like a ricochet.

Blackwater's last conscious thought was to hope turning off the exosuit's EEQ allowed someone to find his beat-up corpse.

CHAPTER 31

POINT INDIA TWO FIVE

BULLDOG 2 PASSENGER SPACEWALK
95 DAYS UNTIL IMPACT

The sudden flare of light from the blast weakly illuminated the others, who had tethered themselves together. Even though concepts like up and down mattered little in space, the group had habitually aligned their orientation to each other so no one was upside down in relation to the others.

Despite being bathed in the weak light, the inky black Marine exosuits remained dark enigmas until Bloodbane motioned for the others to exit the EEQ protocol. The fiery demise of Bulldog 2 was the definitive signal that Perun had been destroyed. They would now be safe from the hostile AI's additional attempts to hack and infiltrate their systems.

Inside her exosuit, Commander Mueller scanned the situational data that began filtering in from the exosuit's scanners. More data suddenly flowed in from Tacnet once all of the exosuit links were interconnected.

Immediately, a collision warning message began flashing inside everyone's exosuit helmets, accompanied by an audible alarm. "Warning, inbound debris. Warning, inbound debris."

Mueller eye clicked the warning icon inside her visor to shut down the alarm and stop it from repeating. There were nervous glances between each of them in the tethered circle because they were totally exposed out in space. They were slowly rotating relative to each other because no one had wanted to attempt a control burn while their suits had been in EEQ and they would have been unable to coordinate the maneuver. Mueller opened a commlink to the group.

"Everyone sit tight. There's nowhere for us to run and hide, so we just have to ride this out and hope for the best. Ten seconds until the debris and shock wave passes by us," she said. Clicks from the others acknowledged her message.

Space around them suddenly filled with the shrapnel remains of Bulldog 2. Some glowed with residual heat; others merely reflected the distant sunlight of this system's star. They were supposed to have exited the shuttle at a safe distance to the planned detonation, but Perun's failed attempts at controlling the maneuvering thrusters had brought it much closer to them.

It was too close. "I think that's it, we're clea…" Mueller had started saying when a larger, slower moving chunk of glowing debris slammed into her leg with the relative velocity of a bullet and the waning heat of recently molten metal.

Despite the somewhat lower velocity, the ragged piece of partially melted hull plating easily sheared Mueller's right leg off above the knee. The crushing impact also severed her tether that linked to the others and she caromed off into the black before anybody could react. Alone inside her exosuit, stars spinning wildly so she couldn't orient herself, Mueller first gasped and then screamed in agony. Her exosuit transmitter suddenly failed and cut short her traumatic cry over the all-team commlink.

"Commander!" yelled Schmidt. Her exclamation was drowned out by an even louder yell.

"Diane!" roared Dr. Mueller. His voice clearly conveyed a complex message of fear for his wife and dread for their family. There wasn't anything he could do, because Dr. Mueller's exosuit was automatically using its thrusters to stop the rotation and spin that began when his wife's tether was torn away by the debris impact. Agonized seconds passed with no further communication, so Dr. Mueller began trying to figure out how to control his exosuit's thrusters to go search for his wife.

Bloodbane overrode Dr. Mueller's exosuit controls. "Doc! I'm sorry, but the Commander's gone! You chase after her, and you're dead, too. You can't …" he said before his voice faltered.

Dr. Mueller looked directly at Bloodbane's exosuit, no emotion visible in either exosuit visor. "You can't, doc. We lose you and the command codes you just obtained from that damn AI, many more will die. And you have to be there for your children. Keep her memory alive for them and speak for her. Only you can do that for her now," Bloodbane added when he found his voice again.

Shoulders somehow sagging while floating in space, Dr. Mueller took a ragged breath and tried to compose himself. Though spoken softly, the honesty and truth in Bloodbane's words hit him like a hammer blow. He reluctantly nodded in grim acceptance.

The effect of Commander Mueller's tether break had created a whip snap effect that traveled downstream, so no two of them were facing the same direction afterwards. They busied reorienting themselves, which also served to divert diverted their attention away from the tragic loss of their ship's executive officer.

Less than a minute had passed when Pena's groan over the all-team commlink was communicated over the frequency. "Ungh," he said, strain evident in his voice. "I'm hit!" Pena's voice sounded more annoyed than hurt.

Bloodbane's eyes checked Pena's status displayed by Tacnet inside his visor as he grabbed the tether and used his exosuit's thrusters to get closer to him. In the dim light, he could see that the lower half Pena's left arm had been torn off, but that image conflicted with the Tacnet data suggesting Pena was relatively unhurt.

"Pena! Umm ... You OK, buddy?" Bloodbane asked over a private commlink as he got close. He could see Pena's exosuit also had a ragged but shallow cut that had been sliced through the left side over the rib cage. The exosuit had resealed the breach to stop the loss of oxygen from both damage points.

Pena nodded and was calming down as he realized he wasn't hurt as badly as he initially feared. "Yeah, mostly just suit integrity worries. That shrapnel tore away half of my mechanical arm, and the slice along my ribs didn't get deep enough to hurt me. My exosuit sealed the air leaks."

Pena held still while Bloodbane continued inspecting the exterior exosuit damage for him. "Now that you're not sporting that thing you call a left arm, we could put you back into the arm wrestling rotation again." Bloodbane spoke distractedly, because he was taking out a can of sealant spray from Pena's emergency pack.

"Ha! You ladies still couldn't take me!" Pena retorted, but in more of a quiet voice than anything else. He was also looking over their situation on Tacnet inside his visor while Bloodbane went to work. "The Commander's already beyond our suit scanners," he said dejectedly.

Bloodbane got busy spraying the sealant over the damaged parts of Pena's exosuit. "I know. I think the impact took out her exosuit's Tacnet links. I replayed the moment of impact on my way over and realized she was gone. We'll need a Bulldog to try to find her." He quickly finished up and returned the sealant to Pena's emergency pack. "Done. Now don't do nothing stupid and get killed 'cause the Corps needs somebody to pay for that suit."

Pena snorted. "Put it on my tab. I'm good for it." It was an old joke.

By now, Bloodbane and Pena had been rejoined by the others as they had been occupied reeling themselves closer on the remaining tethers.

They had nothing to do now, but wait for rescue.

CHAPTER 32

STEEPLECHASE

KITTY HAWK

95 DAYS UNTIL IMPACT

"My God, they're fast!" exclaimed Commander Fisher, shaking his head slightly in amazement. He was watching the plot updates on Tacnet with Captain Nagun as it tracked the breakaway element of enemy warships who were now chasing *Kitty Hawk*.

"Only way we can shake them is with our FTL jump drive," murmured Nagun. "And we're supposed to keep them close enough to think they have a chance at catching us."

A small smile quirked Fisher's mouth for a moment. "That, or outgun them." His sense of humor shone through, because there obviously was no way for *Kitty Hawk* to engage the sizable enemy element and survive a straight up fight.

Nagun snorted. "Their sensors are so good that we've been painted with them the whole time. We can't even use our drive for stealth. They saw right through that imagery like it wasn't even there. So we only have two final options. Run or gun..." he began saying when Tacnet updated with a new image that had entered the *Kitty Hawk's* outer scanner range.

Fisher also saw it and finished Nagun's sentence. "Or go with Option C and play hide-and-seek," he said, a full-on smile breaking across his face. Tacnet had detected an asteroid several miles across that was streaking into their combat zone.

Nagun's face lit up with an idea. "Know what's hidden that can't ever be found, XO?" he asked.

Fisher's eyes flicked over to look at Nagun. "Something that was never there to begin with, Captain?"

Nodding with a cold smile and a gleam in his eyes, Nagun said, "Exactly. We need to vent some plasma. Make it appear as if we're damaged and fleeing towards that rock. Use the plasma cloud to mask another micro jump to get us closer to it. Then leave a trail going round the far side for our pursuers to follow."

"Meanwhile, we jump away before they get to the far side, so they have to assume we're hiding on the rock and waste time trying to find us while we're off causing trouble someplace else," Fisher said.

Nagun snorted again. "So, do you like it?" he asked. It was an old joke in the Navy as well as between themselves.

Nodding, Fisher's cold smile matched Capt. Nagun's. "You had me at devious and sneaky. I love it." He opened a commlink to Engineering.

Kitty Hawk's Chief Engineer, Samuel Nortan, responded immediately. "Go for Chief Nortan."

"This is Commander Fisher, prepare to vent some plasma. We're going to use it to mask a micro jump."

"Aye, sir. We won't have enough for more than a couple of ventings though before we need to recharge the plasma," Nortan acknowledged.

Fisher had expected that. "Just two releases, Chief. Once here, and one in an hour or so. We'll use the second venting to hide our jump out of this mess and confuse our pursuers," Fisher said.

"Acknowledged, Commander. We're ready for venting on your command," said Nortan. He sounded somewhat distracted as he said so because he was busy entering the commands to vent the plasma while he was speaking.

Nagun sent the coordinates of the asteroid over to the navigator and ordered, "Plot a micro jump to get us near that asteroid. Jump on my command." On a smaller ship like *Kitty Hawk*, helm and navigation functions were combined.

"Coordinates ready, Captain," responded the navigator.

Nagun nodded towards Fisher, who opened the commlink to Engineering. "Chief Nortan, we're ready on our end. Vent."

"Aye-aye, Commander. Venting now. The clock is running. Sixty seconds to build up enough outside the ship to become visible on scanners and mask the ship," said Nortan.

Nagun started a timer countdown on lower right corner of the main viewscreen. The bridge was completely silent as everyone focused on both the countdown and their duties until it hit zero. After the minute had elapsed, he looked at Fisher, eyebrows raised in a silent question.

"We're good. Plasma cloud has formed," Fisher noted a few seconds later. He was keeping his eyes glued to the scanner feed displayed on his screen. The plasma would show up on enemy sensors like a beacon.

"Jump the ship," ordered Nagun without a moment's hesitation. The enemy warships were getting too close for his comfort and they needed to be elsewhere.

Behind an expanding cloud of super heated plasma, *Kitty Hawk* vanished.

CHAPTER 33

POINT ROMEO ONE ONE

CERBERUS

95 DAYS UNTIL IMPACT

"Why didn't they hit us with ordnance carrying antimatter payloads?" Ronin asked LeCroy. Ronin was standing next to LeCroy at the tactical station while they sorted out the ship's overall situation after they had arrived at Point Romeo One One to rendezvous with their returning Marine ground force. "If those were antimatter, we would just be glowing dust particles by now."

LeCroy shook his head. "I don't know. We can speculate that maybe we were too close to Forrestal for a blast of that magnitude, but we would just be guessing without any other supporting facts."

Ronin nodded. "Yeah. We can also speculate that they don't have many of those antimatter payloads available, either. The two duds we caught after transiting the jump gate were ancient, pre-Fall relics that had exceeded their shelf life."

Understanding dawned on LeCroy and he nodded slowly. "Only reason to cart around expired weapons is because you might need to use one but can't replace them."

Smiling coldly, Ronin nodded in turn. "Exactly. Readings from the emissions spectrometers also told us those nukes were over a century old, too. Carrying around weapons that far past their sell-by date means they haven't focused on munitions for a long time."

"How does this help us, Captain?"

"Right now, it doesn't, at least from a tactical perspective. It merely is more confirmation that we face a civilization in serious decline due to that AI's mismanagement. But it doesn't help us if we have to take on their navy again. Despite the End of Days, they probably still have many more missiles than they have remaining minutes on the clock. That presumption eliminates running and gunning as an engagement strategy to force them to take potshots at *Cerberus* and use up their ordnance. But maybe it'll come into play in some other way," Ronin said, thinking aloud as he responded.

Delacroix walked over to join them. "Captain, the casualty and damage reports have been sent to your tablet. Damage control teams have fully repaired the connection to the jump drive control nodule."

Ronin nodded acknowledgment of the report. The grave look on his face asked the most serious question for him.

Delacroix had served with Ronin long enough to know that the health and safety of his crew was always paramount in Ronin's mind. "Fourteen wounded, all slight. Four dead," Delacroix said.

A look of confusion flitted across Capt. Ronin's tired face. "More wounded than dead?" Ronin had been in more than enough combat in space to know that typically, the dead far outnumbered the wounded because of the hazards of operating in an unforgiving environment like dark space.

Delacroix nodded. "Yessir. That beam made a quick, clean stab instead of a slice. Had it dragged across the hull, it would have been a lot worse. And had it been a kinetic weapon, it also would have been far worse. Two light nukes weren't enough to do more than rattle our cage. A dozen, and then we would have been in trouble but we could take the hits from just two."

That was small comfort to Ronin, as he thought about his dead crew. The most solemn, difficult task of a commanding officer was to visit their families with the terrible news. It was a task he had dreaded above all others, yet would never consider shirking. The reactions of the surviving families varied from grim grief and acceptance, to outright hostility. Sometimes they refused even to speak with Ronin. As grim as it was, Ronin nonetheless thought that the worst was when a dead crew member had no next of kin. That just added another layer of sadness to the whole situation.

Ronin shook off the sense of grief and refocused. "Our SAR mission ready to launch?" he asked, using the navy's common acronym for Search And Rescue.

"Aye, Captain. They're ready for launch. Deck Chief Taylor reports the Flight Deck was undamaged. They can launch and retrieve the Bulldogs and are awaiting your order, sir."

"Send them. Go get the rest of our people back," Ronin ordered.

"Aye Aye, Captain," Delacroix said, then returned to his scanning station and opened a commlink to the Flight Deck.

"CAG, this is Lieutenant Delacroix. The Captain says you're a 'go' for the SAR mission to find Bulldog 2. Launch your birds and make way for the remaining returning Bulldogs from the ground force away mission." Delacroix unconsciously used the CAG abbreviation to refer to Lieutenant Sunderland, who was the Commander, Air Group aboard *Cerberus*.

***

"Aye, Lieutenant. SAR mission is a go launch," responded Sunderland. He tapped the node on his collar and closed the commlink with the bridge and switched to the commlink channel for his Bulldog pilots. "Bulldog search and rescue, this is Archangel. You have a 'go launch' order from the skipper."

The reply from the waiting Bulldog 5 flight crew was immediate. "Good copy, Archangel. SAR mission to Point India Two Five is a go." The commlink closed, and Bulldog 5 quickly launched from *Cerberus*.

Now all we gotta do is land our incoming Bulldogs, thought Sunderland.

***

"*Cerberus*, this is Bulldog 1, we are in the landing pattern with Bulldog 3. ETA 63 seconds," announced Bulldog 1's rearseater, Chief Patterson over the commlink channel. "Request medical teams meet us in the Hangar Bay. We have wounded Marines aboard."

"Roger that, Bulldog 1. Medical teams are already standing by," responded Delgado from the communications station on the bridge of *Cerberus*. She looked over to Ronin, who was positioned at her scanning station right next to her, to relay the message but he gave her a quick head nod to acknowledge he had overheard the message.

"We can take about 72 hours to lick our wounds. *Pytor the Great* won't be arriving from the Enclave for about a week, give or take a few days. Once they're here, we can rapidly move into the next phase of this operation," Ronin said to Delacroix. "I want to get our people as rested and healed as possible before *Pytor the Great* arrives."

Delacroix nodded. "Repair and rest, aye. Lieutenant Sunderland has his Tomcat pilots rotating their combat air patrols already. They've been investigating and clearing all unknown contacts reported by our forward drone screen and will continue in that effort until we move again. There's a lot of junk in the neighborhood."

Snorting softly, Ronin raised his right eyebrow. "Couple more months, and we'll see a whole lot more junk flying around out there." The End of Days was creating some severe time pressure, and it was weighing heavily on his mind. "I just hope we aren't too late."

CHAPTER 34

NEAR POINT INDIA TWO FIVE

BULLDOG 5
94 DAYS UNTIL IMPACT

"Hey, baby, wanna ride?" asked Chief Akira Nakamura in a sultry and totally insincere voice once they were within commlink range. He had located a single homing beacon from a Marine exosuit and directed Bulldog 5's pilot, Gary Chanson, to its source.

"Ah. I dunno. My mama tried to raise me right and told me not to get mixed up with the booze and the sketchy women," came Blackwater's quick response. He could see the shuttle now as it approached closer.

"Well, your mama was just trying to raise herself a right real gentleman," snarked Nakamura in a poor attempt at a Texas accent. Then in a businesslike tone, he added, "Thirty seconds."

"Gentleman? Why, I'm a damn saint!" said Blackwater, matching Nakamura's blatant insincerity.

Chanson barked a short laugh. "Ha! Saint? I dunno 'bout that. Chief, we try to raise these boys right, and where do we find them? No adult supervision. Slumming on dark street corner's down in the 'hood. Consorting with questionable ladies of the night. Stealing cars. What's next?" he quipped as he maneuvered the Bulldog very close to Blackwater.

Nakamura's voice changed to sound very parental as he readied to open the airlock. "He's a mangy-looking stray, all right. Real questionable behavior. I bet he kicks puppies and runs with scissors, too."

"Hey, I resemble that!" Blackwater said as he closed the outer door of the airlock behind him and sealed it. He turned to eye the red and green lights next to the inner door. When the green light lit, Chief Nakamura opened the airlock from the inside.

"Thanks for the lift, boys," Blackwater said as he stepped inside. His voice sounded tired, prompting Nakamura to immediately recheck Blackwater's health status.

"Grab a seat, Gunnery Sergeant. You look like you're about to fall down," Nakamura said as the shuttle began moving again. "Walk us through what happened. Did the others make it out of the Bulldog?"

Grunting with pain and effort, Blackwater lowered his aching bones into a seat. He removed his exosuit helmet and cracked his neck before he nodded slowly and spoke. "Yeah. After they jumped ship as per the plan, the enemy AI was rapidly learning to gain control over the Bulldog. If we had brought along more of it than just a few primary core cards, I think we would all be dead by now. The thing was fighting to control the thrusters and engines, but only had managed to gain intermittent, partial control. I finished setting the demolition charge and jumped ship, too, only to determine the AI might have been able to stop the explosive's timer as we went well over the zero mark. Made my way back to trigger it manually and the whole thing blew up in my face before I got all the way back there. I didn't catch any shrapnel, though; that went off in other directions."

Nakamura's face registered surprise at Blackwater's casual report about nearly committing suicide through manually triggering a bomb. "Total commitment to cause, Gunny. That's some real John Wayne stuff right there."

Eyes closed and head tilted back by then, Blackwater acknowledged Nakamura's compliment before he fell asleep from sheer exhaustion. "Who the hell is John Wayne?" he quipped, completing the second half of the ancient joke.

Letting Blackwater get some rest, Nakamura returned to his rear-seater station to resume scanning for the others. They had already expanded their search area twice when they stumbled across Blackwater's fading beacon. Who knows where the others were by now?

CHAPTER 35

NEAR POINT INDIA TWO FIVE

BULLDOG 5
93 DAYS UNTIL IMPACT

The silence in the cabin of Bulldog 5 had dragged on for hours. Blackwater sighed softly, too softly for Chanson or Nakamura to hear over the ambient noise of the shuttle's engine whine. Had they been able to hear Blackwater's sigh, they would only have silently echoed it. Despite the pervasive cockiness of Bulldog pilots and rear-seaters, neither of them dared to sigh aloud from the tedium of several long days of searching. Blackwater would mount their heads atop pikes outside the Marine ready rooms as a warning to the other flight crews about getting bored on a SAR mission when Marines and ship's crew needed a rescue.

Nakamura broke the silence at last. "No joy. We need to expand our search grid again."

Chanson wasn't surprised and had an expanded search grid already programmed into the navigation system. They had repeated this process a number of times the past couple of days without success. "Roger that. I have a wider grid ready up in the nav system."

Blackwater hardly paid attention to what they were saying. He sat in the back and started flipping a calorie bar into the air a few times and catching it to distract himself and his temper. *Where are they?* he again wondered to himself.

Minutes passed quietly. The hum of instruments and engine whine again had enveloped the men aboard Bulldog 5, leaving each to their thoughts. Blackwater flipped the calorie bar in the air again, and missed the catch. Irritated, he picked it up and flipped it again. And missed the catch again.

What the hell? he thought. It looked like the arc of the calorie bar in flight had deformed towards the starboard side of the Bulldog. Paying closer attention now, Blackwater repeated the flip and catch sequence. And missed again. The calorie bar was clearly drifting toward starboard a tiny bit.

Blackwater moved to Nakamura's station. "Hey, how strong is the gravity out here?" he asked.

"Which direction? With two planets about to collide, there's a galactic tug-of-war going on out there. Right now it's stronger to our starboard based on our current orientation, and is growing stronger each day from that direction because it's from Celestra," Nakamura replied. He didn't have to explain that Celestra was rapidly approaching because it was obvious, which meant they came closer to the planet's gravity well as it got closer.

"Which gravity well was closest when Bulldog 2 blew up?" Blackwater asked.

Nakamura tilted his head to the side slightly as he responded. "Neither. You were in a temporary Lagrange point where the gravity wells basically zeroed each other out. We've been warping our search grid towards the nearest gravity well to account for drift towards that well."

"How much momentum did I have when you found me?" Blackwater asked. His eyes were unfocused as they looked towards an upper corner of the ceiling as he thought through the idea that was forming.

"Not much. You were only moving at 30 meters per second, relative," Nakamura said, still not sure where Blackwater was going with this.

"I had time to curl into a ball before the shock wave hit me to reduce the force of impact. What if the others didn't, or couldn't?" Blackwater said, now giving Nakamura the missing piece of information that he couldn't have known in advance.

Nakamura shook his head slightly, lips pressed into a line. "Even assuming they were traveling at twice your relative velocity, we've already been searching beyond that range for a while now."

Before either of them could say anything more, they were interrupted by Chanson. "What if they were struck by a piece of debris? Would that result in more acquired velocity?"

Pursing his lips now while he thought, Nakamura replied slowly, drawing out the first few words. "Maybe. If the debris was moving too fast, it would just pulverize them and keep on moving. If there were more than one debris strike, it's possible some kinetic velocity was transferred." He turned back to face his screen and pulled up a schematic of the device used to destroy Bulldog 2.

"It says the explosive you triggered used the Marine 'P for Plenty' formula. What does that mean?" Nakamura asked quizzically.

Snorting, Blackwater knew the answer both from long experience as a Marine, and from having the bomb basically blow up in his face a few days ago. "It means we love to make things go BOOM."

Eyebrows rising at Blackwater's comment, Nakamura replied. "So, assume it contained twice enough explosive as needed to destroy the Bulldog?" he asked.

"If that. Maybe triple. We do love to blow shit up," Blackwater admitted.

Chief Nakamura took a wild guess at the explosive force used for the bomb, ran some numbers to further guess at transferred kinetic velocity, and overlaid it all over a schematic of the Lagrange Point that was India Two Five.

The new search grids didn't even resemble the circular grid they had been using. Depending on which direction they may have been flung, the new grids looked like a bumpy ball with opposing arms extending towards the competing gravity wells.

"Your call, Gunnery Sergeant. Keep searching towards Celestra but get further down into that planetary well like this new grid suggests, or go towards Forrestal," Nakamura said. Right now, choosing a direction was a tossup so gut feelings counted as much in the decision process as did anything else. Blackwater knew that as well as Chanson and Nakamura.

"Forrestal. Let's go down into Forrestal's gravity well," Blackwater said. He just prayed his gut feeling was right.

FORRESTAL GRAVITY WELL

BULLDOG 5
92 DAYS UNTIL IMPACT

Unshaven and smelling fairly ripe, the three occupants of Bulldog 5 were haggard. If it weren't for the onboard clock, terms like day and night otherwise no longer carried any meaning as the shuttle continued to prowl closer and closer to Forrestal.

"Hopefully, no one will notice one little shuttle flying around in all that chaos," grumbled Chanson. His voice carried a little bit of dread.

"Where's their navy? I thought they had more ships on patrol," Blackwater asked, leaning over Nakamura's shoulder to get a better look at his screens. Like Chanson and Nakamura, he had climbed out of his exosuit days ago.

Nakamura pointed out a cluster of ships on a heading that returned them to orbit. "I think this element of ships is the group that *Kitty Hawk* led away from the ground operation a couple days ago. And our drone network telemetry that's up on Tacnet says most of the rest are on the far side of Forrestal at the moment except this ship that's coming closer to our position. Nakamura had previously informed Blackwater of *Kitty Hawk*'s unexpected appearance during the ground mission, so his reference to the ship's name did not require additional explanation.

"Still, we're getting a bit too close to Forrestal for comfort," replied Blackwater, vocalizing what all three of them were thinking. He had fought his way on to the planet, and then off again, only a couple days ago and didn't particularly want to visit the neighborhood again. He was only there to collect their crew and leave the scene.

A sudden beeping emitted from Nakamura's station. "Contact! Intermittent telemetry field detected. It's weak, but it matches the Tacnet signature from an exosuit," Nakamura said, excitement suddenly overwhelming his exhaustion. "Emergency beacons are not activated, presumably to avoid drawing attention to themselves with enemy navy in the vicinity. "Designating contact as Lima-1," he added.

Chanson changed course to vector the Bulldog towards Lima-1. "They're even further down into the gravity well. ETA three hours. Everybody suit up," he ordered unnecessarily because Nakamura and Blackwater were already getting into their exosuits.

After crawling by for days, several hours suddenly seemed to zoom past as they closed with Lima-1. "Telemetry received from five exosuits now. We're still not getting a reading from Commander Mueller though," Nakamura said after he returned to his station. After confirming the three of them were completely buttoned up in their exosuits, Nakamura then drained the air from the shuttle's interior to speed up the process of bringing the away team inside. "The can is drained," he announced, using their slang for emptying air from a ship or shuttle.

Chanson and Blackwater exchanged glances at Nakamura's update. Something was wrong. Blackwater found himself hoping it was just a faulty exosuit Tacnet node that was responsible for Mueller's exosuit being off scans, but the realist in him knew the extreme danger of a space walk in hostile territory all too well, especially as the exosuits out there had to be getting dangerously low on power.

The Bulldog slowed on final approach over the relative top of five exosuits tethered together. The suits were oriented such that they were facing down and away from the approach.

Nakamura decided to risk opening a commlink despite their proximity to Forrestal's navy. "Bulldog 5 to Bulldog 2 away team, prepare for immediate exfil. Confirm missing team member is Commander Mueller?"

The reply from Bloodbane was immediate. "That's affirm. We believe the commander is KIA and her location unknown. We're glad to see you guys. Getting pretty low on most everything here." Despite his sheer exhaustion, Bloodbane's voice sounded surprised at the sudden appearance of Bulldog 5, in addition to grave and exhausted.

Having moved inside the airlock, Blackwater opened the outer door to space as the shuttle finished matching direction and speed with the exosuits. He hooked himself to a tether attached to the shuttle and pushed out into space towards the exosuits. He could see that Pena's suit was badly damaged and his missing mechanical arm was going to make boarding the shuttle challenging. Especially when everyone's exosuits were down to emergency power only, which meant no thruster assist was available as all their dwindling reserves had automatically routed power to life support.

Chanson had done a good job of getting his Bulldog closer to the group, without getting so close that it put anyone in danger. Using his own exosuit thrusters because his reserves hadn't been drained by being in use for several days in space, Blackwater reached the exosuit cluster in a few minutes and began issuing orders. "All right, let's do this by the numbers. Dr. Mueller, then pilot and rearseater follow my tether back to the shuttle. Echo 12 and I will follow along and haul Gamma 7 along with us. Let's do this!"

Traversing back to the shuttle was slow. It suddenly seemed even slower when Tacnet suddenly sounded an alarm, followed by Nakamura's commlink to everyone. "Hostiles! Tacnet is tracking an incoming missile. Acceleration is..." Nakamura hesitated as he double checked the math, "basically off the charts. Time to intercept is a bit over fifteen minutes. They heard our commlink."

Blackwater evaluated the group's progress for a moment. They were just too slow. "We need to unass from this location, pronto. Chanson, what's the book say about minimum safe distance for this sort of thing?"

PO Chanson had also figured out they weren't going to get back to his shuttle in time. "Book? Hell, I can't even read too good. I'll give you kids 30 seconds to brace for impact," he drawled in a country sounding accent.

"Thirty seconds, roger that. Give us a 5 second final count," Blackwater confirmed. He was already reeling in the other members of the away team to collect them together in preparation. "Lock limbs together!" he ordered.

Chanson cracked his knuckles to loosen up his tired hands, then he tapped the controls to spin up the shuttle's FTL jump drive as he eyed the countdown timer that heralded the arrival of the enemy missiles. When he was ready, he counted down as Blackwater requested.

"Enemy cruiser now in Tacnet range. We've got to boogie, people. Beginning maneuver in five. Four. Three. Two. One. Ignition!" he announced over the commlink, then lightly tapped the maneuvering thrusters. Bulldog 5 suddenly closed the distance with the away team.

Closing the distance wasn't so much the issue. Speed, and stopping were, because Chanson couldn't safely fire the maneuvering thrusters on the side of the shuttle facing the away team. Thrusters could scatter and injure the away team, and everyone's suits were so low on power their location beacons had already shut down. If that happened, there wasn't enough time remaining to find and corral them and leave the neighborhood before the inbound missiles ended them.

Bulldog 5 slammed into the away team, hard enough to rattle teeth inside of exosuits and knock the wind out of the occupants. Several seconds passed in silence while they drifted. "Status?" Chanson asked over the commlink. He needed to know if more maneuvering was required and knew it didn't matter if they maintained radio silence now.

The voice of Gamma 1 that answered was nearly breathless as Blackwater attempted to catch his breath and take the pain. "Five by five. Give us a minute to get organized and improve our purchase. Echo 12 managed to grab the airlock hatch with one hand, and I was only able to maglock one foot onto the hull," said Blackwater.

Using his exosuit's power, Blackwater pushed down and mag-locked his other foot onto the hull. The good news is that the tether hadn't broken, mainly because he had not given it a chance to break by reeling in the other team members and interlocking their limbs to one another. It had worked, but just barely. Now Blackwater used his exosuit and helped each into the open airlock by basically shoving them inside whether they were ready or not. While they didn't have to wait for it to cycle because

Nakamura had already emptied the shuttle of air to save time, it still took precious minutes to finish the process.

"We need to hustle up, Gamma 1. Those missiles are going to be the hammer for our nails," urged Chanson. His hand was itching to start the jump drive and get the Bulldog out of this mess.

Blackwater was too busy pushing bodies into the assault shuttle to respond with more than a click. Finally, they were all inside. Blackwater likewise entered the airlock and closed the outer door behind him.

As soon as he saw the indicator light for the outer door turn green, Chanson spoke over the all-team commlink in a tight voice that clearly told everyone he was in All Business Mode at the moment. "We have outer door seal. Hang tight, people. We have less than two minutes before boom time, so get yourselves squared away as of yesterday. Jumping in ten seconds." Chanson proceeded to count down for everyone's benefit, and then added, "Jumping now."

Bulldog 5 executed its FTL transition with a tiny jump flare. With their target having vanished into thin air, the missiles went into their seeker mode to acquire a new target before their fuel ran out.

CHAPTER 37

POINT ROMEO ONE ONE

KITTY HAWK

92 DAYS UNTIL IMPACT

"*Cerberus* reports combat damage has largely been repaired," said the XO, Cmdr. Steve Fisher. He was on the bridge of the *Kitty Hawk*, standing next to the command chair that was occupied by Captain Nagun as the ship flew in formation with *Cerberus* and *Pytor the Great* at Point Romeo One One.

Nagun shook his head slightly. "The war ended a while back, yet somehow *Cerberus* is the only combat ship that keeps getting into actual combat," Nagun said, with a serious expression on his face. "This is *Kitty Hawk's* first deployment beyond the home system with a jump drive, and here we are caught up in another battle involving *Cerberus*. What IS it with Dan's ship, anyway? Seems like they can't go outside the wire without turning into a flying gunslinger."

Fisher's mouth quirked into a sly smile at Nagun's twist on the old joke. "They're a missile sponge. They're also both the most dangerous and prestigious posting in the fleet. The Admiralty generally hasn't transferred anyone off *Cerberus* for several tours, either. Makes other ship's crews talk."

Nagun's eyebrows shot up. "What's the scuttlebutt about that?"

"Seems to be two schools of thought. One is that they're just under-performing troublemakers no one else wants. I call that the 'Pariah' school of thought. The 'Reality' school is they've been kept together for several strategic reasons. They've taken losses, but survived one harrowing deployment after another because of their skill and how well they function as a team. They're also too famous to simply spread throughout the fleet. There's always some petty swabbie out there who will do something spiteful because they're jealous, and that can be pretty dangerous in space," Fisher said.

Nagun nodded slightly. "Obviously you're down with the 'Reality' school of thought, based on the labels you used. And I agree with your assessment. It doesn't sit well with me to hear someone draw the wrong conclusions about that crew. They're not glory hounds.

"I've known Dan for a long, long time. He just doesn't tolerate glory hounding any more than he does someone goldbricking or being an elitist snob. He's always been about getting the job done and his crew functioning like a well-oiled machine. That success also means their missions have been harder, more dangerous. As a result they've become famous, but I happen to know Dan and Commander Mueller absolutely loathe being famous."

An electronic beeping suddenly demanded their attention. Fisher glanced at a screen tablet he held in his hand. "The *Cerberus* SAR Bulldog just jumped back," Fisher noted. A second later, as more information updated on his screen, he added, "They're reporting mission success, 1 KIA, two WIA."

Looking thoughtful, Nagun remarked, "Casualties. I thought they might have some. They were gone for so long, we had speculated they ran into some kind of trouble. Ronin was about to launch another SAR Bulldog because they hadn't returned. Now we can move forward with the next phase of this operation instead of resorting to Plan B."

Fisher looked confused. "Plan B? There's a Plan B?"

Nodding, Nagun half-smiled, knowingly. "Kind of. Now that *Kitty Hawk's* here, Captain Ronin planned to use both ships to shoot our way past the Forrestal navy and commence rescue operations if we couldn't take them off the board by getting them to follow us to nowhere."

Eyebrows raising at Nagun's statement, Fisher couldn't help but blurt out his thoughts about Plan B. "THAT was Plan B? That's it? Doesn't sound like much of a plan."

Snorting, Nagun agreed. "It wasn't. Captain Ronin and I didn't like it either, but there isn't much else we can do. And neither of us thought we could haul away more refugees to safety during Plan B than their navy would do anyway."

"Whew. Sounds to me like Plan B sucked pretty hard. Fingers crossed the codes they brought back actually work." The expression on Fisher's face echoed his words. He felt they'd dodged a bullet by avoiding Plan B.

***

Now that his exosuit was plugged into Bulldog 5's power and his suit's systems were all back online, Bloodbane's tired ears perked up as he listened to the commlink traffic between *Kitty Hawk* and Bulldog 5. *What was Kitty Hawk doing here?* he wondered to himself in confusion. There hadn't been enough time to debrief between their hurried rescue and jumping back to the rendezvous point with the fleet. It's just that he had expected the fleet to still consist of only *Cerberus* and *Pytor the Great*.

Despite still being in their exosuits, Blackwater read Bloodbane's body language like a book. He opened a commlink to the group and said, "Echo 12, *Kitty Hawk* arrived on station while we were gone. The Captain had sent back some sort of new kind of long-range drone asking for assistance from the fleet, and the thing actually worked."

Bloodbane was too exhausted to carry on much of a conversation, so he merely nodded and replied, "Roger that, Gamma 1." After that he added privately in his head, *I'm out of the fight for a while, anyway. We're used up.*

Reading everybody's medical conditions over Tacnet in addition to body language now, Blackwater didn't expect a longer reply. He, too, was worn out and didn't feel too chatty so it would be doubly so for the others. The information from Tacnet merely confirmed the rest of the away team was much worse off. Dr. Mueller's exosuit reported the man to be in an exhausted sleep. Pena was in a stupor that was the next thing to being asleep. Bloodbane, being from a heavy gravity world, was doing better but the vitals being reported from his exosuit clearly indicated he was about to fall asleep as well. Bulldog 2's pilot, Erin Johnson, had also fallen asleep, while the rearseater, Helmut Meyer, was slowly trying to crack his neck and loosen up cramped limbs.

It wasn't long until they would be back aboard *Cerberus*.

CHAPTER 38

POINT ROMEO ONE ONE

CERBERUS

91 DAYS UNTIL IMPACT

"**D**ad, you're cheating!" complained Ronin's teenage son, Eddie. They were sitting at the small dining table in Ronin's quarters with his daughter, Sarah, and wife, Frida, playing cards before retiring for the night.

Busted, Ronin laughed out loud. "I wondered how long it was going to take for you to catch on!" He collected all the cards and re-dealt them, correctly this time. Frida just rolled her eyes at her husband, amused by the family she married into.

The levity vanished when Sarah asked, "Dad, is it true that Commander Mueller is dead?" Dan had welcomed the distraction of a card game with his family to take his mind from Mueller's death on the away mission, but Sarah's innocent question brushed away the diversion.

Sober now, Dan nodded. "Yes, I'm afraid so. She was in command of the part of the mission where Dr. Mueller was hacking into the AI's primary core cards that our Marines retrieved from Forrestal."

Dan didn't offer more detail than that. He was keenly feeling the devastating loss of his longtime friend and first officer. Space was an exceptionally dangerous place, and people often died because of that. Nothing he could do would meaningfully change that terrible equation. All Dan could do was try to reduce the dangers as best he could. It didn't help that *Cerberus* had experienced a long run of missions that had placed the ship into ever more dangerous situations.

While they all knew the risks and reluctantly accepted that some of them would inexorably die, it did little to assuage the pain of losing Mueller. Dan and Diane had long ago bonded as friends and as a team. They had each other's backs through thick and thin.

If someone else could have gone on the away mission instead of her, Dan wouldn't have let her go, but Mueller's command level authorization was essential to maintaining strict EEQ. Putting a Bulldog into EEQ was fraught with dangers because a shuttle could easily become lost while it was shut down. To prevent such losses, the fleet in its infinite wisdom required command level authorization to be present for all electronic emissions quarantines on a Bulldog for away missions. Now that wisdom had resulted in Mueller's death.

Grief over the loss of his friend boiled up inside Dan again. Of all the losses they've suffered the past several years, this one was most personal for him. He was so proud that she was slated for her own command, and that it would have been command of a significant vessel. Possibly even of another heavy cruiser like *Cerberus*. Dan's grief also extended to the rest of the Mueller family. They were all longtime friends, including the children. Dan's own children, Sarah and Eddie, tended to act like older siblings to the twin Mueller children, Sonya and Sophia.

"Will it be OK if we look in on Sonya and Sophia tomorrow?" asked Frida, her warm, dark brown eyes expressing her sadness and empathy for the Mueller family. Her sensitivity continued to surprise her husband since Frida was a combat-tested Ullrian shield maiden. She was a skilled warrior at heart who had mercilessly slain enemies of her Faction in battle, but there was so much more to her than just fighting an enemy. She had a softer side that she revealed to her family, and the juxtaposition of iron-willed, warrior mother and nurturer had meshed perfectly with Dan's protective instincts as a father.

Dan nodded. "They would appreciate that. I spent some time with them earlier when I got word of what happened, but it wasn't just a social call. Karl and the officers from *Pytor the Great* are sorting out the Forrestal fleet's command codes from Perun's primary core cards. Karl is too busy to properly mourn his wife at the moment. They're expecting to finish sometime tonight, and our AI will validate the testing to ensure none of Perun's essence survives to infect any ship in our task force."

Ronin's dubbing the three-ship formation of *Cerberus*, *Kitty Hawk*, and *Pytor the Great* a task force prompted Frida to look intently at her husband. She said nothing, but her raised eyebrows did all the talking for her.

"Informally. Sort of. It's more of a small formation. You know what I mean?" Dan stammered under Frida's gaze.

"I thought a Confederate Navy task force was composed solely of ships from the same fleet?" Frida asked.

Dan nodded. "Traditionally, yes. But primarily because there haven't been any other allied fleets to include. It was just us, and the Collective, slugging it out against each other in the Earth solar system. There wasn't anyone else around to invite to the party."

Eddie yawned. He tried to stifle it to no avail. The corner of Dan's mouth quirked up as he noticed the yawn. "It's getting pretty late. We're all going to have a long day tomorrow. The days after that are going to be even longer. Let's hit the rack and get some shut-eye."

The Ronin kids nodded. They put away the game and secured the table vertically against the wall. That may have seemed strange to teenagers who were being raised on Earth, but to the Ronin teens it was ordinary because they had spent much of their lives on ships in space. Living quarters were extremely cramped, and care was taken to secure anything that could become a deadly projectile. When they finished policing up their game, nothing remained in the open.

Dan and Frida gave the kids a hug as they watched them retire to their tiny rooms. Each was scarcely large enough to accommodate a fold-down sleeping rack, plus a fold-down chair and desk. The desk and chair folded down from the side walls to the longer wall where the rack was, meaning that the desk and chair had to be stowed when the rack was in use.

Dan cracked open a craft beer that had been brewed by Sunderland and delivered to the family's quarters by one of the lieutenant's many minions in his illicit beer-making operation somewhere on board *Cerberus*. He took a swig and paused to savor the taste. It was a brown ale recipe Sunderland had obtained from the pre-Fall archives discovered on Ninebase. The rich, nutty flavor was excellent.

Frida took a tiny sip to sample the brew's flavor. Now that she was pregnant, she would not imbibe, but Sunderland's craft beers were legendary in the fleet. She knew better than to skip testing a new brew from him.

So legendary was Sunderland's brewing fame that even Adm. Jessup Rodding knew of his skill and had a standing "request" for a case of it to be delivered whenever *Cerberus* and Rodding crossed paths. Sunderland was easily savvy enough to recognize that a standing request from an admiral like Rodding was more of an order than a request. In return, neither Ronin nor Rodding put any effort into quashing Sunderland's illicit operation despite that enterprise running afoul of a number of navy regulations. They also made sure Sunderland had access to all the supplies he would need, and Ronin routinely funneled Rodding's gifts of Old Prohibition bourbon back to Sunderland.

Sighing, Dan nodded slightly to himself as he savored the taste. Sunderland's beer temporarily washed down the bitter aftertaste of losing his friend and first officer, but it could do nothing else.

Without saying another word, Frida looked up at him and put her arm around Dan and pulled him in for a kiss. "It's time for us to call it a night too," she said softly.

The next day wasn't going to be easy.

CHAPTER 39

PROCESSING

PYTOR THE GREAT
90 DAYS UNTIL IMPACT

"**D**octor Mueller? Doctor Mueller?" asked Cmdr. Igor Kuznetsova in a tired voice. His face was drawn, and he was nearing exhaustion.

Startled out of his reverie, Karl refocused his eyes back to the screen in front of him. He was sitting at a workstation on board *Pytor the Great* where Mueller and Kuznetsova had spent the night trying to port the fleet command codes that Mueller had previously lifted from Perun's primary core cards.

Karl's face likewise mirrored Kuznetsova's exhaustion, only far worse. He was both physically and emotionally drained and it showed. Karl rubbed his eyes and tried not to think about how much more this mission was going to demand of him. Over the past few days, Karl had been exposed to a ground force combat zone and dust off, hacking a hostile ancient AI which then tried to seize control of the shuttle he was on, survived the shuttle's destruction, saw his wife killed, and barely survived in an exosuit long enough to be rescued days later than planned. Karl didn't have much left in the tank to give, but he was driven by the knowledge that failure would only condemn many more innocent people to a horrible death.

No pressure or anything, Mueller thought morosely. He didn't share his dark mood with Kuznetsova, but he was too exhausted to mask it behind a veneer of detached professionalism so he soldiered on. Kuznetsova had no problem recognizing Mueller's mood and was quite sympathetic for the man and his family. The two of them had already discovered they worked well together as a team.

"Sorry, Igor, I was in another place. There's been a lot to process," Mueller apologized, looking at Kuznetsova, who was sitting next to him at another workstation.

Kuznetsova nodded. Mueller's statement about having a lot to process carried a double meaning that Kuznetsova recognized. They were processing a lot of data that Mueller had hacked from the primary core cards, but Kuznetsova was pretty sure Mueller meant that he was internally having to work through what had happened to the Mueller family in the past few days.

"Da. 'Tis quite all right. You haven't properly had time to grieve. I'm so sorry," Kuznetsova said sincerely. They were quiet for a few moments while Kuznetsova's eyes returned to his screen. "Batch 72 is ready now," he added.

"Send it, and start on Batch 73," Mueller said, returning to focus on their task. "I'll get the Batch 72 lines coded into the command override system."

"Aye-aye, beginning Batch 73," Kuznetsova said absently as he keyed in the commands to begin the next round. They were still busy processing code to cull Perun's malignant AI essence from the fleet command codes the hostile AI had used to control its navy fleet. Regardless of their human crews, those fleet command codes would nonetheless override any human attempt to wrest control of a ship away from the AI's iron grip.

Separating the command codes from the AI's other code is a slow, cumbersome process. Their own systems were analyzing those codes using millions of sandboxed simulations to determine which was which. Perun had existed for an unknown period of time since prior to The Fall, and had tightly integrated the fleet command codes into itself in the hundreds of years that had elapsed since then. Making the process even slower was the fact that the programming language used to create Perun was itself a long-lost language. A retro engineered translation had been provided by *Pytor the Great's* crew, which further slowed their progress.

They were taking great precautions to prevent coding from the hostile AI from contaminating their own systems and recreating itself aboard a ship. Meanwhile, the interplanetary clock was ticking down. If they couldn't finish the job in time, there would be no rescue for the civilians on Forrestal other than those they could take aboard the three ships of their task force.

There just wasn't enough time.

CHAPTER 40

BREAKTHROUGH

KITTY HAWK

88 DAYS UNTIL IMPACT

"How bad was the earthquake?" asked Captain Nagun in a shocked voice. He was sitting in his command chair on *Kitty Hawk's* bridge, and leaning forward towards the image of Captain Ronin on the main viewscreen. *Kitty Hawk's* entire bridge crew could hear the report.

Ronin's face was grave. "Catastrophic. Every city on the southernmost continent was completely leveled. Loss of life appears to be in the tens of millions," he said. Ronin once had been forced to nuke cities to stop the Collective's biological attack from causing another Fall on Earth, but even that paled in comparison to the horrors already beginning on Forrestal. This planet was beginning to experience its death throes because of the oncoming collision with Celestra.

Nagun likewise felt the blood drain from his face. "Couldn't we just use some of those antimatter missiles from the Forrestal fleet to blow up Celestra or something and stop this?" he asked. Ever since *Kitty Hawk* had arrived in the system, the impending doom of the colony had often been foremost in his thoughts. Nagun also had no practical solutions to offer.

Shaking his head, Ronin said, "We thought about that, too. Negative on that idea. Even if they had enough antimatter, and their ancient missiles somehow all detonated, simulations show the resulting meteor shower would just scour Forrestal's surface clean of all life anyway. And that is assuming all those ancient missile payloads actually detonate. Those missiles are from before The Fall and their payloads are unreliable after that many centuries. The AI that controlled the planet had hundreds of years to save Forrestal, but it chose not to by letting the tools needed to save the planet wither away until it was too late."

Nagun slumped back into his chair. Ronin was right. And Nagun knew his old friend would naturally have looked into whether they could simply blow up the planet regardless of how preposterous the idea would normally seem. Ronin was a big picture thinker who would identify the possible solutions, and pick the best of them. Sometimes that just meant Ronin was forced to choose between bad and worse options. When bad situations begin to go down, people often died because the only available options were all differing degrees of horrible so it was a matter of choosing the option in which the fewest died.

"Perun sentenced its own people to death," Nagun said quietly. He shook his head slightly at the enormity of the callous indifference of the ancient artificial intelligence.

"Yeah. And Perun never planned to save more than a handful of its favored elites. Once we take control of their fleet, we're going to try to save a lot more people than that," Ronin said, determination evident in his voice. "Speed is of the essence. That's why we're taking them to Solara."

"Makes sense. How many round trips between Solara and Forrestal can we make with refugees? Our window of time looks extremely short," Nagun noted.

Ronin's face looked thoughtful. "Hopefully three, maybe four trips. Due to the collision and gravity, we're guessing here as to how much time remains before pre-impact earthquakes and meteors eliminate the remaining population."

"All right, Dan. *Kitty Hawk's* interior spaces have been made as ready as we can be. What's the word from Doctor Mueller on board *Pytor the Great*? He give us any sense of when we can move forward?"

Ronin looked at a pop-up message on his screen. "They've finished processing and are about to upload the command codes into *Pytor the Great's* computer system."

Nagun didn't need to ask why *Pytor the Great* had been chosen for the upload of the command codes. It was safer than exposing either *Cerberus* or *Kitty Hawk* to the command codes of a hostile AI that, hopefully, had been cleansed of the AI's software essence. There was still a great risk the code cleansing wasn't entirely successful and that AI could start to rebuild itself inside a host ship. *Pytor the Great* was also a far more practical choice as it the only available ship with the systems built to interface with the rest of their own navy. *Cerberus* and *Kitty Hawk's* own systems were incompatible, and there clearly wasn't time to solve any issues that likely would arise by trying to make the Confederate navy ships become the hosts.

"OK. We'll await your 'go' order. *Kitty Hawk* Actual, out," Nagun said, terminating the commlink. Sighing, he leaned back and traded pensive looks with Fisher.

"You didn't tell him," Fisher noted, right eyebrow raising in surprise. It was a half-question, half-statement.

Nodding thoughtfully, Nagun said, "Dan's got enough on his plate right now. Plenty of time for that later. And that kind of news shouldn't come from his old roommate anyway."

Tilting his head to the side to acknowledge Nagun's statement, Fisher snorted, "He ain't gonna be too happy when someone breaks the news to him."

Smiling coldly, Nagun couldn't help himself. "No. No he won't."

CHAPTER 41

GO TIME

SOYUZ

87 DAYS UNTIL IMPACT

"Fleet-Admiral Kirov, we may have found a way to disable the uplinks Perun used to control the fleet," said First Officer Sergei Drago quietly. Kirov's eyes focused on Drago. Both of them were seated in the small forward mess of the *Soyuz*. The forward mess was empty except for the two of them, and it was filled with the smell of Chifir tea being brewed. It was the bitter, black tea grown on the southern continent of Forrestal and it was the favored tea of Kirov.

Kirov had been born and raised on New Kalingrad, the largest city of the southern continent. At least, it had been until the earthquake leveled New Kalingrad yesterday. The quake was so powerful, his science officer dubbed it a Magnitude 10 quake. The science officer also noted they had not believed a Magnitude 10 was possible. Even the subsequent aftershocks were measured by satellites in the 9.8 range.

"What's our probability of success?" Kirov asked gruffly. His gravelly voice rumbled in the empty mess.

Drago shrugged. "Unknown. We had surmised it was possible because of *Pytor the Great*'s unauthorized actions, but we don't know how they did it."

Kirov was unconvinced by Drago's vague response. "We don't know if *Pytor the Great* was still under Perun's command when that ship collected escaping refugees and departed. They could have received orders which we weren't privy to, although it seems unlikely due to how it played out. We just don't know what we don't know and we're guessing." Glaring, Kirov's eyes seemed to be burning a hole in Drago with their intensity.

Drago met Kirov's glare. "Comrade Fleet-Admiral, what do you suggest? We are stuck in orbit around our colony and it's about to be destroyed." Drago's tone bordered on insolence.

Kirov decided now wasn't the time to dress Drago down for taking that tone with him. They were both exhausted and frustrated. Kirov also happened to agree with Drago's sentiment. He knew they were stuck in orbit just as well as Drago did. Flying around in circles chasing their tails was a death sentence. It was just a question of what killed them first—depleting their fuel, air, food or their rapidly diminishing celestial time due to the End of Days. Privately Kirov was betting that time would kill them. No matter what, time always won out in the end.

"Agreed. You're preaching to the choir, and I don't see any other option. Regardless of how small a chance it is, we still have to take it. Otherwise, our chances of being ended in 87 days or less are 100%. Proceed with the attempt, Commander Drago," Kirov ordered.

Drago stood up and saluted Kirov, who returned it. Kirov watched Drago leave the forward mess. Standing up and smoothing out the wrinkles in his uniform, Kirov left for the bridge.

∗∗∗

"Orders? Seriously?" Lt. Dmitry Sidorov was saying incredulously as Kirov walked onto the bridge. Sidorov's icy blue eyes were locked on the communications officer and seemingly attempting to bore a whole through her.

"What orders?" Kirov asked.

Sidorov and the communications officer exchanged looks in which they silently decided who was going to tell the admiral. Sidorov's face revealed he would take lead here.

Clearing his throat, Sidorov said, "Sir, we've just received new tasking orders from Perun. The entire fleet is now standing by to receive refugees from the surface."

Kirov's eyes flicked over to the forward viewscreen as he said, "Show me."

Simultaneously, power suddenly emanated from the main engines as they rumbled to life. The ship slowly began maneuvering on its own thanks to the orders from Perun.

The forward viewscreen switched from showing the outside view as seen from *Soyuz* to an overhead map of the star system. Symbols representing the Forrestal fleet were moving towards the areas that had previously been designated as rendezvous points for the refugee exodus.

Kirov felt a wave of relief sweep over him as he realized Perun was back in charge. That also meant he had orders to issue. "Lieutenant Sidorov. Get a hold of Commander Drago and tell him Perun has reasserted control over the fleet and he is to cease his efforts and report to the bridge immediately. We can expect to receive the VIPs shortly."

Kirov didn't wait for Sidorov's acknowledgment before he rapid fired additional orders to other officers on the bridge. They had to make the *Soyuz* ready to receive their guests.

It never occurred to Kirov to wonder whether he was more excited at the thought of rubbing shoulders with the most important members of Forrestal's society, or that it meant they were getting out of here before the End of Days. It didn't matter in the end. Perun taking care of him so he could help rescue the cream of their society meant that Kirov was important.

Watching his tactical display, Kirov saw the fleet's ships begin to disperse from their berthings or patrol stations. The Gathering had begun.

CHAPTER 42

THE GATHERING

SOYUZ

85 DAYS UNTIL IMPACT

*S*oyuz had arrived at its designated rendezvous point and its scans clearly painted a busy picture. Hundreds of ships had joined The Gathering. Intership chatter had filled up their channels until Kirov had ordered communications be restricted to clear them up.

"Still no signs of the enemy ships, Fleet-Admiral," reported Drago. He had just joined Kirov at the center of the bridge.

"Good. They'd be foolish to challenge this large of a navy," Kirov said tersely without looking up. Then he glanced at Drago. "Notice anything different about our deployment posture?"

"Da, I did, sir. We're arrayed into three larger rendezvous points over the northern hemisphere of the planet instead of six smaller points that originally included the southern hemisphere," Drago replied.

Asking whether Drago could tell the difference wasn't really Kirov's point. He just used it as an opening for more discussion while they waited for The Gathering to complete.

"That deployment means we've abandoned the southern hemisphere. There will be no Exodus for them anymore," Kirov said, quietly now. His thoughts were on his childhood home of New Kalingrad and the old, painful memories he had of that squalid city. New Kalingrad was a gray, grimy and polluted industrial city filled with identical blocks of run-down tenement housing that was infested by warring gang factions. Like all the other blighted cities on Forrestal, Perun clearly hadn't invested any effort in beautification of the place. Healthy living conditions had never been a concern of the Collective that created and programmed the AI before The Fall.

Despite the grim urban existence, Kirov's parents had done what they could to provide a safe home for their family. His father often sold stolen goods on the black market. His mother illegally cultivated vegetables in their home to supplement their meager food rations, both practices that are strictly illegal in the collective communism system because the government was supposed to own everything and provide for all. In theory, government ownership of all property and the means of production was meant to provide abundance for all. As with so many Utopian theories, it never worked out that way in practice. The only people on Forrestal who had an abundance of food, medicine, clothing and any of the other necessities of life were the elites who in reality controlled the political power on the colony.

To maintain its iron grip on power, Perun had never given the colony the historical knowledge that there always will be a group that is far more equal than the others despite lofty proclamations of social and political equality. Such was the reality that had existed in every civilization ever built by humanity. Perun had instead focused its efforts on controlling the elites, and tolerated small time crimes like black market fencing of stolen goods and private cultivation of food unless they grew large enough to threaten Perun's power. Then Perun would use the military power it controlled to stomp those domestic threats into dust.

In Perun's view, controlling the elites, who in turn tended to keep large swaths of the civilization under their own control for their own benefit, was a logical arrangement. Using elites as its proxy to control Forrestal reduced the amount of effort the AI expended to maintain control by allowing it to concentrate on the smaller group instead of the much larger, at-large population.

It was that small group of elites which *Soyuz* had been waiting to whisk away from the End of Days. Kirov was eagerly awaiting their arrival as it gave him a chance to be their savior and insert himself into their midst.

"Comrade Fleet-Admiral, scans show multiple launch detections down on the surface!" announced Sidorov. He was staring intently at a screen showing the ship's scans. Almost simultaneously, Drago looked down at his own screen. He was receiving a fleet-wide message that his screen displayed in harsh, black lettering.

Comrade Fleet-Admiral, we've received a flash dispatch from Perun," Commander Drago announced solemnly.

"What does it say?" Kirov asked. Perun had been relatively quiet since resuming control over the fleet.

Drago cleared his throat slightly before continuing. "It says, The Gathering has begun. Board your allotted passengers, then depart for your assigned coordinates."

Kirov had been expecting a message containing their destination coordinates. Fifteen years ago, Perun had secretly constructed several luxurious bases in the outer asteroid belt to house elite refugees. Their locations were only known to senior members of the fleet like himself.

"Which base are we deploying to?" Kirov asked. He secretly hoped it was to a base with a decent view of the inner star system. At least there would be something to look at out a window. Despite all his years in the navy, Kirov wasn't a fan of being cooped up inside a hull without a decent view port.

"We aren't. These are the coordinates for the jump gate to Solara," Drago said. He was confused that they weren't heading to one of the secret bases. Going to the old jump gate didn't make sense because they long ago lost the knowledge that would have enabled their ships to transit the gate to Solara.

The confusion on Kirov's face mirrored that of Drago's. "Does that mean Perun knows how to open the gate?"

Drago shrugged. "Perun hasn't seen fit to share the scope of its knowledge with us, Admiral."

Kirov managed to avoid rolling his eyes at Drago's trite statement. It was an old joke, but his improving mood prompted Kirov to echo Drago's sentiment. "We go where, and when, the navy says to."

Drago snorted at being one-upped by Kirov in the worn-out jokes department as his eyes looked down at his screen. "Perun has designated a set of incoming shuttles for *Soyuz*. Our guests will begin arriving shortly."

***

The first shuttle arrived and was being guided into a temporary unloading zone that had been established. As *Soyuz* lacked the interior space to house dozens of shuttles, Perun's evacuation plan was to make way for the next shuttle by jettisoning each shuttle after delivering their passengers aboard *Soyuz*. Kirov had ordered an assembly line approach for this process.

Pausing at a hatchway leading into the *Soyuz* landing bay, Drago suddenly felt overwhelmed by the seeming chaos of the operation. Landing a shuttle was a slow and noisy, carefully choreographed undertaking at the best of times, and the End of Days was anything but the best of times. Now *Soyuz* was receiving incoming shuttles at the breakneck speed of one every ten minutes. It seemed suicidal to Drago to try to land shuttles that fast.

Drago's attention was drawn to a double line of newly arrived civilians who were being shepherded out of the landing bay by a pair of armed soldiers who both wore stern expressions that did little to hide their confusion. Next to the departing line was the angry-looking deck boss who was in charge of this area. The deck boss looked like he was ready to read the riot act to someone.

Sensing something wasn't going according to plan, Drago walked over to the deck boss. "What seems to be the problem here?" he asked.

Surprised by Drago's appearance, the deck boss snapped to attention and rendered a quick salute. "Comrade First Officer! I'm sorry, I didn't see you."

Drago shook his head slightly to indicate it was irrelevant whether he had been spotted or not. The deck boss had other things to worry about. "No worries, Chief. Is there something amiss?"

Before responding, the deck boss whistled loudly to get the attention of the landing crew and he motioned to an unattended piece of equipment. The landing crew got the message. The equipment needed to be secured before the next shuttle arrived.

Attention returning to the first officer, the busy deck boss refocused his eyes on Drago. "Sir, none of the arriving shuttles carried a passenger manifest like they were supposed to. We don't know who any of our passengers are!" he said in exasperation.

Hoping to use them to identify the most important of their new guests, Kirov had let the deck boss know how important the passenger manifest was. And if it was important to the admiral, then it would be important to the deck boss.

Drago's eyes narrowed slightly as his gut began to warn him that something was very wrong. "Thank you, Chief. I will look into it. Carry on."

The deck boss nodded quickly and shifted his attention back to the landing crew. Walking towards them, he whistled to get their attention again. "Quit slacking, lads! If you need something to do, I will find something for you!" he snarled, sending the landing crew scrambling again.

By then, Drago's attention was riveted on the line of refugees. The double line of newly arrived civilians was shuffling forward slowly, stopping at a table manned by two of the female crew members who seemed to be taking down basic information from the civilians. Drago strode over, eyeing the civilians as he walked.

The leaden feeling in Drago's gut that told him something was wrong suddenly crystallized into panic as he finally put his finger on what seemed so off about the civilians. It was their clothes that had triggered his subconscious sense of wrongness. They were the ragged clothes of the working class. Gray, frayed, rough-spun fabric with plenty of mending of various rips and tears.

Furrowing his brows in confusion, Drago and the crew member sitting on the right side of the table exchanged a short glance. Head bobbing up once to indicate he wanted to look over the pad of notebook paper she was writing on, Drago quickly scanned the list and confirmed his eyes weren't deceiving him. Handing the notebook back to the brunette crew member, Drago muttered, "Carry on, Ensign."

Drago exited the landing bay and found a quiet spot in the passageway with an intercom node. He thumbed the transmit button and told it to open a channel with Kirov. "Comrade Fleet-Admiral, this is Commander Drago. We have a problem with the passenger intake."

Kirov wasted no time in responding. "This is Kirov. What is it?"

"Sir, there are no passenger manifests for the refugees that have arrived."

"None? Did Perun transmit them separately?"

"Negative, Admiral. There's more. These aren't the passengers we were promised, either," Drago said, his voice not quite hiding his dread.

"What do you mean?" Kirov's voice had acquired a suspicious tone.

Drago knew Kirov wasn't going to like it, but he soldiered on and delivered his report in the most matter-of-fact tone he could muster. "Sir, it seems they're simple laborers. Farmers, seamstresses and mechanics, that sort of thing. We haven't …"

Kirov's eruption cut Drago off mid-sentence. "What?" he roared. "Where the hell are our party leaders? Who are these clowns?"

"Sir—" Drago tried to say before another eruption from Kirov shut him down again.

"Don't let these laborers get settled in. I'll check with the other ships and find out who has the party leaders we're supposed to have and we'll trade," Kirov snarled before the channel went dead.

Confused, Drago muttered, "Aye-aye, Admiral," into the now-dead intercom node even though he was aware that Kirov had already left the conversation. His eyes fell upon the rapidly dwindling double line of refugees as they were being registered. Almost simultaneously, the next shuttle filled with them arrived in the landing bay.

How am I supposed to even do that? Drago asked himself. He had no answers for that question.

CHAPTER 43

LATE FOR THE DOOR

SOYUZ

84 DAYS UNTIL IMPACT

Drago and Kirov met privately in Kirov's small, but neat and tidy, office next to the bridge on *Soyuz*. They both nursed hot cups of Chifir tea. Its strong bitterness matched their foul moods.

"They're nowhere to be found," Kirov said distractedly. His eyes were unfocused and had dark rings beneath them from lack of sleep while they onboarded shuttle after shuttle of refugees. Many more than they had been expecting, and now refugees were everywhere. Kirov's tiny office was one of the few sanctuaries aboard *Soyuz* that didn't seem to be overflowing with refugees.

"The party leaders?" Drago asked, merely to confirm that Kirov hadn't suddenly switched topics. At first, they were dumbfounded that Perun hadn't sent them the elite members of the single political party that had been permitted on Forrestal since the days of the Collective hundreds of years earlier. Those passengers had been assigned to *Soyuz*.

Eyes focusing on Drago now, Kirov nodded. "Yeah." he grunted. "At first I thought they may have just ended up aboard the wrong ship, but it doesn't appear as if they made it to orbit at all."

Their absence in the entirety was news to Drago. "None of them?" he exclaimed softly in surprise. If anything, the dark rings of exhaustion under his eyes were more pronounced than Kirov's.

With a rueful half smile, Kirov nodded slightly. "That's correct. None that any of the other ships in the fleet were able to identify." Changing topics for real now, Kirov asked, "What's our updated food and water situation?"

Drago tapped on his tablet screen and looked at the data it displayed. "The final shuttle departed an hour ago. We're now carrying three times as many refugees as were originally planned for. If we go to half rations immediately, the ship will run out of food in 34 days. Water is still only an estimate, but we normally should have adequate water for four months. That's the next scheduled maintenance for the recycling system, assuming ordinary levels of usage. The chief engineer says it won't make it that long and will have to go offline for maintenance about the same time we'll run out of half rations. Those are the best-case scenarios."

Kirov's eyes had unfocused while he absorbed Drago's report. It was as bad as he feared. "All of which assumes our air recycling systems are able to keep up with the added strain in the interim."

"Yes sir. If they don't, there won't be anyone left alive long enough for *Soyuz* to run out of food or water." Drago finished the grim thought for Kirov.

Kirov suddenly looked incensed. "Why should we be forced to risk our lives and our ship for a bunch of laborers?" he growled. "They're nobodies!"

"Fleet-Admiral, did you still want a contingency plan for jettisoning the refugees?" Drago asked. His voice betrayed no emotion or empathy in the question.

Kirov thought about it for a moment. "Yes. We need to protect *Soyuz* first. Common laborers are nothing to us and don't bring any prestige or influence that we can use. If we hit the yellow line on any of our life support systems or supplies, round them up and get rid of them."

Drago knew the "yellow line" Kirov referred to was just an arbitrary limit Kirov had set. If they reached those limits on the consumables or recyclables, then they would buy more time by eliminating the extra refugees that were aboard.

Drago nodded, then he shrugged. "I—" he began to say when they both felt a rising rumble begin inside the ship.

"The engines are spooling up!" Kirov snarled. His temper had soured in direct proportion to his increasing exhaustion, which meant he was permanently in a foul mood the past 24 hours.

Both of them rose from their seats and they swiftly walked towards the bridge. On the bridge, Drago and Kirov were taken aback at the controlled chaos. "Report!" growled Kirov as he strode towards his chair in the center of the bridge.

"Perun has taken direct control of navigation and all engines. We have received commands to depart for the jump gate, Fleet-Admiral. The entire fleet is departing!" said Lieutenant Sidorov, without looking up from a tablet screen he was intently reviewing. Kirov could see it was rapidly scrolling through the list of status updates coming in from the rest of the fleet.

All of them felt another rise in the rumbling from their ship's engines as their primary drive increased its forward thrust. *Soyuz* was definitely getting underway and not just maneuvering.

Kirov met Drago's eyes for a moment before Kirov nodded towards the main screen on the bridge. Drago got the nonverbal message and walked to his own station. He tapped a few keys and the main screen switched to display the position of each ship in the fleet on a tactical map. All eyes on the bridge focused on the main screen as they watched the ships slowly form into a long convoy.

"It has begun," Kirov said.

CHAPTER 44

DIXIE STATION

CERBERUS

80 DAYS UNTIL IMPACT

"The ships are ready to jump, Captain," reported Cmdr. Pierre Delacroix. His new rank was reflected on his uniform. Delacroix stoically had accepted his advancement by Ronin to the new rank because he knew as well as anyone that the ship must have an executive officer during a mission. Especially a mission as dangerous as this one had already been. Delacroix hadn't acclimated to the new rank yet, but he tried not to show how uncomfortable it still felt.

Nodding, Ronin indicated it was go time. "Jump," he ordered. The jump drives of *Cerberus* and *Kitty Hawk* were connected by a synced data link for this part of the mission.

Cerberus and *Kitty Hawk* reappeared on opposite sides of Forrestal. Looking over at Delacroix, Ronin raised an eyebrow as he waited for Delacroix's report. It wasn't long in coming.

"We've arrived at the latest rendezvous point designated as Dixie Station, Captain." Delacroix said in a neutral tone. The conflicting gravities of two planets on a collision course had introduced more than a little doubt into their jump calculations. After the jump, *Kitty Hawk* and *Cerberus* were not flying in close formation with one another. They were separated by several million miles of space, bracketing Forrestal in between them. It was perhaps the largest Dixie Station in terms of area that Ronin had ever heard of.

"Text message from Forrestal being received, Captain," Lieutenant Delgado announced, while she scanned the text. "They are confirming the first group of refugees has gathered at the departure site on Forrestal."

"Very well," replied Ronin. He thumbed open a commlink to *Kitty Hawk*. "*Cerberus* Actual to *Kitty Hawk* Actual."

Captain Nagun replied instantly. "Go for *Kitty Hawk* Actual. Our scans confirm the Exodus Fleet has departed. No other threats detected, other than the navigational kind we've already charted."

The data flow from *Cerberus* and *Kitty Hawk* data had already synced Tacnet for the two ships.

"Let's do this," Ronin said. "All ships, launch Bulldogs." The order was swiftly commlinked to the waiting Bulldog flight crews on both ships.

The five Bulldogs quickly launched from *Cerberus*. Somehow a symbolic numbering system for Bulldogs had become the custom among ships in the fleet where the number of a destroyed shuttle was never reused aboard the same ship. Due to the hazards of the prior missions, the *Cerberus* shuttle fleet currently was numbered 1, 3, 5, 6 and 8 due to the prior destruction of Bulldog 2 at Point India Two Five, and Bulldog 7 in the earlier mission to the Solara system. *Kitty Hawk* launched her two shuttles as well.

"Bulldogs away, Captain," said Delacroix. He looked at Ronin before adding, "Seems risky to leverage the comms and controls of a pre-Fall enemy AI to get this operation organized and underway."

Snorting, Ronin's eyebrows shot up briefly as he returned Delacroix's glance. "That might be the understatement of the day. Can't say I like it much either. None of the people left on the surface have any idea that Confederate Navy shuttles will be taking them off planet. We also think they won't particularly care who is giving them a ride when their only choice is go with us, or die in the End of Days."

Ronin didn't need to explain that everyone on the surface was now well aware the End of Days was near. Increasingly frequent earthquakes and the ever larger sight of the dead colony of Celestra in the sky have both heralded the coming extinction of Forrestal for months. No one could miss the disaster coming their way.

Nodding, Delacroix privately wondered what situation will greet the arriving Bulldogs.

***

The Bulldogs short hopped into the night time sky of Forrestal. They had emerged from their jump close to the surface, seven flame trails suddenly shooting downwards from a midway point in the black sky. Each of the flame trails ended in an arc parallel to the surface as their pilots applied full engine thrust to fight the G forces and reorient their birds for atmospheric flight.

"Arrival in 63 seconds. Make ready to do your Marine things," drawled the Texas accented voice of Bulldog 1's rearseater, Chief Hal Patterson. He spoke over the common commlink that everyone in the rescue mission was listening to because Bulldog 1 was acting as the command authority for all seven flight crews on this rescue mission.

Clicks acknowledged Patterson's announcement from the Marines on board the Bulldogs. They were buttoned up in their exosuits, weapons magnetically secured within easy reach. Gamma 2, LCpl. Jefferson Langley, glanced at the other team member with him on Bulldog 1 as the shuttle slowed down for landing. Gamma 8, Pvt. Rick "Rickgun" Desantos, didn't notice Langley's look because he was rechecking that his beloved pearl-handled revolvers were secured.

"Rickgun, hopefully you won't get a chance to use those things," Gamma 2 noted dryly over the commlink the two had open between them. Langley's Wisconsin accent didn't betray the butterflies he was feeling at the uncertainty they would face in just a few minutes.

"That's what I'm hoping, too, Gamma 2. I figure we're either facing hostiles, or a possible stampede. Neither possibility is too comforting," replied Gamma 8.

Nodding, Langley decided to review their procedures with Desantos more as a way to calm his nerves than as a reminder for Desantos. "Just remember the plan. Make sure your translator is active so they can understand us. You stay in the Bulldog and I'll herd them to you to sort out. Tell them to relax but not expect to stay long because this ride will be very short. And remind them we are returning dirtside for more refugees in case any are panicking at being separated."

Rickgun gave Langley a thumbs up. "Roger that, Lance Corporal."

The Bulldog settled down on the surface and began dropping its rear ramp at the same time. "It's go time. I'll herd the first group in," Langley announced.

Shrieks and wails of fear from a crush of frightened humanity immediately carried into the Bulldogs through their still-opening exits as Langley walked down the lowering ramp into the torch lit darkness with his hands raised palms out.

"Your attention please!" he roared, his amplified and translated voice being broadcast over his external speakers. "Give me your attention, right now, people!"

The roar of his amplified voice carried over the huge crowd and quieted them for the moment. "If you want to get off this rock and live, form a double line behind each shuttle ramp and we will board you until the shuttle reaches its weight limit. If you do not follow our directions, you will be left behind. If a shuttle is full, it will deliver its passengers and return for more. Do not attempt to board after a shuttle is full or we will drop you where you stand. If you ignore our orders, we will happily shoot you and leave your corpse behind."

Langley's words quieted the crowd so effectively, the only remaining sound that could be heard was the whining of the Bulldog engines that the pilots had kept spun up for quicker departures.

"Follow the directions of the soldier when you get inside the shuttle. Line up, now!" Langley ordered. Although his words had been translated into the language of the crowd, the translation hadn't affected the commanding authority in which he delivered his orders. The shocked crowd jumped at his sharp tone.

The smarter members of the crowd quickly formed the double lines as ordered, while the slower members of the herd didn't react quickly.

"Get your heads out of your asses and get in line. Right now!" roared a Marine with one of the other Bulldogs. Like Langley, his voice brooked no dissent. "Do it and live. Do not, and you WILL die. Unfuck yourselves and figure it out."

The double lines swiftly finished forming under the verbal encouragement of the Marines that was meant to cut through the mental fog of the more confused refugees. The scared crowd suddenly, and brutally, had been given a sharp new clarity of their situation.

Loading the Bulldogs went swiftly, as the refugees now understood they needed to cooperate to survive at the moment. Suddenly, each exosuited Marine acting as a Bulldog loading boss turned to face the refugees waiting to board and shouted that the Bulldog was full. Their ramps simultaneously began raising, lifting the Marines standing at the end of each ramp into their interiors.

One refugee attempted to ignore their instructions and tried to barge past Langley, who has having none of it. Langley reached out and grabbed the frightened man with the strength of his exosuit enhanced arms. Turning back to face the panicking refugees still on the ground, Langley roughly tossed the man deep into the crowd. The refugees were shocked into submission by the sheer physical power they had just witnessed. Langley had disdainfully tossed the man 20 yards as if he were no more than a rag doll.

The Bulldog began rising into the air as the ramp finished closing. "Now, that was downright disrespectful," noted Rickgun dryly over the exosuit commlink he had with Langley so none of the refugees could overhear them.

"What do you mean?" Langley asked. He wondered if Rickgun was commenting on Langley's body language or something else.

Snorting, Rickgun's dry humor was irrepressible. "A man goes to all that trouble to ignore your instructions like that, and you only bothered to throw him 20 yards downrange. You could've thrown him for twice that."

Langley smiled inside his exosuit. It was definitely something else. "Yeah. Wasn't throwing for distance. The ramp was closing too quickly."

"Maybe next time," Rickgun said. He sounded somewhat distracted as he was busy getting their new passengers situated.

Their conversation was interrupted by the rapidly rising roar of Bulldog 1's thrusters as the pilots pushed power through them so they would gain altitude. Seconds ticked by before they heard the all-team commlink carrying the away message.

"All players, jumping in three. Two. One. Jump!" announced the Chief Patterson over the all-team commlink. As one, all the Bulldogs vanished with small jump flares even though they were only a mile above the planetary surface.

CHAPTER 45

POINT, CLICK AND SHIP

CERBERUS

80 DAYS UNTIL IMPACT

"**B**ulldogs have returned to Dixie Station, Captain. They'll begin landing on *Cerberus* and *Kitty Hawk* in two minutes," Delacroix reported without looking up as he watched the tablet screen he was holding. Delacroix was standing next to Ronin, who was seated on the bridge in the command chair.

Ronin quietly acknowledged Delacroix's report as he drummed his fingers on the arm of his command chair. It was the waiting that Ronin always had trouble with, and waiting for the first group of Bulldogs to arrive home wasn't any different. He didn't even have the distraction of giving orders or asking questions because all that had already been done during their mission planning. Everyone knew what to do, and he felt like a fifth wheel.

The bridge was relatively quiet while each crew member focused on their jobs. Ronin followed the progress of the Bulldogs on Tacnet. He could imagine the organized chaos on the ship's flight decks now.

***

"Get this bird back into the launch bay, right now!" yelled the ship's Deck Chief, Adam Taylor. He was a busy man with the rapid launch cycles of the Bulldogs fleet aboard *Cerberus*. Three landing bay "tugboats" sprang into action and latched themselves to the hardpoints on Bulldog 1 and rapidly began maneuvering the shuttle towards the launch bay. Officially named the YS300, the small towing vehicles on all navy flight decks had long been dubbed "tugboat" by the deck crews in the Confederate Navy because they served the same functions of maneuvering small spacecraft aboard a larger vessel as does a tugboat in a harbor.

A ship's flight deck was a dangerous place to be at the best of times. The carefully choreographed dance of the flight deck crews had to be performed with precision. Crew who fail to observe the necessary precision risk getting sucked into an engine intake or being gruesomely ground into jelly by heavy machinery. Adding confused civilians into the mix just added to the chaos. Factor in that these scared civilians mostly just realized the signs in the landing bay were written in a foreign language using an alphabet they did not recognize, and it was a recipe for trouble.

Trouble was what the ship's Marine teams specialize in, and exo-suited Marines were present in force.

"People! Give me your attention!" roared Bravo 1, GySgt. Brett Mackey with his hands raised high to provide a visual cue for the civilians who were clustered together into a mob surrounded by Marines. Mackey's amplified voice was translated into the language of Forrestal and boomed over the background noise of the landing bay. The civilians traded a few terrified and confused glances among themselves before quieting down.

Mackey wasted no time as they needed to clear the landing bay to make way for the next round trip. "Form into a single file and follow me inside the ship. We need to exit this area to make way for the others," he ordered.

The Marines began herding the civilians into a line. Within seconds, the large group formed into a long line. "Follow me!" Mackey roared again, and he marched them out of the landing bay into the ship.

They led the civilians into the ship's Mess before Mackey stood before them once again. "Give me your eyes, people!" Mackey said, still using the booming amplification despite the quieter surroundings. "Welcome aboard. We don't have much time, so I'll make this short. The shuttles you arrived here on will be returning several times with more refugees before this ship leaves orbit. It will get very crowded on board before we depart, and none of you will remain aboard this ship for long. Because of this, you must cooperate with orders when they are given or ...” he was saying when an angry looking man stepped forward and yelled at Mackey.

“You can’t take us prisoner!” the man snarled. He had an acne-scarred face that was poorly covered by a scraggly beard and watery blue eyes. He was taller than the average male. “We know you’re the enemy!” He glared defiantly at Mackey.

Mackey’s head slowly turned to face the man. His inky black exosuit and black visor were normally menacing enough, but even the cockiest of Marines recognized the slow head turn as a clear warning of imminent danger. The slow reorientation of Mackey’s attention to this defiant civilian promised a whole different level of suffering.

The man’s defiance blinded him to Mackey’s anger, and he took several steps forward to poke Mackey in his chest. His finger never made it that far.

Just as the man began to shout something, Mackey’s left arm brusquely brushed aside the man’s hand and he grabbed him around the neck. Not bothering to use his other arm, Mackey simply lifted the shocked civilian straight up, causing the man to choke and start turning blue.

Mackey’s booming growl left few doubters as he held the man suspended in the air with little discernible effort while he turned his attention to address the remaining civilians. They had fallen silent and all eyes were on Mackey. “I have your attention now, yes? Then listen up! This mission is to rescue as many of you as possible before that rock you call home turns to dust. It does not matter to us who is rescued. If you can’t follow orders while aboard our ship, we will be happy to replace you with someone who wants to live. As to who we are and where we are taking you, those are not going to be kept secret. This ship is from Earth, and you are being taken to the colony of Solara while we find a safe place you can call home.”

The large crowd of stunned civilians began to trade confused looks with each other and a small roar of shocked comments filled the room while Mackey commlinked his Marines. “All right you apes. Move these people to their assigned spaces and show them where to find the facilities and how to use them."

Mackey disdainfully dropped the man he had been holding in the air and he looked down at him while the rest of the Marines began herding the civilians out of the Mess to their temporary new quarters. He dialed down his external speaker so only those near the gasping man could overhear his next comments. "And you have to make a choice, right now. Cooperate, and you'll get to stay alive and go make a new home somewhere else. Do not cooperate, and we'll simply replace you with someone smarter."

Despite gasping as he regained his breath, the man remained defiant. "Pfft. You are our enemy and just want to kill us. Perun will save us and continue to provide as it always has." He began to stand up when two Bravo team Marines suddenly "helped" him to his feet by lifting him into the air and suspending him there.

Mackey didn't have time for anybody's brainwashed stupidity, conditioned dependence and learned helplessness. None of them did, and such people only endangered everyone else aboard *Cerberus*. "If we wanted you dead, all we had to do was just leave your dumb ass on that rock back there because your rescue fleet already left."

Switching over to privately commlink the two Marines who held the man suspended in the air between them, Mackey simply said, "He chose poorly. Flush him."

The defiant man began struggling against his fate, but he could not do anything to counter the crushing powered grip of the exosuited Marines who easily dragged him out. The last few civilians who were waiting their turn to exit the Mess saw the scene play out, which only confirmed in their minds the deadly seriousness of what was happening.

Minutes later, the man's hoarse screams abruptly stopped when he realized the Marines had stopped at an airlock, and he began begging and pleading while Bravo 6, Pvt. Steve Cupper, used his free arm to cycle it open. Cupper and Bravo 4, Pvt. Carlos Guthrey, were the Marines who had dragged the now sobbing man out of the ship's Mess.

Once it cycled open, Bravo 4 and 6 simply tossed the man into the airlock without further ado and shut the inner hatch as the man crashed into the far wall of the outer hatch. "Punch it." said Guthrey. Cupper pressed the button to open the outer hatch and initiate an explosive decompression to flush the man out of the ship.

Neither of them was going to get too worried about airlocking useless civilians who preferred to believe propaganda over what their own eyes were telling them. The ship's life support systems were going to be under too much strain to waste it on someone too dumb to accept being rescued from certain death. Without saying anything more, they returned to the ship's Mess. The next group of refugees was arriving and they were certain they would encounter a few more in need of airlocking throughout the day.

CHAPTER 46

LAST CALL

FORRESTAL

79 DAYS UNTIL IMPACT

The ramp of Bulldog 1 began lowering again, which again exposed the tired Marines aboard the shuttle to the now familiar roar of the next disorganized mob who had been directed to gather outside. After repeated trips to the surface, the fearful shrieks and wails of panicked civilians had become little more than a discordant soundtrack playing in the background. The only difference was that it was now daylight.

The latest mob had again been electronically summoned by what they had been led to believe was the omnipresent AI which had ruled this planet their entire lives. None of them knew the same AI which had secretly abandoned them before it was destroyed so this rescue mission could be carried out by strangers posing as the AI.

Gamma 2, Jefferson Langley, walked down the still-lowering ramp into the sunlight with his hands raised palms out to repeat the same performance he had already given multiple times over the past 18 hours. His speech to gain the crowd's attention followed the same abbreviated crowd control formula each time. There was no need to establish a security perimeter, no crowd leaders to identify or interact with, and only the most transitory of mobile staging areas with the Bulldogs. That merely meant the skeleton force of Marines was to maintain security for themselves and the flight crews while projecting enough power to keep the civilians compliant during their loading and short transit.

Their brief time on the surface with a skeleton force also meant there was essentially no policing of the civilians amongst themselves before the shuttles arrived and left again. Langley could see that some of the civilians had already suffered at the hands of a few other members of the crowd. He had already made enough trips to the surface to no longer wonder why some people chose to prey on the vulnerable at times like these. He figured such predators thought they could get away with it due to the world ending and taking everyone along with it. While such despicable behavior offended his sense of right and wrong, the harsh reality of the end of the world meant they had to ignore it and just focus on saving as many civilians as they could.

"Your attention, please!" Langley roared. His amplified and translated voice rumbled through the crowd. "Give me your attention, people! Right now."

The huge crowd and quieted down as the civilians focused on the strangely dressed human who had descended down a ramp from an unfamiliar type of shuttle with equally unfamiliar writing on its side. Once he was sure he had their attention, Langley spoke again.

"This colony is dying, and these shuttles are your only ticket off this rock," Langley rumbled, then he paused for effect. "Time is short, and our resources are scarce. That means we can only spend them to rescue those of you who want to be rescued. If you do not want to leave with us, then return to your homes and may God be with you."

Mentioning any form of deity other than Perun had long been illegal and punishable by death or imprisonment on Forrestal. Langley didn't know that, and wouldn't have cared even if he had been made aware. He was the type of Marine who enjoyed breaking ridiculous norms and taboos when it suited him, and right now, it suited him if it shocked brainwashed civilians into cooperating so he could get off this doomed planet faster.

Langley continued. "If you want to live, follow our instructions. We will board as many of you as we can and leave this rock behind. If you do not follow our instructions, you will not be allowed to board or you will be forcibly removed. We will make no exceptions, nor will we waste the time that no one here has left just to negotiate with you." The whine of the Bulldog engines in the background only served to underscore the importance and urgency of Langley's words.

The crowd had fallen dead silent, shocked by Langley's message. All they knew before Langley spoke was they had received an electronic summons from Perun to appear at this location, carrying only a fresh change of clothes. By now, it was common knowledge that the colony of their ancient enemy had been growing larger in their sky for months. Everyone could see that, plus some earthquakes recently which their local media assured them were nothing to worry about. A few of them were also aware that travel to New Kalingrad and several other cities had suddenly been restricted, but no official explanation had been given for the cancellation of flights and rail travel to those destinations. Nothing in their media had hinted at the total destruction of those destinations.

After being assured for months there was no danger, there were still a few dozen who refused to believe Langley's words, despite the evidence of seven unfamiliar spacecraft sitting right in front of them. Heads began shaking with disbelieving expressions on their faces. Several of them simply turned and began to walk away. Only a few chased after them because they had spouses or children in the crowd.

In every crowd, there are inevitably some closed-minded sheep who are dimwitted enough to believe propaganda over evidence. Langley briefly watched them walk away, thinking these folks definitely had just earned the Darwin Award for being so dumb, their absence could not help but improve humanity's gene pool.

"If you want to live, line up now behind each shuttle ramp in a double file. If you want to go to your homes instead, do so now and walk away. Make your choice because we will be leaving, with or without you!" Langley barked.

His amplified and translated voice had also been re-transmitted over the external speakers of other Marines who were standing alongside their own Bulldogs, but most in the crowd hadn't noticed the same drama was concurrently playing out at each shuttle because of the distance separating them and their shock at what was happening. At some point during the earlier trips, the Marines had figured out that it was more efficient to simultaneously broadcast Langley's instructions through an exosuited

Marine at each Bulldog location, and to ensure adequate space separation between each Bulldog to avoid confusion.

Now that the chaff of the disbelieving souls who refused rescue were separated from the remaining wheat of those wishing to live, the Marines began herding the smarter civilians into the waiting Bulldogs. For once, it seemed to go smoothly. The evacuating civilians cooperatively began to walk up the shuttle ramps, and the Marines collectively breathed a tired sigh in relief. This was their final time with their boots on the ground before *Cerberus* and *Kitty Hawk* departed for Solara with the current crop of refugees because the ships had been filled up with far too many people. The ships would keep returning to evacuate more civilians until the clock ran out when the End of Days arrived, but for now, it was time to go.

The first hint of trouble didn't really register with any of them at first. "Gamma 2, Echo 12. You seeing this?" said Echo 12, Pvt. Jagr Bloodbane, from one of the other Bulldogs over the all-team commlink to Langley. Bloodbane's voice indicated the Ullrian Marine from Solara was in All Business Mode and clearly not joking around.

Langley's eyes quickly scanned the civilians before glancing at Tacnet. He didn't see any threats. "Negative, Echo 12. What is it you're looking at?"

"Gamma 2, eyes to the skies. Something's wrong with this picture. If it flies, it's in the sky and they're flying the same direction. ALL of them," reported Bloodbane as he emphasized the word, "all." His voice was definitely beginning to sound very concerned. "Something's wrong with this picture," he repeated.

Langley looked around. His attention had been on the civilians and he hadn't noticed millions of flying animals had just taken flight in the same direction. It was a sight that confused all of the Marines.

Langley never got a chance to respond when they were suddenly interrupted by Hiro "Gung Ho" Gozen on the commlink. "All players, this is Echo 8. Be advised, ground-based wildlife is likewise headed the same direction."

Despite the crowd of civilians and the whining engines of the Bulldogs at the departure site, fleeing local wildlife suddenly appeared and heedlessly began charging headlong right through them in a panic. Langley thought he saw something resembling several Earth-like deer who simply smashed through the refugees unfortunate enough to stand in their way, sending several of them sprawling. Cottontail rabbits imported from Earth centuries ago skittered between legs as they ran like the devil himself was after them.

"Uh, I think we need to get the—" one of the Marines started to say, no one had time to figure out who, before they were overridden on all commlinks by Lieutenant Gustav. His authoritative voice was unmistakably in All Business Mode. It also carried a strong note of urgency.

"All players, dust off, dust off, dust off!" yelled Gustav. His last repeat of the order was nearly drowned out by the sudden roar of the Bulldog engines as their pilots pushed power through their vertical thrusters. Within 10 seconds, the heavily loaded shuttles began lifting off the ground, all of them with their rear ramps simultaneously closing as they clawed for altitude. Langley barely had enough time to leap back aboard the shuttle as his ride suddenly ascended. It happened so fast, he had to use the power of his exosuit to clear the rising horizon of the ramp before it was out of his reach. Bloodbane similarly found himself doing the same thing as Langley.

Shrill screams and scared shouting suddenly seemed to erupt from everywhere. Langley couldn't tell if it was coming out of the Bulldog, or rising from those left behind on the surface, and he was too busy to find out. On their respective Bulldog ramps, Bloodbane and Langley both realized some civilians had fallen off the half-closed ramps while others had spilled onto the ramp floors and were dangerously close to tumbling off those ramps and joining the other lost souls on a terrifying return trajectory back to the surface.

Grunting with the strain, Langley dived forward and used his exosuit's power to grab the hands of two refugees who had been in a slide going past him on an uncontrolled return trip out of the ramp into the sky. He felt the shoulder of one of them, a younger female in her mid-20s, pop out of joint as he arrested her departure into the Great Beyond. As her terrified scream turned into a gasp of pain and surprise, the ramp on Bulldog 1 finished closing.

Using his exosuit amplified, heavy-gravity Ullrian muscles over on Bulldog 2, Bloodbane's remarkably similar rescue of three female civilians from a bad case of imminent gravity poisoning broke the shoulder of one of them, dislocated another and sparked a romantic intrigue with the third. Not that Bloodbane particularly minded the attention as she was his age and quite pretty. Regardless of joining the Confederate Marines, Ullrians like Bloodbane still liked to enjoy the spoils of victory and bravery.

On Bulldog 1, Langley released his death grip on the two civilians he had saved and he quickly rolled to his feet. Civilians had tumbled all over the shuttle's interior and were attempting to untangle themselves.

Langley lifted one of the older males to his feet and pointed to the female whose shoulder he had dislocated. "Help her, she has a dislocated shoulder. I will go forward and find out why we had the emergency dust-off," he said over his external mike. The gray-haired man nodded, and moved to help the wounded young woman.

As Langley worked his way to the front of the Bulldog, he could feel the shuttle accelerating and transitioning into forward flight mode when his commlink suddenly crackled to life.

"Gamma 2, PO Johnson. Chief Patterson is patching the external camera feed to you. You gotta see this. It's unbelievable." The pilot's normally unflappable voice was shaking slightly, while the rearseater, Chief Patterson, patched all the Marines into the shuttle's external feed.

Langley stopped right where he was and watched the stunning video feed on the inside of his visor. He had expanded it from his usual feeds to virtual mode, so it looked like he was flying above the planet without need of an aircraft. Even from this height of several miles, he could see a massive undulation in the planet's surface heading towards their landing site. It almost resembled a tidal wave coming ashore from the deep sea. Behind the wave, a nearly impenetrable cloud of dust and debris obscured the destruction on the surface.

Chief Patterson zoomed the optical gain to focus on the departure site they had just left. Hundreds of abandoned civilians remained on the ground, unable to regain their feet on the unsteady surface. They watched in horror as the massive seismic wave rolled through 30 seconds later, inexorably crushing everyone and everything in its path.

No one spoke for several minutes. There was simply nothing to say after they had watched hundreds of innocent civilians die, and there was nothing at all any of them could have done about it. If the Bulldogs hadn't lifted off, none of them would have survived.

The spell of silence was finally broken by PO Johnson, when she alerted the rest of them the Bulldog was jumping in 20 seconds. Langley simply clicked once over the commlink to acknowledge the update.

Langley couldn't help but wonder if they should have left sooner, or stayed a little longer to save more civilians. He also knew playing the what-if game wouldn't do any good. The order to leave came directly from Lieutenant Gustav, and it was an emergency order at that. Marine training was to immediately execute emergency orders that are repeated. Second guessing about how many more could have been saved by risking everyone for a few more seconds wouldn't change anything in the long run.

It was time to leave. And they were alive. That would have to be enough.

CHAPTER 47

DIXIE STATION

CERBERUS

79 DAYS UNTIL IMPACT

"With respect, we need to get the hell out of here, Captain." said Delacroix quietly. He was sitting across from the desk in Ronin's ready room next to the bridge while he gave his report on the ship's status. It wasn't good.

Ronin nodded slowly. Delacroix had only voiced what they both knew to be true. They were both tired, very tired. The stress of bringing thousands of civilian refugees aboard and cramming them into every available nook and cranny was weighing on the entire crew.

Delacroix continued with his report. "The ship's sanitation facilities are ..." he paused, looking for an apt description as he wiped away another trickle of sweat, "...overwhelmed, for lack of a better word. We will run out of water in seven days because our water and waste recycling systems cannot handle the volume.

"That's not even the worst of it. The rest of the critical Life Support systems have begun failing already. Internal temperatures are rising faster than our ability to regulate it, which is obvious as it's already eighty-five degrees in here." He paused again, this time to sip the coffee that Ronin had made for them.

"Well, as you know, I'm most worried about our air. *Cerberus* is one tough bird, but none of that matters if everyone aboard has already suffocated to death,"Ronin said, cracking a half-smile that contained little humor.

Delacroix's eyebrows raised briefly as an acknowledgment of the truth in Ronin's observation as he finished sipping some coffee. "Aye, no argument here, Captain. Our latest calculations give us almost four days before our air becomes too fouled for the crew to operate effectively. Carbon dioxide is building steadily. We hit too many parts per million of CO_2, and hallucinations will begin. I've sent countdown timers for each of our critical systems to your tablet."

Before either of them could say anything further, Ronin's collar commlink chimed. He tapped it with his fingertip and answered, "Ronin here."

It was Lieutenant Delgado, still at her communications station on the bridge. "Captain, incoming message from the last flight of Bulldogs. They had to scramble an early dust-off from the surface due to a seismic event before the shuttles were fully loaded. They're bringing them in and will begin arriving in 3 minutes."

Delacroix and. Ronin exchanged alarmed looks before Ronin responded. "Acknowledged. Tell Lieutenant Perez to prepare to jump the ship once they're aboard."

"Aye-aye, Captain. Delgado out."

"It's getting worse down there faster than we thought it would," Ronin said quietly.

Nodding now, Delacroix agreed. "Yessir. It won't be getting any better on our return trips, either."

The stark truth of that statement spoke volumes about their immediate future.

CHAPTER 48

GO TIME

DIXIE STATION

79 DAYS UNTIL IMPACT

"All shuttles down and secured, Captain. Their passengers have not been offloaded into the ship," reported the Deck Chief, Dan Taylor, over the commlink.

"Very well, Ronin out," replied Ronin before the closed the commlink. He was sitting in his command chair in the bridge of *Cerberus*, and he took a moment to look around. His crew were attentive to their duties, but Ronin noted more cups of navy coffee than usual. They were borderline exhausted, and it was time to get to work.

Ronin caught Delgado's eyes, and he nodded in her direction. She acknowledged the unspoken, but expected, order and opened a ship-to-ship commlink.

Delgado looked back at Ronin. "Ship to ship commlink is open, Captain."

Nodding his thanks, Ronin thumbed open his collar node commlink. "*Cerberus* Actual to *Kitty Hawk* Actual."

The crisp reply from his old friend Captain Nagun was immediate. "Go for *Kitty Hawk* Actual." Nagun sounded like he was completely refreshed and working on another full night of rest.

Since their days as roommates together at the academy, Ronin had always envied Nagun's ability to sound chipper and fresh despite long hours and a lack of sleep. It had always annoyed him, too. Ronin had long secretly suspected Nagun had a private cache of coffee with near-magical powers of potency squirreled away somewhere. Nagun, knowing his old roommate was an insatiable coffee hound, swore on his life and the life of his sainted mother that there was no such cache of coffee.

Dropping the formalities since it was just the two of them, Ronin continued. "Hu, is *Kitty Hawk* ready?"

"That's affirmative, Dan. We've tied in our navigation system to *Cerberus* and have synced our jump drive with your ship. Ready when you are," Hu said without a moment's hesitation before taking a sip of the coffee that he always claimed had never existed.

Because Ronin and Nagun knew each other so well, Ronin had no trouble reading Nagun's eagerness to leave. His overcrowded ship was as stuffed to the rafters with refugees as was *Cerberus* and the living conditions aboard both vessels were rapidly deteriorating.

"We'll be jumping momentarily. Ronin, out." Ronin closed the commlink and glanced at Delacroix, who was grinning broadly despite the building heat and humidity.

"He's drinking his magic coffee again, isn't he?" Delacroix said. Nagun's energy had to have come from a steaming cup, and the navy ran on coffee.

Nodding, Ronin raised his eyebrows. "He has to be, that bastard. We need to get our people onboard his ship and tactically acquire that coffee for our own use."

Still grinning, Delacroix bobbed his head to the side slightly for a moment. "Not sure our Marines would get too excited about infiltrating another ship just to grab a cup of coffee instead of something bright and shiny that goes boom."

Snorting softly, Ronin couldn't help himself. "They would take on that challenge if properly motivated. We'd just need to find something that would light their world on fire. Maybe a free pass into our mad scientist's armory?"

"Might be safer to just offer up a couple cases of Old Prohibition as the prize. I don't want our ship getting blown up by Marines playing with their new toys without any adult supervision," Delacroix noted wryly, as his attention was drawn down to the tablet he was holding when it beeped. "All stations report ready to jump now, Captain."

"Acknowledged. And good point," Ronin conceded. His eyes focused on Perez at the helm. "Lieutenant Perez, jump the ship."

"Aye-aye, Captain. Jumping the ship in five. Four. Three. Two. One. Jump!"

Cerberus and *Kitty Hawk* disappeared with tiny jump flares.

CHAPTER 49

TRANSITION

JUMP GATE

78 DAYS UNTIL IMPACT

Delacroix was busy taking in the information displayed on his scanning station screens. Finally, he was satisfied he knew what their situation was. "Gate transition complete, Captain." he announced at last.

Before Ronin could do more than nod in Delacroix's direction, Delgado answered an insistent beeping that suddenly emanated from her communications station. "Captain, we're being hailed via video commlink!" she said, trying not to sound surprised at the swift receipt of a message.

"Receiving automated friend or foe data now, Captain. It's the *Cygnus* and *Ceres,*" LeCroy reported from his tactical station. Simultaneously, Tacnet updated to plot the positions of the other spacecraft.

Ronin glanced at Delgado, and ordered her to open a commlink to the other ships. A moment later, she announced, "Video commlink open, Captain."

Ronin thumbed open the commlink from the node on his collar and the main viewscreen image was replaced by images of the other three ship captains. "This is *Cerberus* Actual. Report."

"*Cerberus* Actual, this is *Cygnus* Actual. It's good to hear your voice, Dan. We got your drone message in time to recall *Cygnus* and *Ceres* to the Solara system. We were about to transition through the gate when our ships were somehow moved to one side to make way for the arrival of *Kitty Hawk* and *Cerberus*."

Ronin immediately recognized the slightly German-accented voice of Capt. Alfred Jurgenson, in command of *Cygnus*. Like Ronin, Jurgenson was a veteran of many hard-won fights during the long war to end the Collective, and he had earned his reputation as quite an innovative tactician and strategist. Jurgenson's piercing blue eyes conveyed his concern that his voice didn't quite articulate.

About the same time as Jurgenson was speaking, Tacnet updated the rest of the fleet with the current situational status of *Kitty Hawk* and *Cerberus*. That caught everyone's attention.

"Dan, we're reading battle damage on *Cerberus*. And both your ship's life support systems are failing! What happened to y'all out there?" exclaimed Capt. Michelle Rodgers from her command chair on *Ceres*. She and her first officer were aghast at the shaky conditions aboard *Kitty Hawk* and *Cerberus*. Like Nagun, Ronin and Jurgenson, Rogers was an experienced veteran of numerous naval battles. She was also old friends with Ronin and Nagun dating back to their academy days together.

Half-smiling ruefully, Ronin figured he better bring the other captains up to speed as fast as he could. "We're sending you a data packet containing our logs and rescue information. The lost colony of Forrestal is on a collision course with the former colony of Celestra. *Kitty Hawk* and *Cerberus* are packed with refugees from the surface of Forrestal, and a rebel ship called *Pytor the Great* is standing by to help transmit orders to bring more refugees through the gate in their own evacuation fleet."

"Understood, Dan. We were following some remarkably broad orders of our own to jump to Forrestal system and participate in Taskforce 4 under the overall command of Commodore Ronin," Rodgers said with an unmistakable note of wry humor in her East Texas accented voice.

Since Rodgers was good friends with Ronin and Nagun, she couldn't help but take a good-natured dig at them. "Although, putting you boys in charge of anything more complex than flying a garbage scow seems pretty questionable." Framed by her curly black hair and ebony skin, Rodger's dark eyes sparkled with mirth and she cracked her megawatt smile that always lit up the room.

The four captains snorted with laughter, along with most of their bridge crews who overheard the wisecrack. Nagun didn't even bother trying to tamp down his reaction. He just laughed out loud instead and took a sip of coffee.

Everyone's eyes immediately locked onto Nagun's image on their viewscreens as they simultaneously wondered if Nagun was deliberately tormenting them by drinking his magically strong coffee that he nonetheless denied even existed. Nagun was indeed tormenting them with his coffee, as he smiled broadly in satisfaction after his sip. It wasn't the coffee that provided him with the most satisfaction, though; that came from openly drinking it in full view of the others.

Rogers' simple sounding statement about their orders left Ronin speechless for a few moments. It wasn't just one bombshell to unpack in that statement, but two. For the second time in the careers of Rogers, Ronin and Jurgenson, they would be serving in a Confederate naval taskforce, an event so rare that it happened only three times.

Before they had participated in Taskforce 3 during the Battle of Earth and end the Collective, the last time such a taskforce was assembled was 75 years earlier. Taskforces were powerful groups of warships, but required a huge undertaking in terms of commitment, resources, and war fighting capability.

Confederate task forces were also legendary in the lore of the Navy, as Taskforce 1 had wrested control of Mars away from the Collective, and Taskforce 2 had done the same with Mercury. The losses of Mars and Mercury had represented the beginning of the end for the Collective, because losing those planets choked off the Collective's easy access to massive mineral resources and forced them to rely upon asteroid mining, which was far more speculative and less efficient.

The second surprise was that Ronin had been elevated to the honorific rank of Commodore as the overall commanding officer of Taskforce 4. The Confederate navy did not use Commodore as an official rank as its use instead derived from an ancient naval custom. For modern day purposes, that custom merely served to quickly differentiate which captain was in overall command of a taskforce if it were not actively under the immediate command of the Admiralty like Taskforce 3 when it was commanded by Adm. Jessup Rodding.

Since Ronin had been put in overall command of what was now a small but formidable fleet taskforce, it was time to make things happen. "What's the status of the refugee camp I requested in my drone message?" he asked as a way of refocusing on their mission. *Cerberus* and *Kitty Hawk* had mostly been out of contact with the fleet while the ship was in the Forrestal system.

Jurgenson was ready with the answer. "A camp with full facilities is ready and waiting on Solara. Navy personnel from Earth, Terra Station and Solara have been making it ready since your message first arrived. The Solaran Factions have each supplied hundreds of aid workers to assist that effort. Security for the refugees is being provided by a mix of Marines, navy shore police, and Faction personnel, including two full military brigades from Ullrian Faction."

Nagun chuffed softly. "Anybody getting uppity will be in for a heck of an unpleasant surprise when they encounter Ullrian military. Empathy isn't their style."

Nods and knowing smiles answered Nagun's blunt observation. While fiercely loyal to their friends and allies, the bloodthirsty warrior Faction from the heavy gravity world of Solara also wasn't known for getting overly concerned about an enemy's hurt feelings.

"Here's what we're going to do. I want *Ceres* and *Cygnus* to transit through the jump gate and contact *Pytor the Great* to coordinate the next rescue. There is still time to transit because the evacuation fleet is several days away from their side of the gate. Time is of the essence as the planets are on a collision course in the next 78 days.

"We have significantly less time than that to evacuate as many civilians as we can, and bring them to the refugee camp on Solara before the competing gravitational fields make it impossible to rescue any more. Pack them in like sardines.

"We don't have time to reason with anyone or spend time we don't have trying to get refugees to follow orders or behave. Use your discretion to take trouble making players off the board immediately and replace them with refugees willing to be evacuated to Solara.

"In the interim, *Kitty Hawk* and *Cerberus* will offload our refugees, re-stabilize our ship systems, and begin the next round trip to Forrestal and take the place of *Ceres* and *Cygnus* as you return here with civilians. Questions?"

These were experienced captains, and all long-time friends or acquaintances, yet there were still questions because Ronin's bluntly stated orders reflected the cold, harsh situation *Cerberus* had found on the other side of the jump gate. Ronin had expected questions, but he was nonetheless taken by surprise when Rodgers asked him about uncooperative evacuees.

"Dan, how much 'discretion' are we to exercise when they're uncooperative? I'm not clear there," Capt. Rodgers asked.

Ronin and Nagun locked eyes for a brief moment before Ronin looked back at Rodger's in her corner of Ronin's viewscreen. He blew out a small sigh before answering, "These people have lived their entire lives ruled by an old legacy, pre-Fall artificial intelligence created by the Collective. If they panic, or try to rebel because they believe we are their ancient enemy, they endanger both your ship and everyone aboard it. *Cerberus* airlocked dozens of them. *Kitty Hawk* likewise airlocked several dozen, plus the Marines aboard *Kitty Hawk* had to put down another dozen with Mag-rail rifles. All were then replaced with additional refugees."

Surprised eyebrows rose on both Rodgers and Jurgenson's faces, and they traded slightly shocked glances at each other's images on their respective viewscreens for a brief moment. The unforgiving security measures taken aboard *Cerberus* and *Kitty Hawk* drove home the scope of the desperate situation in which *Ceres* and *Cygnus* were about to find themselves. Nonetheless, for these civilians it was a race between getting evacuated or dying, and dying was always going to be in the lead. There were no other options.

"Make no mistake. As rescue missions go, this is a snatch-and-grab of refugees. No matter what happens, we will lose far more of them than we can ever save. There isn't time for finesse here. All these civilians had been abandoned to die by that ancient AI, so every life we manage to save goes into the plus column of our accounting ledgers," Ronin added, then his attention focused on Perez at the helm.

"Captain, our jump drives have finished spinning up. We're ready to jump to Solara," Perez stated.

Nodding towards Perez, Ronin then issued his final orders. "Our jump drives are back online, so *Cerberus* and *Kitty Hawk* are ready to deliver our passengers. Remember, there is a sublight evacuation fleet headed towards the jump gate from the other side, but it will be a while until they arrive. We've enabled a ship named *Pytor the Great* to activate the gate and shepherd them through it once they arrive. Until then, our four ships will ferry as many refugees as we can in a round robin of two ship rotations. We won't stop until it gets too dangerous to approach Forrestal. Any other questions?"

There were, but none that the other captains were not willing to spend time they don't have in asking them.

"Godspeed, then. Ronin out."

CHAPTER 50

THE END OF DAYS

DIXIE STATION

67 DAYS UNTIL IMPACT

"Commlink the Taskforce and advise them *Kitty Hawk* has jumped to and is holding at Dixie Station per Commodore Ronin's orders," ordered Nagun. He never broke his intense concentration on the image displayed on his forward viewscreen as he issued the order. Nagun never even paid attention to whether his report was subsequently commlinked to *Cerberus* or not.

Every eye on the bridge of *Kitty Hawk* was riveted onto the same video. They were safely holding station several light hours from the cataclysm playing out on their screens, so the horrifying and fascinating images they were currently watching were likewise several hours old.

For a long time, no one spoke unless it was necessary to fulfill a duty. Everyone sensed breaking the heavy silence with something as mundane as speaking would only serve to diminish the awesome magnitude of the stellar horror to which they now bore witness. The crew seemed to silently have agreed upon an unwritten rule that you don't speak while witnessing a world ending catastrophe—just shut the hell up and watch it.

Standing next to Nagun, who was seated in his command chair, Commander Fisher seemed as if a stone statute for long stretches of time. The spell which seemed to hold him in a trance was finally broken by Nagun while they both watched the maelstrom of destruction of two planets' tearing themselves apart because of their colliding gravitational fields.

"No humans have witnessed the complete destruction of planets in real time before," Nagun said quietly, almost reverently. He was as awe-struck as everyone else to witness the End of Days.

Fisher nodded wordlessly. He had no words to describe what he was seeing. Titanic forces tearing apart two planets. Intense heat. Immeasurable kinetic energy. Atmospheric lightening storms from the skyrocketing magnetic influences preceding a global firestorm that subsequently burned away the atmosphere. Volcanoes. Earthquakes. World-ending tidal waves. Melted polar ice caps. Biblical disasters wiping out every last vestige of life from the surfaces of both planets before rending the planets apart.

When Fisher finally found his voice, he answered Nagun in little more than a ragged whisper. "All those disasters, rapidly striking all at once. And yet the overall cataclysm will take months before it is all over and the remains actually collide."

As Fisher's words sank in, Nagun tore his eyes from the main viewscreen and focused on his XO. Nodding thoughtfully for a few moments, he quietly murmured, "Yeah. Sudden planet-wide destruction, but it takes months to finish anyway."

A soft, electronic beeping indicating a ship-to-ship communication emanated from his commlink. He thumbed it open. "Go for *Kitty Hawk* Actual."

"This is *Cerberus* Actual. Hu, there's a trio of Confederation science vessels which have arrived on station through the jump gate to monitor the End of Days in this system. We're no longer needed here," said Ronin.

Nagun's eyebrows rose up slightly. He wasn't aware science vessels had been deployed to replace the Taskforce and its End of Days vigil at Dixie Station. At the same time, it also wasn't surprising since the science vessels were better equipped to study interstellar phenomenon than warships. Right ships for the right job.

Ronin was right. It was time to go home. Nagun cleared his throat slightly before replying. "That's affirm, *Cerberus* Actual. We'll meet you at the jump gate."

Nagun closed the commlink and looked at his helmsman. "Prepare to jump the ship to the jump gate."

As *Cerberus, Ceres, Cygnus,* and *Kitty Hawk* jumped away from Dixie Station, Nagun couldn't help but wonder if they would ever return here.

There was no way to know.

CHAPTER 51

SOLARA

CERBERUS, ORBITING SOLARA

63 DAYS UNTIL IMPACT

"How many were lost, Admiral?" asked Nagun. He and Ronin were sitting in Ronin's ready room next to the bridge along with their executive officers, Commanders Delacroix and Fisher. The small ready room was slightly crowded with the five officers in it.

Sighing to buy time, Admiral Rodding leaned heavily with his back against the wall. He was standing behind Ronin's small desk with the four ship's officers sitting on the other side. Rodding couldn't help but see the exhaustion plainly written on their faces. They looked like coffee addicts on the wrong side of a three-week caffeine bender, which was a fair description at this point. Even the famously chipper Nagun looked strung out.

Rodding crossed his arms, and bit his bottom lip. There was some bad news which just couldn't be softened, and these men led crews that had risked everything to save as many lives as they possibly could. It wasn't enough.

"I'll level with you boys. Tens of millions died in the Forrestal catastrophe, and there was no changing that outcome, ever. Dan could've commanded a fleet containing every ship ever made in the history of the Confederacy, and the lives-to-deaths ratio would only have shifted a little bit.

"The number you should be focusing on is how many your ships and crews saved. That's north of 200,000 civilians. Add in the refugees carried on the Forrestal evacuation fleet, and the number rises to over 300,000. That includes those ship crews that were still trying to figure out how to break free of the enemy AI's command control over their ships, a control system which you neatly hijacked in order to save several hundred thousand additional refugees." Adm. Rodding's West Virginia accent had softened in the decades since he had left the mountains he still called home, but it still sounded comforting to the officers in the ready room and his informality by using their first names only added to their sense of comfort.

The hatch to the ready room opened and Frida Enginnsdottir walked in. Her pregnancy was beginning to show, but she still walked as powerfully as ever. Rodding smiled broadly when she entered, and he nodded to acknowledge her arrival. "Frida's here, good!"

Enginnsdottir flashed a heart attack inducing smile at Rodding and her husband for a moment. "Admiral, it's good to see you, as always. You wanted to me to be present?"

"I certainly did, and thank you for coming. This next bit of news concerns both you and Dan," he said, reaching into his pocket. He withdrew a small, black velvet box, and handed it to Ronin.

His voice grew deadly serious. "Captain Ronin, you served with great distinction as a temporary fleet Commodore for the evacuation of Forrestal. I know you hate ceremonial pomp and circumstance as much as I do, and I'm happy to accommodate your preference. You've been promoted in rank, effective immediately. Congratulations, Admiral Ronin. Or, my condolences, your choice on how you want to look at it," Rodding said as he and Ronin shook hands.

Ronin's exhaustion didn't mask his surprise at the promotion. Even though it had been long delayed because of the importance of having their most famous captain commanding Cerberus during perilous times, it wasn't something Ronin had dwelled on.

In fact, it was the last thing on his mind. Rodding's wisecrack about extending his condolences also brought a half-smile to his face along with everyone else as it was an ancient joke. Ronin opened the velvet box and saw admiral stars inside.

"Son, I'd be honored to pin those to your collar, if you're agreeable to that," Rodding said while the other three officers clapped and whistled their approval of the promotion.

"Yessir, I'd appreciate that very much!" Ronin drawled while Enginnsdottir gave him a rib-creaking hug. He handed the velvet box to Rodding while Enginnsdottir removed the captain's rank insignia from his collar. Rodding pinned the stars to Ronin's collar, and the two men shook hands again.

The hatch to the ready room opened again, and Rodding's aide stepped in with a worn, leather briefcase that he held out to Ronin. "Admiral Ronin, congratulations, sir! Admiral Rodding wanted this delivered to you."

Taking custody of the briefcase, Ronin looked questioningly to Rodding, who merely raised his eyebrows and nodded to the briefcase before answering Ronin's unasked question. "You should pass the contents of that briefcase around now."

Ronin opened the briefcase. Inside were five glasses and a bottle of Old Prohibition bourbon. He smiled broadly, and distributed the glasses.

Nagun was grinning broadly as Ronin filled his glass. "It's five o'clock somewhere. Time for a snort of the good stuff."

The five officers raised their glasses, touching together in a circle. "To our lost shipmates, to our new shipmates in the future, and to some new beginnings," said Rodding before they took a hearty drink of the expensive bourbon. It was Rodding's tradition to commemorate important occasions with Old Prohibition, and he would be damned if this small celebration would have been excluded from that tradition. Even Enginnsdottir took a tiny sip from Ronin's glass, both as a show of solidarity with her husband, and because it was the good stuff. She wouldn't imbibe more than that though because she was pregnant.

"Well, Admiral, what's our next steps?" asked Nagun as they returned to their seats and Enginnsdottir left the ready room now that the small ceremony was over. Rodding sat in Adm. Ronin's chair behind his desk since there really wasn't room for any of them to shift around.

Rodding leaned back in his seat, bourbon glass still in his hand while his eyes suddenly seemed to focus on something far away. He took another sip before answering. "Resettlement. Those refugees have had a lifetime of malnourishment and poor healthcare. They aren't strong enough to adapt well to Solara's heavier gravity, and Solara isn't in any position to try to absorb hundreds of thousands of refugees anyway.

"Thanks to our ongoing discoveries at Ninebase and several expeditions to confirm viability, our first colonization mission is about to launch. The new planet is more than habitable, it's downright hospitable. The colony ships are all equipped with jump drives, and the refugees from Forrestal will be resettled on the new planet along with the other colonists." Rodding paused to take another sip of his bourbon before continuing.

"Colony? We're launching a mission to establish a new colony?" exclaimed Ronin. He hadn't heard anything about such a mission before.

"That's correct. Earth's first new colony expedition since before The Fall. Hopefully we don't screw it all up as badly as we did before," Rodding stated, sounding both hopeful and somewhat cynical at the same time.

Rodding's remark gave pause to the other four officers as each of them contemplated what had been discovered the past few years. The discoveries at the old Western Coalition's secret, pre-Fall facility called Ninebase that orbited a dark gas giant at the edge of the Sol system near a destroyed jump gate.

Those discoveries lead to *Cerberus'* exploration missions to find the mythical Lost Colonies of Solara, Forrestal and Celestra. Instead *Cerberus* first made the surprise discovery of the unknown colony of Terra Station and the unjust, class-stratified society that had evolved on that planet.

Then the re-discovery of Solara, itself marked by warring Factions, and a working jump gate that in turn led to the now-dead colonies of Forrestal and Celestra. Four colonies, two of which were destroyed on such a massive scale that none of them could truly comprehend it. The apocalyptic scale of destruction wrought over eight centuries earlier by The Fall had remained the overarching constant through it all.

Ronin took a contemplative sip of Old Prohibition. "The longer I've been out in The Dark, were even out here the horror of The Fall continues to wreak interstellar havoc, the more I've come to appreciate our ancestor's desperate fight to survive it. We were that close to snuffing our race out," he said, making a pinching motion with his fingers to indicate how close it truly was. His eyes locked onto Rodding's. "What's next for my crew, Admiral?"

Rodding's face lit up a bit, shaking off the faraway look that had taken over each of them as they had mulled the deeper, darker implications of The Fall. "Both *Cerberus* and *Kitty Hawk* are returning to Wayside Station for the moment. I'm sorry gentlemen, but your ships stink. And I truly mean that, they literally smell bad!"

Rodding's half joke caused the others to snicker a bit. They knew damn well how foul the air had become aboard *Cerberus* and *Kitty Hawk* after stuffing their ships with so many refugees that their sheer numbers nearly overwhelmed the life support systems. It had become better since the rescue phase of the operation had concluded, but the air systems needed new filters and the ships needed a thorough scrubbing.

"Commander Delacroix will remain aboard *Cerberus* as its first officer going forward. Captain Nagun and Commander Fisher will continue in their roles aboard *Kitty Hawk*. After a short refit at Wayside Station, *Kitty Hawk* will be escorting the colony expedition and performing long range scouting missions out there. *Cerberus* will also undergo a refit, and her latest battle damage repaired. The Admiralty has a deep space mission in mind for *Cerberus*, and they need Admiral Ronin's input for it," Adm. Rodding added.

"Admiral, any idea who my replacement aboard *Cerberus* will be?" Adm. Ronin asked. Since he was losing command of his beloved ship, it was a natural question.

"Somewhat. I'm forwarding the list of candidates to you. The Admiralty wants your confidential recommendations for each candidate. Your opinion will carry a lot of weight for the final decision," Adm. Rodding said, his eyebrows arched slightly. He had been expecting Ronin to ask that exact question.

Rodding tossed down the last of the bourbon in his glass. "All right, gentlemen, it's a big universe out there and time's a wasting. Let's make it happen."

CHAPTER 52

NEW BEGINNINGS

WAYSIDE STATION—MARS ORBIT
POST IMPACT

Ronin took a few moments to appreciate the stunning view of Valles Marineris and Olympus Mons. The 2,000-mile-long canyon and 13-mile high super volcano were both visible from the current geosynchronous orbit of Wayside Station, and his office was located on a part of a wing of the gigantic space station that faced down towards the planet below.

The commlink node on his collar chirped to announce an incoming communication. He tapped it to accept the message from his aide. "Admiral Ronin, your family is here. And you asked to be notified when *Cerberus* was ready to leave the space dock."

Dan smiled. While he did not own *Cerberus*, he would always think of the ship as his. And he knew exactly when *his* ship was ready to depart, which is why he timed his family's arrival to coincide with it.

"Send them in. Thanks, Lieutenant." Dan closed the commlink as the door whooshed open. His children, Sarah and Edward stormed in. Moments later his very pregnant Ullrian wife, Frida, followed them.

"Dad, is it really launch time?" Edward said excitedly. Sarah was much more subdued as her attention was distracted by the spectacular view of Mars.

"That it is," Dan said with a grin that only grew larger after Frida planted a light kiss on him. Moments later, the family gathered in front of the large view port.

Dan's collar node chirped again and he tapped it to open the channel. "Admiral Ronin, this is *Cerberus* Actual. Just give the word, and the ship is ready to depart."

Half-grinning with anticipation, Dan replied, "*Cerberus* Actual, the word is given. Godspeed and good hunting."

"*Cerberus* Actual confirms departure orders," acknowledged Capt. Tomias Miller, before adding in a cocky tone, "I'll bring her back in one piece for once, Admiral."

Dan barked a laugh as they watched the giant doors on this wing of the space station slowly open. "Try not to blow up any planets while you're at it," he deadpanned.

Miller snorted. Under Dan's command, *Cerberus* had a well-earned reputation for repeatedly getting shot up in combat, and bombarding planets. Like everyone else in the navy, Dan was the object of good-natured ribbing. In Dan's case, it was for finding interesting planets and showering them with ordnance from orbit.

"No promises about that, Admiral. Traditions must be upheld. *Cerberus* Actual, out."

For the next few minutes, Dan and his family quietly watched *Cerberus* emerge from space dock. Once it was free of obstructions, the ship maneuvered away from Wayside Station and soon vanished from sight. Dan's thoughts were of his crew before Sarah brought him out of his reverie.

"Dad, do you think we'll ever be stationed aboard a ship again?" Sarah asked in a quiet voice.

Shrugging with a tilt of his head towards Sarah, Dan could only say, "No idea. You never know what the future will bring."

Minutes later, Dan sat alone in his office. He had a partial answer to Sarah's question, but it wasn't one he had been willing to share with her. A Confederate Navy spacecraft is no place to raise a family. *It's dangerous enough without going into combat. I'll really miss commanding my ship and crew, but I'm so thankful my family doesn't have to face all that danger with me now*, he thought.

AUTHOR'S NOTE

Thank you for reading the *Cerberus* quadrilogy! I hope you enjoyed it. I have read science fiction for as long as I can remember, but never really encountered a series which told the particular post-apocalyptic story I wanted to read. So, after the success of my first nonfiction book, I wrote such a series myself. I just didn't expect it to stretch into four books!

ABOUT THE AUTHOR

John Filcher is a recovering attorney who graduated from law school back in the days when we walked to school barefoot in the snow. Uphill. Both ways. After many years of toiling in the corporate legal department of massive corporations, he finally had the time to "write something fun" as his son once quipped to him after looking over a chapter or two of his first nonfiction book, *Red Herrings*. While normal people would normally note decades of toiling away as a corporate attorney is pretty much the opposite of fun, writing the *Cerberus* series definitely was entertaining.

Finishing *Forrestal* was extra challenging, so it took longer. It was more complex than the other books in the Cerberus series, and life events provided a constant challenge to finding the time to write. My next literary adventure will be a murder-mystery that will incorporate my legal background. Such adventures are what life is all about. Thanks for reading!

www.ingramcontent.com/pod-product-compliance
Lightning Source LLC
Chambersburg PA
CBHW031232210726
48287CB00003B/761

9 781955 622080